THE

Glass

DOLPHIN

WENDY DEWAR HUGHES

THE
Glass
DOLPHIN

WENDY DEWAR HUGHES

Summer Bay Press

Summer Bay Press

The Glass Dolphin

Copyright 2013 © Wendy Dewar Hughes

www.wendydewarhughes.com

Published by Summer Bay Press.
Agassiz, British Columbia V0M 1A2
www.summerbaypress.com

Editing, Interior Design and Cover Design:
Wendy Dewar Hughes, Summer Bay Press

ISBN: 978-1-927626-24-5
Digital ISBN: 978-1-927626-25-2

For my lovely and beloved cousin,
Julene Hodges Schroeder,
without whose encouragement, enthusiasm, prayers, and
editorial help this book
and my writing career would be nowhere near
where it is today.

ACKNOWLEDGEMENTS

I was particularly blessed to grow up in a family of readers and creative thinkers. This tradition spread throughout my extended family, too.

My first and biggest thanks goes to my editor, Julene Hodges Schroeder for her sharp eye, not only for grammatical problems but also especially for her deep insight into spiritual matters and incredible knowledge of the Word of God. What a resource!

For inspiration and plot brainstorming, thanks go to my friend, Dale Sigurdson, who thinks of things that I never would have and is not afraid to suggest I put them in a book.

Special thanks and big hugs to two of the loveliest and smartest young women I know and love, Bethany Dewar and Sarah Amrein Sarissky. They generously offered to proof read this book for me. It makes me happy to have them both for my nieces.

I am also greatly blessed to have a husband who truly gets why the house is messy and the furniture is covered in books; who understands what it's like to live with a writer and artist (me) and says, "Go, write. Do what you have to do." My appreciation for Gordon Hughes goes beyond words.

Most of all, I thank God for filling my head with exciting stories and enticing me to do more of what I love. Jesus is my hero.

PROLOGUE

I can't do this.

My fingers gripped the twisted strand of vine as I leaned out over the edge of the precipice. Far below me, the raging river crashed over boulders and flung itself against the steep canyon walls.

My heart banged against my ribs.

At my back, a wall of jungle loomed, dripping with the aftermath of a recent downpour. Muck sluiced past my boots in coffee-coloured streams, becoming ragged plumes as they plunged over the sheer drop.

I braced my feet against a boulder where another cord, the thickness of a man's arm, stretched across the chasm and disappeared into the underbrush on the other side. Stepping away from the edge, I turned back to the jungle, my knees like jelly.

"No way!" I brushed past my uncle, Neil Bryant, the intrepid Meso-American archaeologist and official leader of this terrifying expedition. "There is no possible way I'm crossing that!"

Neil grabbed my arm and stopped me. "There is no other way, Jill. If we don't cross here you may never see Marco again."

I swallowed hard and glanced back over my shoulder toward the swinging rope bridge. Mouldy tendrils of ragged vine hung from the broken strands of the structure. Where the two hand cords attached to the main cable, several strands no longer even existed. Above our heads a heavy mist trailed through the jungle canopy, obscuring treetops and threatening more rain. Steam rose from my filthy, soaked shirt.

I ran the back of my hand across my forehead, swiping away a rivulet of cold sweat.

He was right.

"We can't go back, can we?" It was a statement, not a question. I knew, just as Neil had said, that if we did not go on I might not ever see the man I loved again. The kidnappers already had four, maybe five days on us.

Hitching my backpack up, I took a deep breath. "What do we need to know about these rope bridges?" I turned to our guide, a small, brown-skinned man with two missing incisors.

"I go," Gutierrez answered, stepping around me. "After, you come."

"I'll take up the rear." Neil patted my shoulder.

The guide slipped off his sandals, tied them together by the straps and flung them over his shoulder. He stepped onto the twisted vine cable, his bare feet curving around the cords. I watched, heart pounding, as he set off over the chasm, nimbly navigating the space with a hand on each side cable. The bridge seemed sturdy enough but I wasn't taking any chances until he reached the far side.

What am I doing here? I thought. *I should be reclining on a sugar-sand beach right about now, not slogging through a snake infested jungle.*

"Off you go." Neil nudged me as the guide scrambled up the slope on the other side of the chasm. "You'll be fine."

Still not convinced that the bridge would hold me, I followed Juan Carlos's lead and unlaced my boots. Pulling them out of the sucking mud, I tied the laces together and looped them over a clip on my backpack. I placed my bare feet sideways to the main rope and gripped the cord with my toes.

Grasping the hand ropes, I set off across the crevasse. In the centre of the expanse a blast of wind blew down the canyon. The ropes sang. Frayed ends lashed at me. The bridge swayed, snapping as it rocked. I stopped walking and clung with my hands and my feet, gasping in short, sharp breaths.

"Keep going." Neil's voice echoed across the abyss. "I'll start out when you get to the other side."

I could see the guide, Juan Carlos Gutierrez, waiting under a giant fern on the far side of the chasm. I bit my lower lip and edged forward. Damp strands of my dark hair whipped across my eyes, obscuring my vision.

With each step, the agonizing refrain of, "If only…" tapped like a metronome in my head. *If only Marco had come a day earlier. If only Lord Wardley had called Neil a day later. If only we'd planned a morning wedding instead.*

None of it mattered now. I shook my head and for a second I glanced down.

Mistake.

White water crashed and roiled over knife-edged boulders and jagged rocks, splashing and tumbling down the gorge and disappearing in a cloud of mist in the tropical rain forest. The world spun as the bridge rebounded.

Vertigo engulfed me. I sucked in a deep breath and squeezed my eyes shut. My aching arms stiffened as my fingers gripped the prickly strands. On my back, my boots swayed in the gusts of wind, unbalancing my pack and intensifying the dizziness. My stomach clenched.

Neil's voice floated from somewhere behind me, faint and hollow, "Keep going."

I wanted to scream, "I can't!" Instead, I exhaled a prayer. "God, I need your help here. Get me across this."

When I opened my eyes, the bridge had stopped heaving and for the moment at least, hung still between gusts. Moving hand-by-hand and step-by-step, I crept along the knobby rope, my bare feet throbbing with pain at every knot.

One more minute, I told myself.

Then I was there. At the far wall of the canyon, I leapt away from the precipice, grabbing for Juan Carlos's outstretched hand. Gasping in relief, I lunged into the slippery undergrowth and turned back to watch as Neil started toward us. Within minutes he had reached our side.

"Well, that's one more hurdle behind us," he said, sounding almost gleeful. "Let's see what else this land has in store. Get your boots on, Jill."

Chapter One

I eased into my favourite living room chair and laid the bouquet on the polished antique table at my elbow. Slipping my feet out of my pearly leather heels, I leaned back and heaved a deep sigh as a hot tear trickled down the left side of my face.

The day was perfect, or at least it was meant to be. The weather, sunny and fragrant with the scents of late summer, had set the stage. The armloads of flowers, the flowing chiffon dresses, the chairs with giant taffeta bows on their backs, even the aqua carpet unrolled down the centre of the terrace at the Ivy Cottage Tea House had added to the perfection of the afternoon. The food had all been prepared, the cake decorated with sugar blossoms, the guests had arrived. My bridesmaid daughter, Julia, looked beautiful in layers of creamy chiffon accented with an airy aqua sash. My father, who had spent the entire morning wiping his palms on a handkerchief, had been ready to walk me down the aisle to meet my long-legged, bronze-skinned Spanish groom.

But three o'clock had come and gone, and still my son Tim had not shown up with the groom in tow.

At half-past three, while the guests fidgeted under the ivy-covered trellis at the charming, neighbourhood café, I saw the car pull up on the street outside. Tim had been dispatched to the airport to pick up my soon-to-be husband, Marco.

Marco, I thought now, *with that perfect dimple in your cheek and your tender heart.* My Marco. Tim had leapt from the car and ran toward the doors of the restaurant, alone.

"You're late," I remonstrated under my breath when Tim burst through the door. "Where is Marco? Why is he not with you?"

"I couldn't find him, Mom." Tim's voice had a frantic edge, like a little boy in a mess of trouble. "I looked all over the airport. I checked with the ticket counter and everything. He wasn't on the flight."

"How could he not be on the flight? He's getting married today!" I knew my voice was rising but I couldn't help it.

Tim backed away, gently removing my clutched hands from the front of his jacket. "I did everything I could, Mom."

"Why didn't you phone?"

"I did," Tim said. "I guess you didn't have your phone in your dress."

"That's not funny, Tim."

"No, I guess not," he replied, glancing at my father for help.

"There has to be a reasonable explanation," my dad said, launching into rescue mode.

"What's reasonable about not showing up for your own wedding?" By now, my voice had risen to a wail and guests had turned to glance toward where I stood inside the café door.

When it was clear that my intended would not be coming to his own wedding, explanations and apologies had been made. I suggested they all stay and eat anyway as there was no point wasting all that good food. Uncomfortable, they left soon after, saying good-bye, kissing my cheeks and fixing me with looks of such profound sympathy it was almost too much to bear. My little family had walked me home, clustering around me for protection against curious stares as we trudged the two blocks from the tea house to my house.

Now my parents had gone home and Tim had gone upstairs for a nap. Julia hovered in the kitchen, cleaning up nothing in particular.

He didn't come. The thought stabbed me again as anguish knotted my insides. The phrase kept ringing through my brain like a bell that wouldn't stop. *He didn't come, he didn't come, he didn't come,* I mourned, turning in my chair to stare out the multi-paned window. How could it be that Marco Alejandro Ibarra de Jimenez, with his flashing dark eyes and wrap-around-your-finger curls, had pursued me all over Europe, Mexico and even the Holy Land and now, after convincing me that my life would never be complete without him, left me sitting here on our wedding day, all alone?

Barely four months before as I picked up a collection of rare artifacts for my uncle, Marco had been there, always turning up in the most unlikely moments, steadfastly shadowing me through my travels. By the time we had rounded up all the pieces of the Mayan find, dispatched a Mexican Mafioso and a band of Middle-Eastern extremists, I had fallen profoundly in love with him. It was a feeling I had expected never to have again.

"Would you like me to put those flowers in some water?" Julia's soft voice broke through my thoughts and startled me. She squeezed my hand as she picked up the bouquet.

"It's going to be okay, Mom," she said giving me a sympathetic gaze.

It was too much and I sobbed. "You don't know that."

"Yes, I do," she replied. "There has to be an explanation. And God will help you find it and help you through whatever happens. You know that."

I nodded as I watched her move toward the kitchen, still dressed in her wedding finery.

Why had Marco not come to marry me? More tears slid from the corners of my eyes and rolled down my cheeks. I didn't even bother to wipe them away. By now, the evening sun slanted through the blinds, turning the floating dust motes into flecks of gold. I could hear Julia in the kitchen, taking far too long to stick a bunch of flowers in a vase.

Suddenly, loud rapping at the front door shocked me from my gloom. The door crashed open and my uncle, Neil, sprinted in.

"I think I've found him," he gasped, throwing himself onto the nearby sofa and grabbing my hand. "At least, I think I know why Marco didn't show up."

"What do you mean?" I grasped his arm. "Where is he?"

"Well, that part I'm not sure of right now," he replied, easing my nails out of his forearm. "He stopped off in Britain like I asked him to..."

"You what?"

"Oh, dear," Neil said, rubbing his jaw. "I was afraid this might not go well."

"What are you talking about?" I shrieked. "He was supposed to show up this morning to marry me, coming directly from Madrid. What do you mean he 'stopped off in Britain'?"

Neil had the grace, at least, to look sheepish. "I'm sorry, Jill. It was a simple request. An old friend called last week to tell me that he had come across a bit of family history and thought I'd be interested in having a look at the artifacts. I asked Marco to pop in and pick them up on his way here. He had a stopover in London anyway and Wardley Hall isn't far from the airport. I just spoke with Lord Wardley and he told me that Marco was there last night."

"Where is he now?"

"No one seems to know."

"Who is Lord Wardley?"

"Cardiff Wardley and I have known each other ever since I spent that stint at Cambridge years ago."

"Why on earth did you send Marco on a wild goose chase on the day before his wedding?"

"Jill, honey, I'm sorry. It wasn't supposed to turn out like this. He had plenty of time between flights to dash up to Wardley Hall, pick up the articles and still catch his overseas flight. You knew that he wasn't due to arrive until this morning because of his business schedule anyway. It should have all worked out just fine."

"Except that it didn't," I cried.

Neil ran his hands through his hair. It was still thick, dark and streaked with only a few strands of grey, even though he was in his sixties. "No, but he wouldn't just *not* show up. You know that. Something had to have happened. I've been on the phone for the past two hours calling every agency and police department in the whole of England. They have nothing. He seems to have vanished and you know as well as I do that Marco wouldn't do that."

No, he wouldn't, I considered. *Would he?* "What are we going to do?"

"We're going to find him, of course."

"How?"

"We have to go to the last place he was seen and figure out what happened."

"In that case, we have to fly out tonight," I announced, leaping up from my chair. "You find the flights. I'm going to pack. And to pray."

CHAPTER TWO

A grey mist speckled the windshield of the tiny rental car as we peered into the darkening evening at the dimly lit road signs flanking the hedgerows. We had left the motorway and found ourselves driving on smaller and smaller roads until now we crept along a paved track hardly wider than the car.

It must be here somewhere," Neil muttered.

"I thought you'd been there before." I swiped the inside of the window with a tissue and searched the road ahead.

"I have," Neil replied, "but that was in 1985. Ah, there it is." A massive set of wrought-iron gates appeared out of the gloom on the right and Neil slowed the car. Gravel crunched under the tires as we rolled through the opening and onto a long winding lane leading through a copse of dripping trees. We took a curve to the left and the big house loomed ahead, dark and foreboding except for the few lights that glowed from the main floor windows.

"Cardy is expecting us," Neil said. "I warned him that we'd be here around eight. I hope he hasn't given up on us." He pulled the car up in front of the sandstone façade of the house, which was streaked with black mould and soot. The front door opened and a pack of dogs exploded from the lighted portal as an aged man in a black suit stood holding the door open, his back stiff. "Good grief," Neil exclaimed, "that must be Burton. I thought he'd have kicked off eons ago."

I opened my car door, unfolded myself from the miniscule vehicle, and shooed the sniffing dogs away from my ankles as Neil came around the front of the car and headed up the mansion steps.

"Good evening, sire, milady," said the man at the door with a stiff bow. "The master is expecting you."

"Hello, Burton," Neil said, pumping the butler's hand.

"Good evening, sire. A pleasure to see you again." Unsmiling, Burton withdrew his hand as though he had taken Neil's familiarity as a personal affront.

Burton led the way and we found ourselves in a sizeable entrance hall lit by a glowing chandelier and several wall sconces. The round room had black and white marble-tiled floors and a broad staircase that swept upward along the wall on one side, with steps covered in worn crimson carpeting. Looking up, I could see a domed ceiling that ballooned skyward up to the third floor.

"If you'll follow me," Burton intoned after a brief introduction. He led us through a set of soaring, carved doors into an expansive room lit by lamps and with a crackling fire in a magnificent hearth at the far end. Massive portraits, no doubt of the ancestors, scaled the walls up to a ceiling painted with images of angels, clouds and swags of roses. A thick, patterned rug covered the gleaming wood flooring and an enormous vase of flowers stood on a grand piano next to a pair of French doors that appeared to lead onto a terrace, though at this hour all I could see was the glow of lamplight on wet flagstones.

"Ah, there you are." An elderly man rose from the depths of a wing chair next to the fire and strode toward us with surprising vitality. "I was beginning to wonder if you would come up here tonight in this ghastly weather," he said, throwing his arms around Neil and thumping him on the back. "And this must be your delightful niece." He reached for my hand and pumped it vigorously between both of his while smiling down at me with eyes that crinkled so tightly at the corners that they nearly disappeared. "I'm Cardiff Wardley," he explained, leading us to seats by the fire. "You must call me Cardy, my dear. That's what all my friends call me. The people who call me Sir or Lord Wardley are not generally my friends."

"I am sorry to intrude on you like this," Neil began.

"Stuff and nonsense," Cardy interrupted. "Mrs. B, that's Burton's wife who runs the kitchen," he explained as an aside to me, "has prepared a lovely little meal for us. I'm sure you must be starving after your long trip and having to eat that dreadful airline mess they try to pass off as food."

The doors to the room opened just then and a round lady with a halo of white curly hair entered pushing a tea trolley laden with trays and platters. She reminded me of what Mrs. Santa Claus might look like with her rosy cheeks and ample waistline. The contrast with her towering, almost cadaverous, husband, who had entered behind her, was striking. She smiled up at him affectionately as he set out side tables and poured drinks.

"I thought we'd have a bite in here," Lord Wardley explained. "It's much warmer by the fire on a dreary night like this." Plates of petite sandwiches and warm meaty tarts, plus an assortment of local cheeses, pickles and a bowl of chutney appeared. The light meal was accompanied by china cups of hot tea with milk and, in Lord Wardley's case, a heaping spoonful of sugar.

"Off with you two now," Wardley instructed his staff, waving them away with a bony hand. "Neil will help me clean up this lot. He's had plenty of experience roughing it." They silently vanished, backing out the double doors and pulling them closed behind them with a barely audible click.

I studied Lord Cardiff Wardley for a few minutes as he munched his meal, taking in his long arms in cuff-linked sleeves and brown velvet jacket with shiny elbows. Steel-grey hair started far back from where his hairline used to be and great bushy eyebrows loomed over eyes of piercing blue, separated by a long hooked nose.

"We must talk about your man, Mr. Jimenez," he said

12

between bites of bread spread with peach-ginger jam.

I gulped. "So you saw him? When was he here?" Neil reached over and squeezed my wrist.

"Yes. He was here only two days ago, or was it yesterday? Never mind, he appeared just as we'd arranged." He nodded toward Neil. "When I spoke with your uncle about the surprising little find I'd made, I thought he would like to see it right away. Since it turned out that your man was passing through so nearby, we thought it would be a fine time to send it along with him. That way we wouldn't have to trust it to the post."

"What was so important that you had to have it on our wedding day?" I turned brimming eyes on Neil while I tried to swallow past the lump in my throat.

"I don't know how many ways I can say I'm sorry, Jill. It wasn't meant to turn out this way."

Lord Wardley spoke up. "My dear, regardless of the current circumstances, which will no doubt be resolved post-haste, the fault is not your uncle's. I accept full responsibility because, had I waited even a few days to inform him of my good fortune, none of this would have happened. You see, it came to my attention recently that a small box of artifacts had surfaced at a nearby village auction, discovered in someone's attic clean up. The items belonged to my great aunt, a formidable woman in her day, and I wanted to bring them home, so to speak. I attended the auction and managed to outbid the desultory efforts of my neighbours by a few pounds and brought home this collection of what appeared to be Great-Great-Aunt Cecilia's things."

"What sort of things?" I pulled a tissue from my purse and dabbed my eyes.

"Nothing much of interest, really, as I discovered," he replied, picking up his teacup. "There was a sextant, a few pressed flowers of unknown species, some field glasses and other paraphernalia a traveller might have used or collected in her day. The item of most importance was a map. Cecilia Wardley never married, you see. She was, to her family's horror and wonder, an explorer, and one of some renown, as it turned out. She was responsible for uncovering some of the most important Inca sites in Peru. Oh, nothing so grand as Machu Picchu or that one up above Cusco…what's it called?"

"Sacsayhuaman?" Neil offered.

"Yes, that's it. Nothing so grand as all that but she did find a tribe in the jungles out there that had never encountered anyone from the outside world before. Given the era we're talking about, that's not too surprising either." He set his teacup down and helped himself to a sliver of shortbread. "The map was of her own making and presumably of what was until then completely uncharted territory. I knew that Neil would be particularly interested in this piece. He suggested that your man, Mr. Jimenez, might be able to help. I can't think what could have happened to him." His voice trailed off.

"But he was here," I stated, looking from Cardy to Neil and back again. They both nodded.

"Oh, yes. He arrived right on schedule. We had time for a quick cup of tea. I offered lunch but he said he'd get take-away at the pub in town. Then he was off to the airport with the artifacts tucked up safely in his hand luggage. There wasn't much to it, after all, just a few bits and bobs, this and that. And that map, whatever it may mean. I thought Neil might be able to make something of it."

"But what happened to him? Where did he go? He couldn't just have disappeared," I said.

"If you saw Marco come here then leave in one piece," Neil said to Cardy, "then something had to have happened after he left here." He rubbed a hand over his chin and frowned, turning his head to gaze through the glass doors and out onto the terrace. "We're going to have to do some investigating, Jill," he stated.

14

"In the morning we'll have a word with the gardener and a few others who drift around the estate. It's possible one of them has seen something," Cardy suggested.

"Can't we start now?" I asked.

"Oh, no. They've all gone home for the night. I did talk to Burton after Neil called but he had nothing out of the ordinary to report."

I finished my tea and set my cup back on the saucer with an unsteady rattle. The thought of having to wait until morning to start looking for my darling Marco made me want to sob. My shoulders sagged and I let out a long, deep sigh.

"You must be exhausted after your long trip, my dear," said Cardy, gently. "Let me show both of you to your rooms. Burton has already delivered your bags."

CHAPTER THREE

My small rolling suitcase and tote bag had been placed in a spacious room on the second floor of Wardley Hall, the estate of the Wardley family since 1720 or thereabouts. Even though it was still just late summer, the inclement weather left a damp chill in the air and either Burton or Mrs. B. had seen fit to light a fire in the hearth. I lowered myself into a big, comfy old chair next to the fire and laid my head on its arm.

Marco and I had met while picking up the pieces of the Mayan artifact that Neil had discovered in Mexico and sent to colleagues halfway around the world. The value of the find was inestimable, and as it turned out, to more people than just himself. He had been forced into hiding for his own protection and had begged me to pick up the sections of a ring of stones, one piece at a time. Marco, the son of one of Neil's oldest and most trusted colleagues, the late Dr. Jimenez of Madrid, had driven me across Spain in order to keep ahead of the vile Menendez, a thug with the persistence of a bulldog, working for some Mexican organized crime syndicate.

Sitting here, staring into the flickering fire, I remembered how we had been ambushed in an ancient monastery in Barcelona and I gently ran my fingers over the scar left from where I had been shot and injured. For some reason that it took me a long time to comprehend, Marco always seemed to be there when I needed him. I knew there was something strange going on and yet, distracted as I had been with the job at hand, I could not decide if he sided with the villains, of whom there were many, or with Neil.

I sighed and watched the sparks glimmer upward as a

charred log broke and fell and I tugged a heavy, woollen throw up over my legs.

I knew that God had brought Marco into my life. I had expected that I would never love a man again. My first husband, Roger, had passed away a few years earlier after an early morning bicycle accident that left a hollow gap in my life and the lives of my children, Julia and Tim. In their teens, when the accident had taken place, they had gradually gathered up the threads of their young lives and finally carried on – Tim to travel Southeast Asia and Julia to leave our small town and take a job in the city.

I had intended never to marry again. That was, until Marco came along. Though I hadn't known it at the time, it turned out that he had been working for Neil all along as undercover security during the whole rescue operation. Once the sixteen stones had been rounded up and delivered, Marco was free to go home and so was I. By then, of course, it was too late for me to stick to my never-marry-again policy. I had found a wonderful man and I didn't want to live the rest of my life without him. A vision of his brilliant smile drifted into my mind, the dark laughing eyes, the dimple indenting his left cheek. I wanted to savour the picture; to reach out and touch his softly waving hair; to be folded into the embrace of his strong arms.

But now, he had disappeared. I felt sure that he wouldn't simply skip out on marrying me. He couldn't do that. He wouldn't. *Would he?* I rubbed the tense muscles along the tops of my shoulders and glanced at my watch.

I had switched it to London time just before the flight had landed at Heathrow Airport and was surprised to see that it was already nearly ten o'clock locally. A tidal wave of fatigue swept over me. Whatever had happened to Marco, we would not be able to discover tonight. I pushed myself out of the chair and across the room to unpack my night things from my case. As I leaned toward it, my foot caught on the carpet and I half tripped, catching myself but knocking my upright suitcase over with my knee. The bag toppled sideways and the extended handle rapped against the wall panel with a thud, a peculiarly hollow sound.

Tilting the suitcase back on its wheels, I reached for my tote and my elbow clumsily knocked the wall on the next panel. It made a dull sound, not at all like the other panel had. *How odd*, I thought, staring at the two identical panels. Using my knuckles, I tapped first one panel then the other. The sound was completely different. I tried the rest of the panels along the wall. They looked identical to one another – about waist-high, dark burnished wood with ornate trim. They sounded identical, too, except for the one that my suitcase's handle had knocked.

It's probably nothing, I concluded, dismissing it as I dragged my things into the adjoining bathroom to ready myself for bed.

Once tucked into the big four-poster bed, I slathered cream on my hands and switched off the lamp. The wind had risen and the rain that a few hours ago had been a miserable drizzle now slashed against the windowpanes like needles. Somewhere far away the low rumble of thunder echoed across the countryside.

I pulled the bed covers up under my chin and closed my eyes. *Heavenly Father*, I prayed, whispering into the dark, *please, please help me find Marco. You know what happened and you know exactly where he is. Please keep him safe and help us find him.*

I rolled onto my side. Exhaustion pulled my bones into the mattress and made my muscles ache with weariness. Listening to the sounds of the night storm, I lay still, taking long, slow, deep breaths to calm my troubled mind. I waited for sleep to overtake me but it would not come. For more than an hour I flipped from side to side, rolled onto my back and stared up at the ceiling and watched the flicker of light from the dying fire. I couldn't get comfortable, no matter what I tried. It felt like the elusive hope of a deep sleep had shunned me.

The thought of that odd-sounding wall panel kept sliding unbidden across the corners of my mind. Not a stranger to the nudging of the Holy Spirit, I began to sense that I lay awake for a reason and that there was something about that wall panel I needed to know.

I switched on the lamp, squinting against its sudden brilliance and threw my feet over the side of the bed and onto the old patterned rug. Padding to the section of wall I had examined earlier, I tapped on the panels until I located the hollow-sounding one. With my knuckles, I rapped gently on the wood, here and there. There was no doubt that the entire panel sounded hollow compared with its neighbours, as though it were the only one not stuffed with insulation of some kind. I ran my fingers around the inside periphery of the ornate trim. It was completely smooth. Puzzled, I then tried sliding the tip of my index finger along the outside perimeter of the panel.

At first I could feel nothing. About to give up and go back to bed, I sighed. Yet something compelled me to try one more time. I fetched my ultra-bright little flashlight from my tote bag and shone the beam along the edge while examining the rim. Up in the top right corner I found what I suspected was there. A simple notch in the wood revealed a tiny latch. With the flashlight beaming into the notch, I flicked the latch. *Snick.* The panel popped away from the wall with a high-pitched squeak. Drawing it open I peered into the gloom.

At first I was not sure what I had discovered. The cavity resembled a small closet, which looked empty until I shone the light around the space. A small box about the size of a shoebox stood on the floor of the cupboard. Leaning over, I blew the dust from its top, coughing from the powdery cloud that billowed out of the enclosure. The flashlight beam caught the glow of polished wood and I reached in and drew out the box, took it across the room and set it on the carpet near the faint radiance of the fire. Grabbing a tissue from the bathroom I wiped the grime off the surface and examined the fine craftsmanship of the inlaid wood.

It looked very old. When I pressed a tiny latch, the lid popped open. Inside, I found only one item. A small, leather-bound book lay in the bottom of the chest, wrapped in worn thongs and bulging with more than the binding had been meant to contain. I lifted it out and turned it over, running my fingertips over the tattered surface. Sitting cross-legged on the cold floor, I unwound the stiff leather thongs and opened the front cover. Inside, a faded hand-written inscription read, *The Journal and Exploration Records of Cecilia Margaret Wardley, 1835.* Ever so carefully, I began to turn the pages.

An hour later, chilled and stiff, I closed the book, crawled into bed and slept for ten hours. The sound of a pair of doves cooing in a tree outside my window woke me. When I pushed the heavy brocade draperies back, dazzling sunlight burst into the room. The storm had passed and though I could see broken branches and leaves strewn about the drive and gardens, everything looked washed clean by the rain.

After splashing my face in the bathroom and pulling on a pair of jeans and a light top, I brushed my dark hair back into a low ponytail and secured it with an elastic band. Flicking on a dusting of blush and a coat of mascara, I considered myself presentable and went downstairs.

I found Neil and Lord Wardley in the dining room deep in conversation over the remains of breakfast. They sat at a small table in a spacious bow window and both men looked up when I tapped on the door and entered.

"Good morning, my dear," cried Lord Wardley, rising and taking my hand. "All the breakfast things are still here and warm." He led me to an ornate sideboard laden with covered dishes. "Please help yourself to anything you would like and do join us."

"Thank-you, sir."

"Please, 'Cardy' to you."

"All right," I replied, smiling. I filled a small plate with scrambled eggs and a few pieces of fruit, poured a cup of coffee from a carafe and joined the two men.

"Jill, we've just been discussing what could have happened to Marco," Neil said, turning to me as I sat down. "Cardy told me that Marco arrived here around noon and left about forty-five minutes later. He had mentioned to me that he had some business to do in London before continuing on for the wedding. Everything was fine then."

My shoulders sagged and tears sprang to my eyes before I could stop them. "Don't cry, honey," Neil said softly, putting an arm around my shoulders and pulling me into a hug. "We're going to find him."

"I've been wracking my brains to find a reason why he might have gone missing," Cardy said, drumming his fingers on the table. "The only thing I can think of is that there was something in that collection of Aunt Cecilia's that someone wanted."

"Like what?" I wiped my eyes with a napkin. "I thought you said there was nothing of any consequence in her things." Neil and Cardy exchanged a glance. "What?" I nailed Neil with a look he couldn't get away from.

"Remember when I told you my next dig was going to be in Peru? I got wind of a site on the eastern slopes of the mountains from an old pal of mine and we thought there was a lot more to it than had already been discovered. The university decided to send me down for a look and when Cardy called to tell me that his great-auntie's belongings had surfaced and that he was willing to let me have a look at them, I jumped at the opportunity."

"You see," Cardy interjected, "as far as we know, Great-Great-Aunt Cecilia may still be the only white person known to

21

ever have explored that particular area. When she came home, however, she was a changed woman, and not in a good way. According to family stories, she never talked about what she had seen except to say that no one should ever go there again."

"What else did they say?" I asked, forcing down another bite of eggs.

"She went into a sort of semi-seclusion here at Wardley Hall and died a few years later from unknown causes. She was thirty-eight."

"Good grief, that's younger than I am," I said, getting up to pour myself another cup of coffee and offering to re-fill the others' cups. "What happened to her in Peru?

"No one ever found out. She never spoke of it again," Cardy reported. I thought of the diary I had discovered the previous night but for a reason I didn't quite understand, I said nothing about it. It seems almost like a dream now. In the meantime, I have had a more pressing problem on my mind than Lord Wardley's long-dead relative. We had to find out what happened to Marco and if there was any connection between his disappearance and the box of Cecilia's belongings.

"When Marco came to see you," I asked, turning to Cardy, "did anyone else see him here?"

"Of course. Burton and Mrs. B. saw him."

I glanced at Neil. "We should talk with them. Perhaps they noticed something, anything that might help explain what happened after Marco left here. We have to start somewhere." I had been holding it together pretty well up until then but when I thought of Marco again, I started to cry. "I'm sorry. It's just that I'm supposed to be on my honeymoon today, not trying to find my groom."

Neil stood to his feet and came around behind me. He wrapped his arms right around me and held me tight. "We'll find him, sweetheart," he said. "Don't you worry. We'll find him."

22

Chapter Four

I found Mrs. B. in the back garden gathering chives and butter lettuces into a trug basket hanging from one arm.

"Oh hello, love," she said brushing soil from her knees as she pushed herself to her feet. "I hope you're feeling well this morning. It's a beautiful day after that storm last night."

"Yes, thank-you," I replied, falling into step beside her as she headed down the carrot row. "I was wondering if I might talk with you for a moment."

"Of course, dear. How may I help?"

"Did you see my fiancé, Marco Jimenez, when he was here?"

"Yes, I saw him. He's a lovely young man. So good-looking. You're ever so lucky."

"I hope you're right," I replied, feeling a stab of pain in the middle of my chest. "Did you notice anything unusual about him when he was here? Did he seem distracted, or did he say anything that might tell me what happened?"

"Let's see." She stopped walking and pulled off her gardening gloves. "He arrived around noon. I offered him some lunch but he said he would just get take-away from the pub in the village. He was here only about a half hour, no, more like forty-five minutes, and he spent the entire time speaking with His Lordship. When he left he carried a box under his arm. I never thought much of it since I don't meddle in His Lordship's business." She pursed her lips as though the very idea of discussing her employer's affairs left a bad taste in her mouth.

"Did he say anything? Did you notice anything unusual or odd?" I pressed.

"No, I don't think so." She thought for a moment. "Well,

there was something but I doubt that it means anything. No, I'm sure it doesn't." She shook her head and started walking again.

I reached across the vegetable row and grasped her wrist, stopping her. "What was it? Please tell me anything you know, no matter how insignificant it seems."

She gently extracted her arm from my grip, patting my hand as she did. "As he said goodbye to His Lordship, he said that he hoped there was nothing in the box that anyone else would want. I wasn't eavesdropping, you understand, just passing by to clean up the tea things."

"Was that all?" I didn't want to sound demanding but I could feel my anxiety level rising. Neil had gone off to talk with the groundskeeper and Cardy's groom. After breakfast, we had spoken first to Burton who had assured us that he had neither seen nor heard anything out of the ordinary. As he had reiterated, Marco had been at the estate only a short time. Burton had served tea in the same room where we had met with Cardy the previous evening. He had left the room while the two men talked, then reappeared as Marco prepared to leave. He hadn't mentioned the comment that Mrs. B. shared with me now but perhaps he considered it too insignificant to notice.

"Yes, that was all," Mrs. B. assured me. "I don't know what was in the box but I suppose he must have known. I'm afraid that's all I can tell you, dear. Now, I really must get on with this. I have lunch to prepare before I run off to a library society meeting. I am sorry."

I made my way back through the vegetable gardens and the flower garden and when I came around the corner of the house found Neil talking with a man I didn't recognize. Before I reached them, however, the other man hurried away, leaving Neil standing alone looking out over the vast lawns of the estate.

"I've spoken with the others," he said, turning, "but no one seems to know anything. What have you found out?"

I shook my head. "Only that he was planning to pick up something to eat at a pub in the village on his way back to the airport. It's not much but it may be a start. Who was that man you were talking with?"

"His name is Gerald Jones. He's the groundskeeper and general landsman here. He also looks after Cardy's horses. Unfortunately, he didn't have anything to share with me that I didn't already know."

"Oh, Neil, what are we going to do? No one seems to know a thing."

Neil jammed his hands into his pants pockets. "We don't have much to go on. I suggest that we start by visiting the pubs in the village and see what we can find out. Cardy has invited us to stay as long as we need to."

Fifteen minutes later, Neil pulled the little car into a parking spot in front of a pub called The White Rose. Several other vehicles sat in the lot and on the street in front of the ancient, half-timbered building, including a tractor with a sheepdog guarding its seat. We pulled open the heavy timber door and as it was nearly lunchtime now, the pub echoed with conversation and the clatter of dishes. We wove between the wooden tables and the farmers standing with glasses of beer in their meaty hands, and slid up to the bar.

"What's your pleasure?" The burly barkeeper said, looking over a pair of reading glasses clinging to the tip of a bulbous nose. He dashed back and forth behind the counter filling orders with both hands.

"We would like to ask a few questions, if you don't mind," I said over the noise.

"Make it quick, dearie," he replied, bracing his elbows on the polished bar in front of me.

I pulled a photo of Marco from my purse and handed it to him. The photo was one I had taken only a few weeks before of

Marco standing in my garden next to a fading hydrangea bush. "Have you seen this man in the past few days?"

He wiped his blunt fingers on a splotched yellow apron and gingerly took the photo from my fingers. "Oh, aye," he said. "He got some take-away a couple of days ago, or maybe it was yesterday. I rarely forget a face and he kind of stood out because he looked a bit foreign. Not that we don't have plenty of foreigners here-about but he had a Spanish accent. I recognized it because the wife and I like to go to Spain on hols." He handed the photo back to me.

"Did you notice anything peculiar about him, or anyone else around who might have been interested in him?" Neil asked.

The bartender thought for a moment before another patron hollered for service. He dashed away, filled a couple of glasses with beer from the tap and came back. "There was something I thought odd," he said, glancing around the room and dropping his voice. "For most of the mornin' there was a little guy sitting over there in the corner all by himself. All he ordered was coffee. He was of the brown persuasion, if you take me point, like an Indian but," he scratched his cheek, "he didn't look like the India kind of Indian. More like those pictures you see on the telly of those Indians in the Amazon jungles or somewhere."

"Yes? And what happened?"

"Well, when your fellah, the one in the picture, came in, this guy perked right up and when your man left, the other bloke got up and followed him out. That's about all I can tell you. Sorry, but I've got to run."

We thanked him and I turned to Neil. "Now what?"

Before he could answer another voice spoke. "I saw him, too." Neil and I both swivelled toward its owner. A young lady of perhaps eighteen with a streak of purple hair tucked behind one ear stood behind me. "I'm Sherry," she said, holding out her hand. I shook it and so did Neil. "I can tell you what he

26

looked like, that little guy. I've got a picture."

"You have?"

"Yeah. I like to draw and he was an interesting character. I'm an art student at the college. It wasn't very busy that morning so I was sitting behind the bar with not much to do. Me da's the owner, see. So I sketched that guy. He never saw me. I was discreet."

"Do you still have the sketch?" Neil asked.

"'Course I do. I'll go get it for you."

Sherry ducked into a back room and returned a few minutes later. She handed me her sketchbook, the usual heavy volume with a hard black cover. The drawing was remarkably good, a detailed sketch in fine strokes of black ink. I could see what the barman meant by the man's looks. He did indeed look South American and I said so to Neil.

"May I keep this, or make a copy?"

"Oh, you can have that," Sherry answered, tearing the drawing out of the book. "It was just for practice. He were a strange one, that. The only word he said was 'coffee' and when that other fellow came in for take-away he perked up like a foxhound. Got up and ran out after him, he did." She handed me the sketch. "Got to run. Lunch rush. I hope that helps."

We thanked her and walked out into the summer sun, squinting against the sudden brightness.

"What do you make of this?" I asked Neil as he led me to a bench in front of the pub.

Taking the drawing from me, he examined it. "If this is accurate, his features indicate that he's South American, possibly from Peru or Bolivia or maybe somewhere along the Amazon into Brazil. He looks to be middle-aged but sometimes those indigenous people look older or younger than they are so I'm just guessing." I stared at the picture. The face showed a long nose, a wide mouth and flatness around the eyes under heavy brows. The hair lay slicked back from a low forehead.

Sherry hadn't included the details of his clothing, only the turned-down collar of an ordinary shirt. I couldn't see where this would lead us.

"Well, we'd better get at it," Neil said, folding the page and stuffing it in his shirt pocket. He stood up and reached for my hand.

"Where are we going?"

"Where do you think? To find Marco, of course."

CHAPTER FIVE

A bell jangled over the scuffed black door as Neil pushed it open. I followed him, stepping over the sleeping yellow dog that lay across the hall rug of one of the three small inns in the village. The dog opened one eye then closed it again, not even moving when a tall narrow man appeared from behind a faded red curtain and stepped up to the small desk in an alcove. A computer monitor stood next to a stand of rack cards advertising the hotel. A pen on a ball chain anchored to the wood countertop dangled over the edge of the counter.

"Good afternoon," he said, without smiling. "May I help you?"

Neil explained that we were looking for an individual and showed him the drawing. The man pulled his wire-framed glasses down his nose and peered over them at the picture, his lips forming a tight circle as though drawn taut by a drawstring.

"Yes, I've seen him." He handed the paper back to Neil.

I stepped forward and leaned toward the man, smiling sweetly. "Can you tell us his name? He must have stayed at your lovely hotel."

"Our guest information is confidential, madam," he replied, his mouth growing tighter and nostrils twitching. Evidently, I needed to crank up the charm or try another tactic.

"You don't understand," I said, placing my fingertips on his arm. "This man is responsible for ruining my wedding. I was supposed to get married yesterday but," I sniffed and blinked rapidly, hoping that a tear would materialize, "something terrible has happened to my husband-to-be."

"I'm afraid I can't help you." He lifted my wrist between a

thumb and finger and dropped it on the polished counter. "I'm not at liberty to divulge personal information regarding our guests."

Well, that didn't work either, I thought. However, I wasn't about to give up yet. I turned sad eyes toward Neil. "Now what will we do?" I whimpered. "Maybe we'll never find him."

Neil placed an arm around my shoulders. "There, there, honey. We'll just have to think of something else. Come on." He took one long step backward and landed squarely on the dog's hind foot. The animal erupted from his dormant state with a yowl, leaping into the air with ear-spiting yelps.

The man sprinted from behind the counter and hollered, "Look what you've done, you oaf!" He ran to the dog and gathered it in his arms. Neil spun me around the counter and jerked his head toward the computer. While Neil made a fuss over the dog, gushing apologies and purposely making things worse by clumsily knocking the man over, I ran my finger down the guest list displayed on the screen. Fortunately, the program also listed the addresses. One from France, two from Germany, and one from, bingo! Peru. I read the name, silently sounding it out then stepped from behind the counter.

"I'm so sorry about your dog. We'll be going now." I gave Neil's sleeve a tug. We slipped past the glaring hotelier and closed the door behind us.

"So? What did you find out?"

"There was only one guest from South America," I told him as we headed down the sidewalk. "A Hector Huanaco, from Cusco, Peru. Who knows whether that's his real name or not?"

"Well, he'd have to produce a passport at check-in, no doubt," Neil speculated, "but you're right. Those can be faked."

"He checked out this morning. That means he might still be around."

A motorcycle buzzed past, hugging the curve of the street. For some reason, the sudden sound rattled me even more, setting my already agitated nerves on edge. "So, what do we do?"

Neil put a hand on my arm and stopped me. "We take this one step at a time. If Marco has been kidnapped that means there is something that someone wants and they think that Marco either has it or can help them get it."

"But Marco has nothing anyone could want." I stopped talking. I had known my fiancé only a few months and most of that time we had spent apart, communicating by phone or Internet. Even though we'd talked for hours at a time nearly every day, I had to admit that there was plenty that I still had to learn about him. "Has he?" I squinted at my uncle through the bright sunshine. "You've known him longer than I have, Neil. Is there something I should know about him?"

"Oh, Jill," Neil said, chuckling as he slid an arm across my shoulders. "That's not what I meant. I'm thinking about that little satchel of Cardy's that was meant for me. Is there something in it that someone could want? If they found out that Marco had it, getting it from him would not be easy."

"I see what you mean. He wouldn't let something of yours go without a fight, would he?"

"Then there has to be something about that case or whatever is in it that is mighty important to someone." We continued down the street, back toward where we had parked the car.

"Shouldn't we alert the police?" I asked, trying to make my voice sound calm.

"Maybe. But let's wait a little while. If the kidnappers don't find what they want in that jumble of old artifacts they may toss it *and* Marco out before we can do anything else."

"Or they might not." I grabbed Neil's coat sleeve. "Oh, Neil. What if they decide to kill him?"

He didn't answer that. Instead, he had turned his head away from me and was staring down the street, his forehead

31

furrowed. I followed his gaze and saw a black car parked at the curb opposite the direction of the traffic. A man in a dark jacket had opened the driver's door and the passenger door on the same side of the car. Presently, two other men emerged from the nearest building, a tall, narrow brick house with a flight of a half dozen stairs leading to the front door. No, there were three men, I realized — two shorter men and one tall one. The two short ones had the tall man between them and seemed to be rushing him toward the car. They glanced about, jerking their heads to look up and down the street. Dark glasses covered their eyes.

When the trio reached the car, one of the men ran to the opposite side and opened the passenger door while the second man, with a hand in his jacket pocket, pressed close to the tall man, clearly meaning for him to get in the car. Instead, the tall man stiffened and glanced around the quiet village street. Almost no one was around except for Neil and me and when his head swivelled in our direction I caught sight of him and for only an instant our eyes met. It was Marco.

I let out a choked squeak and began to run toward him. I made it almost to the corner when Neil caught up and yanked on my arm.

"Jill, stop right now!"

"It's Marco," I cried, tears streaking down my cheeks. I tried to wrench my arm from his grasp.

"I know, but wait," he commanded in a harsh whisper. "Those men are armed. If you go running up there they're likely to shoot you or kill Marco. We can do him more good if they don't know we saw anything."

By this time they had managed somehow to fold Marco's long-legged body into the black Mercedes. The doors slammed shut and the glossy vehicle roared away from the curb, tires squealing as it rounded the curve near where we stood. Through the windows I could make out four heads and as the car sped past the one in the middle of the back seat turned and looked out the back window at me. His eyes held mine until the sunlight reflecting across the car window obliterated him from view.

Frantic, I wrenched myself from Neil's grip and ran after the disappearing car. As it vanished around a curve in the road, I drew to a stop, panting. Neil caught up with me and folded me into a firm embrace. "They have Marco," I cried into his shoulder. "They got away."

"I know, honey. But we'll get him back, you'll see. Marco won't stand for much and he's as smart as a fox. Come on. Let's go back to the manor now. There isn't anything we can do here right now and I've got the license plate memorized."

We had been at Wardley Hall not ten minutes and had just been ushered into the sitting room by Cardy when the telephone jangled in the front foyer. I could hear Burton's muffled voice answer it before he appeared in the doorway. "It's for you, sir," he said to his employer. "I think you had better take this call."

Cardy hoisted himself from his worn armchair with a groan. "What is it this time?" he grumbled, hitching up his pants as he tramped across the floor and disappeared into the entry hall. Neil glanced at me then rose to follow him. Puzzled, I followed, too.

Cardy stood next to the hall table with one hand gripping the telephone receiver. His face had turned the colour of newsprint.

"I see," he said. "I'm sure I have no idea what you're talking about. I've never heard of such a thing." A pause. "My good man, if you'll let me just speak with him for..." He ran a hand across his forehead and turned to Neil. "That's impossible! Preposterous!" He was shouting now and he motioned for Neil to come closer. "I'm going to put someone on who might know what you're talking about. Just hold on, hold on, I say..." He snatched the receiver away from his face and glared at it. "He's hung up on me, the miserable wretch." With tight lips he slammed the telephone down on its cradle.

"What is it? What's happened?" I had to know.

Cardy drew in a long breath and let it out slowly before answering. His eyes snapped from mine to Neil's and back again. "They're demanding ransom for Marco's life," he said.

My hands flew to my face as I gasped. "What do they want? Are they after money? How much?"

"No, not money."

"What then?" Neil demanded. I could see the cords in his neck, taut with tension. "What is it these thugs want?"

Lord Wardley sighed and his brow puckered in a deep frown. Then seemed to steel himself. "They want something called the glass dolphin."

CHAPTER SIX

The room had taken on a chill yet I felt loath to crawl between the damp sheets to try to sleep. I picked up the iron poker and jabbed at a crumbling log in the dying fire. Pulling the woollen blanket closer around my shoulders, I tucked my feet under me, my knees drawn up into the overstuffed chair. I could hardly have taken up a smaller space. Snuggling deeper, I leaned my head against the chair's arm and closed my eyes. I could still see Marco's face as the car sped past where Neil and I stood on the sidewalk. *What were his eyes saying?*

My eyelids drifted closed and I had just slid into that twilight of sleep when a knock on the wood-panelled door startled me back to wakefulness.

"Come in," I called, clearing my throat and pushing my hair away from my face.

"You can't seriously tell me that you intend to spend the night in that chair," Neil said, smiling down at me. "You'll wake up with a kink in your neck. Besides, I've brought you something." He held out a bulging hot water bottle wrapped in a plaid flannel jacket. In his other hand he had a small tray with two steaming mugs of hot chocolate. "This English weather," he said, setting the tray on the hearth and slipping the hot water bottle between the sheets on the bed, "could freeze even the most stalwart polar bear. They haven't clued in to forced-air heating here."

"Mm-hmm," I replied. "And it's only September. How do they survive January?"

Neil pulled a matching chair closer to mine and poked the fire, tossing another log in and leaning back to sip his drink. He

35

reached over and patted my hand. "Tomorrow is another day," he said.

That afternoon, after the kidnappers had called with their demands, Cardy, Neil and I had simply stood and stared at each other for a good minute or more. Stunned.

I broke the silence. "What are they talking about? Do you know what the 'glass dolphin' is?

"I'm sorry, my dear," he replied. "I haven't the foggiest. It must have something to do with that case of stuff that belonged to Great Aunt Cecilia. That's the only thing I can think of."

"How can we give them something we know nothing about?" I cried.

Just then, Burton stepped forward. "I believe a cup of tea would be in order," he pronounced. "If you would all care to assemble in the drawing room, I shall bring it in presently."

It sounded like a good idea to me, if only so I could sit down. I think better sitting down. Neil wandered over to the French doors and stood looking out while I lowered myself into a high-backed, drawing room chair. Cardy removed an aged Yorkshire terrier from a worn armchair and plunked himself into it instead. Burton appeared a few minutes later pushing a teacart loaded with china cups and more shortbread cookies. A tea cozy decorated like a thatched cottage covered the pot. He poured the tea as Lord Wardley relayed to the rest of us the details of the telephone call in which the abductors demanded that we hand over the glass dolphin in exchange for Marco's freedom.

"The fellow spoke so quickly that I hardly had time to think," Cardy explained. "And he had some kind of accent, Italian or Spanish or something." He gave a dismissive wave of his hand.

I leaned forward. "But what did he say?"

"He said that if we wanted to see your Mr. Jimenez again we were to produce this glass dolphin. We're to meet him at Hyde

Park in London. There's a pavilion in the Italian Gardens at the end of the Serpentine and he insisted that we produce this object and hand it over to him there at precisely three o'clock tomorrow."

I gasped. "But that gives us barely twenty-four hours! And we don't even know what they want. Maybe it's time we called in the police."

"That's the other thing," Cardy said. "They said 'no police'."

"There were three men in that car, besides Marco," Neil mused, turning from the window and breaking into my tumultuous thoughts. He ignored the comment about the police. "If I were guessing, which I am, I'd say they're South American. Let's assume that's the case. We also know that at least one Peruvian stayed at that hotel in the village last night."

"Yes," Cardy said, "and we know that the artifacts, if you can call them that, were from Aunt Cecilia's Peruvian explorations. Assuming that there is a connection, the glass dolphin must be somehow related to all this. I wonder what makes it so valuable that those rogues would risk kidnapping."

"The news of Auntie Cecilia's belongings had to have been announced somewhere," I reasoned out loud. "They had to have found out about them by some means. You said that the list of auction articles had been printed in the local paper, right?"

Cardy nodded. "There's no telling where else it went, though. Attic cleanings are immensely popular with the antiquing crowd. They're always hoping for the find of a lifetime from some aristocrat's mouldy trunk. That listing could easily have gone out to all the trade papers and to Internet sites as well. Literally anyone in the world could have seen it."

I groaned. "If someone thinks there is a link between your aunt's explorations and this glass dolphin, there's no telling who might come out of the woodwork, or why."

"No, it's simpler than that," Neil stated. "Whoever wants

this artifact had prior knowledge. They had to have already been looking for it; otherwise, why would they have turned up so quickly to nab Aunt Cecilia's things?" He snapped his fingers and turned to Cardy. "You wouldn't by any chance have seen someone at the auction who might fit into this picture, would you?"

Cardy ran a finger over his chin and stared at a worn patch in the carpet. "As I recall, there were only seventy or eighty people there, mostly dealers and a few curious locals. Only one other buyer even bid on Aunt Cecilia's things, which pushed up the price for me, unfortunately."

"Who was that buyer?" Neil wanted to know.

"No idea. He seemed like one of those second hand dealers who like to call themselves antiques experts. Scruffy character, really. When the price went up a bit he dropped out."

"There may be no connection but we should check him out and see if he knows something we don't," I suggested. "It's possible he was working for someone else."

"I can call the house where the auction took place," Cardy offered. "I know the owner. Not well, mind you, but well enough to inquire." He pushed himself to his feet and headed back out to the foyer to use the telephone. The Yorkshire terrier looked up from its place on the carpet then promptly leapt back into the vacated chair and curled into a tight circle.

"There is something bothering me," I said, turning toward Neil.

"What's that?"

"Why would the kidnappers wait until today to make their move; to phone about the ransom? If it was only this glass dolphin they wanted, and it had something to do with Lord Wardley's great-great-aunt, they could have made their move yesterday, before we arrived."

"Maybe they're trying to get at me."

I looked at Neil sharply. "Why? Is there something I should

know that you're not telling me?"

"I've never heard of the glass dolphin, Jill, but I have spent time at archaeological sites in the Andes – Peru mostly. There are still many sites that have never been excavated. We know they're there but for various reasons, want of money mostly, we've been unable to go in. The Peruvian government has become touchy about foreign archaeologists marching into their country and digging up their past. I have recently obtained permission to trek into the mountains farther than most expeditions have in years. There is a site that I heard rumours of ten years ago but have been keeping quiet about, for obvious reasons."

"Such as?"

"Looters are the biggest threat. Word can travel pretty fast when a find with burial remains or hidden tombs is discovered and the minute your back is turned they can be in there and have the place stripped of valuables before you can document any of it. You can't hire guards to stay at a dig for months on end, especially if it's in a remote location. They won't stay and you can't feed them. They have families they want to see, so they drift off and leave the site unattended. Or, they loot it themselves and sell the goods to their own connections. There is no shortage of opportunity to fence antiquities and no lack of black market buyers."

"How do you handle that?"

"Maximum preparation, then get in, do the work and get out. There are plenty of hoops to jump through to satisfy the government's antiquities departments, and there should be, but it means that preparation time can be lengthy. It's hard to keep secrets about everything."

"Are you telling me that you know something that they don't? That they may be using Marco to get to you?"

"It's possible. I still don't know where the glass dolphin fits but I have a couple ideas."

Before he could elaborate, Lord Wardley strode back into the room and displaced the Yorkie once again. "I've made a little headway," he announced. "Our Mr. Perkins had the foresight to insist that all attendees to the auction sign in and show identification. I had forgotten that. He's agreed to email me the list."

The remainder of the afternoon now seemed like a blur to my jet-lagged brain but what had emerged had at least blunted the edge of fear that clung to my every thought of Marco. Now Neil sipped his hot drink and stared into the dying fire and I pulled the woollen throw up around my shoulders again. Putting my cold feet on that hot water bottle in my bed was starting to appeal to me. *I wonder where Marco is sleeping tonight*, I thought drowsily.

A cinder crackled in the fire and broke with a sprinkle of sparks, throwing the room into deeper darkness.

"Well, my dear. I guess I'd better head to bed." Neil got up and took my mug, placing it on the tray with his own. "Pray for God to reveal a plan for us in a dream, will you?" He kissed the top of my head and went out, closing the door behind him.

CHAPTER SEVEN

Anthony Sims Antiques occupied a narrow piece of commercial space in a strip mall on the main street of a town called Prestwood, which thankfully, was only about a half-hour drive from Wardley Hall. A bell above the door tinkled when we entered and a lazy cat that had been sleeping in the window raised its head and glared at us before lapsing back into unconsciousness. The place was cluttered with dusty junk, most of which looked like garbage gleanings from a '60s back alley. Here and there something stood out as possibly having value, like a carved picture frame hanging crookedly on one wall and a tall dresser with unpolished brass fittings. A radio with a yappy, high-speed announcer played somewhere in the back.

"See anything you'd like?" I asked, giving Neil a sideways glance. "Your birthday is next month." I held out a pink Bakelite piggybank.

He sniffed as he picked up a book from a small, scratched end table and blew the dust off its cover. "This doesn't look like the kind of place that would be looking to sell Andean artifacts," he said.

"Perhaps our Mr. Sims didn't go to the auction for that." Before Neil could comment, I heard the rattle of a beaded curtain and a man appeared out of the gloom. His skin had the pasty pallor of someone who had been sick for a long time and his eyes were so pale a blue as to appear almost white. His shirt looked as though it had spent the night on the floor, with him in it.

"May I help you?" he inquired, giving us an obsequious smile.

41

Neil set the book down and approached him. "I have a particular interest in South American art, especially the Inca or other Andean cultures. Would you have anything like that?"

The man shifted his weight from one foot to the other. "South American," he repeated. "I have very little from that region, only a few baskets, not very old and, hmmm," he stopped and rubbed his hands together. "I've recently come upon some small figurines. I believe they are from Peru or Chile. Let me get them for you." He slipped between the strings of plastic beads and appeared a moment later with a small cardboard box. Removing the lid, he gently unwrapped the little figures from wads of tissue and laid them on a dusty velvet pad. There were three of them, all clay and coloured with faded designs. They didn't look particularly ancient to me.

"Do you have the provenance for these?" Neil asked, picking one up and turning it toward the light.

Sims backed up a step. "You'll find that they're very old, probably from around 300 A.D," he sniffed. I peered over Neil's shoulder to look at the pieces. A bird figure with a hole in its head sat in Neil's palm and the short figure of a man in a fancy headdress lay on the velvet pad. The other piece looked like a small goat or a deer, I couldn't tell which.

"So you don't know the origin?" Neil said, putting the piece down.

"I'm sorry sir, but pieces like these are difficult to trace."

"Do you have anything in glass?"

"Glass? No, I don't think those South American cultures used glass. I've never heard of that."

"I understand that there was an auction that took place recently, about a half hour drive from here. You didn't happen to pick anything up there, did you? I heard that there were some South American pieces included but wasn't able to attend myself," Neil eyed the man closely.

"You mean the Perkins sale. Yes, I was there and bid on a

box of trinkets that was once owned by some woman who had travelled in Peru or Bolivia but there was nothing of much interest in it aside from a pair of old field glasses. One other person bid up the price so I let it go. You can't make any money on those things if the buying price gets too high, you know."

"True, true," Neil replied, giving the man a tight smile. "Well, thank-you anyway." We turned to go when the man stopped us.

"I have something else that your wife might like," he said, reaching into the cabinet by his knees. Neil and I exchanged a glance but didn't correct him. He drew out a small wooden box the size of a cigar box and opened it to reveal a pale blue cameo necklace on a tarnished silver chain. "This lovely piece is from 16th century Italy. Notice the delicate detail, madam."

"It is lovely," I said, "but not what we're looking for. Thank-you anyway."

Back in the car a few minutes later, Neil pulled out onto the road leading back to Wardley Hall.

"That was a dead-end," I said, sighing.

"So it seems."

There was something about Anthony Sims that made me feel that he was not a man given to telling the truth. By now it was nearing four o'clock and I realized by the growl of my stomach that we hadn't eaten anything since breakfast. When I mentioned it to Neil, he agreed to stop at the first restaurant or pub we found. We came upon one only a mile down the road and pulled in. The place was nearly deserted so we took a table in the corner and ordered sandwiches and cold drinks.

"We've got to figure out how we're going to deal with these kidnappers tomorrow," Neil said, sipping on a sugary drink. He made a face and went on. "We can't show up with nothing in hand or Marco's going to be in trouble."

I shuddered. "But we can't give them something we don't

have. If we had an inkling what the glass dolphin was, that would help."

"Let's pray about it. Your turn."

"Lord," I said, taking Neil's hand, "we need your guidance and direction here. Please tell us what to do, whether we should go to the police or not and what to do about this artifact. Keep Marco safe, wherever he is. And bless this food, in the name of Jesus. Amen. I think maybe we should talk to the police, Neil."

Neil set his sandwich down and sighed. "I can see why you'd want to," he said, "but I have a pretty good reason for not involving them just yet."

"What?" His serious expression unnerved me.

"Remember what we have been doing at the complex in Israel? The testing and the breakthroughs we've made?" I nodded. "Well, I believe that this find I've made in Peru may link to some of that. I'm not sure how yet but I think there is a scientific connection and I can't afford to have that jeopardized. If we bring in the police, the media won't be far behind. When they get a whiff of story about an archaeological find in the Andes, the next thing you know, every newspaper in the world is trumpeting that a lost city has been discovered in the jungle. Before we know it the place will be crawling with teams looking to get their piece of the pie, not to mention looters, charlatans, black marketeers and those infernal new age loons wanting to worship the sun or something." He shook his head and looked at me. "I know that Marco's life may be in some danger but there are bigger things at stake. I have to step very carefully right now."

"Oh." I took a bite of my chicken salad sandwich.

"I've been in touch with Bobby."

"Really? That's fantastic. Is he coming to help?"

"He should be here tonight." Bobby Buckingham, built like a line-backer and with a heart of pure marshmallow, ran an international security company out of an office in Galveston,

Texas. Neil had consulted with him or called in his team before when things had become dicey. "That's not all," Neil continued. "Quentin McSweeney is already working on things on that side of the pond."

"The Quentin McSweeney that I know?" I asked in disbelief. Neil's friend, Caribbean treasure hunter and Ernest Hemingway look-alike had come through for both Neil and me more than once during our last expedition while rounding up the Mayan stones.

"He's getting bored," Neil said with a grin. "He was more than happy to have something crazy to do."

I took another bite of my sandwich then thought of something. "Mmph." I banged on Neil's arm as I swallowed my mouthful. "Oh, my goodness! How could I have forgotten to tell you this? Last night I found something that might help us. I was getting ready for bed and knocked over my suitcase. When the handle hit the wall panel, I thought it sounded funny – the panel, not my suitcase. I tapped around on the other panels and sure enough, one of them sounded different, sort of hollow, so I got out my flashlight and felt around the edge. The panel popped open when I pressed on a hidden latch and inside there was an old wooden box. I found...you won't believe this!"

"Yes."

"Cecilia Wardley's exploration notes. It's an old leather diary with a flap and thongs to hold it closed. It's bulging with details of her travels. I read it for a while until I got so tired I couldn't see straight and was freezing from sitting on the floor. I only just thought of this but maybe she makes reference to this glass dolphin or gives us some kind of hint. If not, there might be something in there that would appease the kidnappers enough to release Marco."

Neil stared at me. "And you forgot to mention this?"

I shrugged. "I was pre-occupied with Marco. Remember, I was supposed to marry him the day before yesterday."

"Look, I'm sorry. But this could be just the breakthrough we need. Grab the rest of your sandwich and let's get out of here."

CHAPTER EIGHT

"I'll be down in a minute," I said, dropping my bag by the front door of Wardley Hall and dashing past a blinking Burton. I took the long, curving staircase two risers at a time and ran down the hall to my room. Pulling Cecilia Wardley's worn book of field notes out of my suitcase where I had tossed it the night we'd arrived, I leaped back down the stairs, certain I looked like an ibex on a mountain slope. Okay, maybe not quite but I wasted no time. Neil and Cardy stood waiting in the lofty-ceilinged drawing room where the afternoon sunlight streamed through the tall windows. Cardy placed a small table next to a faded-red, silk-covered settee and pulled up a chair on one side.

"Let's take a look at that," he said as Neil and I slid onto the settee and I unlaced the leather thongs of the journal. The leather binding crackled as I spread the front cover back and showed the inscription to Lord Wardley. "It looks like the real thing," he said, grinning like a boy in a candy store with a handful of change.

As we slowly turned the dry, old pages, we perused the notes that Cecilia Wardley had made – paragraphs in tiny, cramped script written with an inked pen or quill and punctuated with elegant drawings of plant life, birds, mountain scenes and even the faces of the native peoples she encountered.

"She was a pretty good artist," I observed.

"You'd know," Neil answered. In my real life, the one where I wasn't chasing around the world doing something crazy for Neil, I had a solo business as a professional artist. My specialty was portraiture but I made a good living selling my watercolours and oil paintings through a local gallery.

We took turns reading passages aloud, often resorting to the use of a large magnifying glass that Cardy had produced from the drawer of a nearby table. The detailed text told of daily adventures from the procurement of food by the native guides to the reptilian dangers of using the makeshift latrine at night. Every several pages, Miss Wardley included a map of the area where she travelled or stayed. Her goal did not seem to be the discovery of ancient ruins so much as simply exploration of the unknown regions of the Andes and the eastern slopes leading down to the Amazon basin.

Cecilia Wardley's expeditions had taken place decades before Hiram Bingham had stumbled across Machu Picchu. She had travelled alone, hiring guides and teams as needed. At one point her expedition included more than eighty people, mostly locals who knew the Inca roads and passages over, around and sometimes even through the mountains. We turned the pages one by one, scanning for any reference to glass or dolphins or artifacts of any kinds. Cecilia had sketched the crafts produced by the people who lived where she stayed. Her main station for sourcing help and supplies seemed to be Cusco but she spent long periods of time in remote villages until she became well known by the inhabitants, mentioning different individuals by name.

"This is interesting," Neil commented after we had perused about half of the volume. "She talks about this tribe taking a pilgrimage to the sea. Look at this." He pointed at a passage with his finger. "The tribe had some ancient tradition of trekking over the mountains and going all the way to the ocean."

"It says they only did this once a generation in order to renew the spiritual power of their current leader." I ran my own finger down the page and flipped over to the next one. "Oh, my goodness! Here it is." Neil and Cardy leaned in closer. "She writes, 'they took with them the glass dolphin mounted on a ceremonial platform carried by four men. At first the purpose of transporting this depiction of a fish was unknown to me but as I had spent considerable time with these indigenous people I had come to recognize some of their language. They seemed to believe that the glass figure held spiritual power that was bestowed on the tribe's chief. When the old chief died, the new one was required to transport the glass dolphin back to the sea from whence it had come in order to renew its power for the duration of the reign of the new monarch. The processional exhibited a great deal of pomp and circumstance, including fancy dress costumes replete with vibrantly coloured feathers and much gold. Gold or silver breast-plating and tall, ornate headdresses decorated all but the smallest children.'"

"Well, I'll be!" Cardy leaned back in his chair and blinked at me over his glasses. "How extraordinary!"

"What else does it say?" Neil demanded. "Any indication of what happened to the glass dolphin?"

"Let me see…" I skimmed the text. "This trek took weeks. She tagged along with the tribe out of curiosity. Apparently, they allowed this, as she had been with them long enough that they had come to accept her. She says that when they finally reached the sea," I flipped another page, "they held a big ceremony Hmm, it seemed to take her a while to figure out the significance of this glass dolphin and the whole ceremonial rigmarole. It turned out that the dolphin had been part of the tribe for what she estimates might have been several hundred years or perhaps even a few thousand. She isn't clear about that. She finally…" I stopped talking and had to use the magnifying glass to make out the tiny scrawl. I was about to go on when a tap sounded on the drawing room door and Burton entered.

"Yes, what is it?" Lord Wardley demanded, clearly impatient to find out what came next in the diary.

"There is a gentleman here to see Dr. Bryant and Mrs. Moss,

sir. He says his name is Bobby Buckingham."

Bobby's brown face, split by a wide grin, appeared over Burton's shoulder. Neil leaped to his feet and headed for the door. I dropped the diary on the small table and followed him. Neil and Bobby had already pounded each other on their backs in a warm hug by the time I got there and flung my arms around Bobby's neck. He spun me around before setting me down on my feet again.

"Forgive me, ma'am," he said, his brown skin taking on a flushed tone. "It's just nice to see you again."

"Oh, Bobby," I cried. "It's great to see you, too. I was so upset when you told me you couldn't come to the wedding..." I stopped myself.

"Don't you worry, ma'am," he said, taking my shoulders and looking me in the eyes. "We're going to find Marco."

I gave him a weak smile and squeezed his arm. "I'm sure we will now that you're on the case. But how on earth did you get here so fast?"

Neil interjected with introductions then led us all to sit again. "I was in Barcelona working on another case," Bobby explained, "when I got the call from Neil. I had to wrap up a few things before I could leave or I'd have been here earlier."

"Bobby, how is your arm, where you were shot last spring?" While acting as my bodyguard in Mexico that May, Bobby had been shot by a Mexican Mafioso intent on getting his hands on Neil's Mayan find. We had managed to elude them with God's help but Bobby spent several pain-filled hours riding across the Yucatan in a rust-bucket of a car we'd procured from an old army buddy of his. I finally deposited him in the hospital in Merida.

"It's all healed up," he replied, rolling up his sleeve to show me where a faint line of scar tissue puckered his muscled flesh. I was relieved to see that the damage had been slight and told him so. Still, I couldn't help remembering the panic and desperation I had experienced when the bullet had shattered the windshield and ripped through Bobby's upper arm.

"So tell me, what have y'all got so far on Marco's situation?"

"We've discovered a diary, field notes actually," Neil explained, "written by Lord Wardley's great-great-aunt, a Miss Cecilia Wardley. She was something of an explorer in the Andes and Amazon around the mid-1800s. We're short on clues about this artifact that the kidnappers have demanded and we're hoping that the diary will enlighten us." Turning to me, he said, "Why don't you carry on reading from where you left off."

I picked the book up again and leafed through the fragile pages. "Let me see. She talks at length about the costumes and the preparations leading up to this expedition across the mountains, hmm, hmmm. Oh, here it is," I grabbed Neil's sleeve and gave it a tug. "She writes: 'The glass dolphin had originally been created by lightening striking the sand at the beach. According to the tribal legends, a priestly ancestor had been in attendance during a violent storm and when the lightning struck, the priest miraculously withstood the blast and emerged unscathed from the shock. What remained, melted by the lightening and subsequently hardened by the cold rain was a piece of glass that resembled the shape of a dolphin leaping from the sea.' She goes on to say that the people concluded this was a sign from the gods that this priest had otherworldly powers and was destined to be their mighty spiritual leader."

"Let me see that for a minute," Neil said, carefully taking the diary from my hands. On the open page in front of us, Cecilia Wardley had drawn a meticulously detailed sketch of the glass dolphin figure. The shape of the dolphin, complete with a jagged blade of glass resembling a dorsal fin, rose from a frothy clump of glass and sand. Cecilia had noted the features, including the narrowed snout and crude representations of what might be construed as pectoral fins. The tail flukes dissolved into the clumps of dull glass at the base.

"Remarkable." Neil passed the book to Bobby who studied it for a moment before handing it on to Cardy. When it came back to me, I picked up the magnifying glass once more and examined it more closely.

"Do you see what I see?" I asked turning to the others. Within the confines of the dolphin's jagged body we could clearly see the shape of a perfect six-sided crystal.

CHAPTER NINE

As a child, I was the quiet one, the one who never gave my parents any trouble – well, almost never. The thinker. I always needed time, preferably alone, to think things through before deciding what to do. Now, as I peeled off my jacket and deposited it on a coat stand in Wardley Hall's grand foyer, I had done that. Outside, the evening sun lingered, throwing lavender rays across diaphanous bands of cloud as the birds chirruped in the trees, fluffing their feathers against the cool of the coming night.

The moment we realized that the glass dolphin held a strange six-sided crystal in it, that is, if Cecilia's notes were to be believed, a hush came over us as we glanced at each other and back at the drawing. Without anyone saying a word, we knew that this would be no ordinary archaeological find, like a shard of pottery or a dirt-crusted axe-head. Neil's work with ancient technologies and their present applications had become legendary, if you happened to travel in the right circles. I remembered the impact that the Mayan ring of stones featuring the three ancient and unrelated languages – Mayan, Olmec and Hebrew – had produced. Accessing the technology revealed by the stones had aided in the development of devices and systems that defied gravity, among other things too complex for most people to begin to grasp. The mere fact that some person or group was desperate enough to kidnap someone in order to get their hands on the glass dolphin indicated to us that there was more to this find than met the eye.

With three men in the room, all spouting ideas and arguing about the artifact, what it meant and what kind of strategy to employ before meeting the kidnappers the next day, my head began to ache. I could feel the tension arc across my shoulders and creep up the back of my neck. These three seemed to have forgotten that the life of my husband-to-be was at stake, that I had just lost him, on my wedding day no less, as their shouting blasted my ears.

Finally, I could stand no more. Excusing myself, I grabbed my jacket and headed out into the fading day. The estate, located far from the nearest neighbours, lay quiet and serene. Burton and Mrs. B. had disappeared, much to my relief, and the man who groomed the stables and did the fieldwork seemed to have gone home as well. Two of the dogs, a friendly old golden retriever and the diminutive Yorkshire terrier, chose to accompany me but the retriever soon wandered back to the house to lie down on the warmed stone of the back terrace. The Yorkie grew tired and sat down on a gravel path along a row of privet and whined so pitifully that I went back, picked the animal up and carried her for the rest of my walk. Somehow, holding that warm little body close to mine comforted and calmed me as I strolled around the grounds.

Because the past few days had been a mad rush to prepare everything for the wedding, followed by the crushing shock and disappointment of Marco's disappearance, then a frantic trip across the ocean ending here in the English countryside, there had been almost no time when I could be alone and awake enough to think straight. I had hardly prayed at all. Or so it seemed, even though I was in the habit of praying on something at a subconscious level almost continuously. More precisely, I had hardly had a moment of stillness in which to listen to the voice of the Lord.

So, while I walked, I talked a little but mostly I listened. Even though my apprehension about what tomorrow would bring never left – about how things would turn out with the kidnappers – a sense of peace settled over my troubled mind, peace that, under the circumstances, shouldn't have been there. It seeped into my jumbled thoughts and calmed them all down. By the time I returned to the house, I felt like I had tapped into my source of strength again, because indeed I had. But I also had a distinct sense of warning – but about what, I didn't know.

"Whatever we do," I heard Neil say as I stepped back into the drawing room where the three men sat on the edges of their chairs, "we can't let that glass dolphin fall into anyone else's hands. There is something more than meets the eye about that artifact. We have to get to it first."

"Where do you think it is?" I asked. Three heads twisted around to where I stood.

Neil shrugged. "There's no telling, really. It could be anywhere But if these guys who have Marco think it still exists, then it probably does. Chances are it's still in Peru but if it was looted from its original location and sold through the antiquities black market, it could be anywhere in the world."

"And we're supposed to find it and hand it over to the kidnappers tomorrow?" I sat down next to Neil on the small sofa. "We don't have it and we don't have any idea where it is. All we know is that it existed in 1837 when Cecilia Wardley documented its existence and by three o'clock tomorrow we're supposed to hand it over. We all know that's impossible, so what are we going to do to get Marco back? Have you guys come up with a plan?" I glanced at Bobby and Cardy then back to Neil.

"We've been working on some ideas," Bobby answered. "Obviously, we can't hand over the artifact so we'll have to do some bargaining."

"What have we got that they could possibly want?" I turned to Lord Wardley. Did he have something belonging to Cecilia Wardley that would suffice? He shook his head. "We can't give them the diary if we're ever going to find the glass dolphin," I continued. "I know the kind of work you're doing in Israel, Neil

– you and Dr. Silverman and Dr. Ben Shalev. I read a bit of that diary last night, as it happens. There's a lot in there."

Neil sat with his elbows on his knees and stared down at the floor between his feet. Bobby leaned his head back in his chair and looked intently up at the ceiling.

"It might be our only way to get Marco back," Bobby said softly. "They might go for it."

"What you mean is that you're putting me in the middle of this. Am I the one who has to decide between saving the man I love and possibly upsetting the balance of power in the world?" My voice was rising but I didn't care. "If this diary and the glass dolphin mean what you're implying, how can I do that?" I stood up and paced around behind the sofa where Neil still sat. My fingertips swiped at the tears running down my cheeks. "How can any of you ask that of me?"

Neil turned in his seat and reached for my hand. He didn't look at me. "There is one other alternative," he said. With his other hand he plucked at a thread in the worn sofa's seat.

"What? What else could we give them in exchange for Marco?"

He took a deep breath and looked into my eyes. "Me."

CHAPTER TEN

The Italian Garden in Hyde Park is situated near Lancaster Gate, the north entrance to the park. In the glaring afternoon sun, even its fountains and flower plantings seemed to droop sullenly in the heat and humidity. The water in the geometrical ponds bloomed with algae, coating the brackish water in a layer of bubbling green slime. Tired mothers packed up their babies' and toddlers' belongings, to take their whining offspring home for afternoon naps before tea. I took a seat on a bench along the west side of the pond nearest the pavilion, next to an elderly man in a fedora who muttered aloud while he read the financial pages of a folded newspaper.

Bobby sat opposite me on the far side of the two pools and the centre walkway. At the north end of the set of four classically-designed pools stood a pillared, white marble pavilion crowned by an ornate cupola festooned with a flock of pigeons. Not a breath of breeze disturbed the sticky air. I pulled a spring clip from my tote bag and twisted my hair up high on my head then mopped my neck with a tissue.

The previous night we had stayed up late discussing plans for meeting with the kidnappers. Another telephone call had informed us that Cardy was to come alone and bring the glass dolphin with him. The exchange of the artifact for Marco would take place in front of the pavilion exactly at three o'clock and in full view of anyone who happened to wander by or be lounging in the sun at that time.

"They can't seriously expect you just to show up alone and hand over a priceless artifact in broad daylight," I fumed, tossing strips of bacon onto my plate that morning. "They have to know that I will be there, don't they?"

"Not necessarily," Neil reasoned, irritatingly calm under the circumstances. Lord Wardley's kitchen had put on another copious breakfast, far too much food for himself, Neil, Bobby and me to eat. The breakfast room faced east and sunlight streamed through the tall windows and splashed glaring patches of brightness onto the polished wood floor. "Though it doesn't seem likely, it is possible that these people didn't know that Marco was on his way to be married. There is also a chance that they don't know me. If they haven't done their homework and simply heard about the auction and decided to act, they may not even know either of us exists."

"That would be all the better," Bobby remarked. "It means that you can be there without even being noticed."

"I hadn't thought of that," I said, taking my plate and sliding into a chair next to Neil. "Regardless, even if I have to come in disguise, I'm coming. There is no way that I'm going to be left here languishing in the country while you go off alone."

Neil chuckled. "It's not like I haven't gone 'off alone' before, Jill. But, be that as it may, I believe that our plan should proceed like this: You and Bobby will take up positions near the pavilion and Cardy will drive the car. He knows the city."

"I have a better idea," Cardy interjected. "I do believe that traffic is not allowed in that area of the park except for service vehicles. As it happens, I have a nephew who owns a plumbing company and would be a good man to have on the job. He can drive instead." After discussing the ramifications of calling another person in and possibly risking his life, we agreed that Cardy could put a call in to his nephew and see if he would be willing to help. Kevin Tarnquist arrived half an hour later, explaining that he'd been installing a toilet not far away and just had time to "pop round and see what the excitement was all about."

"Call me Kev," he announced as he pushed past the perpetually-composed Burton and strode into the morning room, hand extended. Kev had the build of a pit bull on steroids and looked like he'd be an easy match for Bobby any day. In contrast to Bobby's mahogany brown, Kev had the pink-white skin of an Englishman who didn't dare go out in the noonday sun. His ashy-blond hair stood up in a crew cut and a tattoo depicting a dragon coiled around his neck.

While waiting for him to show up, Cardy had explained that Kev was one of his few remaining relatives and had been particularly congenial to his uncle since discovering that he'd been named in Cardy's will. He had agreed that his afternoon appointments could wait until tomorrow and had jumped at the chance for a little excitement and adventure.

Neil and Bobby rose to shake his hand as introductions were made. I did too, once I'd washed down a mouthful of dry toast with a slurp of milky tea. My own hand disappeared in Kev's catcher's-glove hand as he pumped my arm and grinned.

"I've had breakfast already this morning but that was hours ago," he said to his uncle as he eyed the laden sideboard.

"Help yourself, dear boy," Cardy offered, "then come and sit down. We have a difficult situation to untangle. Perhaps you can offer your penny's worth."

Cecilia Wardley's diary had included the approximate dimensions of the glass dolphin and though we had no idea whether the kidnappers knew its size and shape, we decided to substitute something similar for it in the hopes that they'd be fooled long enough for us to snatch Marco and make a run for it. Mrs. B. had rounded up a box about eighteen inches tall and a foot square and Cardy offered a heavy glass vase that vaguely resembled a swan and fit easily into the box. We wrapped the thing in bubble wrap and then with a towel so if the kidnappers wanted to look before they made the trade it would take them a few minutes to find out that it wasn't a dolphin after all.

The plan required Neil, accompanied by Bobby and me, to arrive first and leave his car along the nearest road that allowed parking. There was no telling how far we might have to walk because it all depended on how busy the park might be on a weekday afternoon. Neil was to pose as a tourist taking photographs. He always carried a camera when he travelled so he would hang his digital SLR around his neck and wander around the grounds gawking at the sights. Cardy even managed to unearth a print shirt and a fisherman's hat to complete the day-tripper costume. While he feigned curiosity and snapped photos of the park's sights, he would actually be watching for the arrival of the kidnappers and recording every moment of the action that he could convincingly pull off. We needed to learn as much information as possible about the kidnappers.

As for Bobby, there was no way he could be inconspicuous as his size alone made him stand out so we agreed that he would get as near to the action as he could while still trying to maintain the look of disinterest.

My role would be similar except I would appear to be a secretary on a break from the office. I already had the tote bag and with a simple skirt and blouse and a pair of flat shoes, I looked credible enough. My face would be disguised behind a pair of large, black sunglasses, which I also happened to have in my tote. Red lipstick completed the look.

Cardy would ride with Kev, whose job was to convince the gatekeepers at the park, should they encounter any, that they were there to repair the waterworks. Fortunately, he knew all the right phrases and terms to use and just enough obscure ones to go over the average layperson's head. They would manoeuvre his plumber's van as close to the pavilion as possible and park at the side of the narrow road designated for foot traffic only. The proximity to the pavilion offered a quick getaway vehicle should it be necessary.

Cardy would appear at the appointed time in front of the

pavilion, alone, and would not hand over the box until the kidnappers let Marco go. The kidnappers had called again in the morning with renewed threats and warned that no one was to be armed.

"I'm not going anywhere without my gun," Bobby proclaimed. As a security man, he considered his weapons part of his clothing. I didn't even want to know how he had brought his weapon into this nation where private gun ownership was illegal but presumably, as the owner of an international security firm, he'd already hopped through all the appropriate hoops.

Kev informed us that he too, would be armed. "I've got some pretty wicked tools in my van. Nobody'll ask why a plumber 'as spanners 'anging from 'is belt, now will they? Plumbing is a dangerous business," he added with a sly grin.

"I'm handy with a short length of lead pipe myself, when called upon," Neil said, grinning. "But let's hope it doesn't come to that."

Over the dregs of breakfast we attempted to envision every possible scenario and anything that could go wrong. The kidnappers had chosen to meet in a public place in the middle of the day so they must be feeling confident that detection or recognition wasn't going to be a problem for them. Why not?

We had seen three men take Marco away in the car. Were there more? Were they from Peru, as we suspected, or were there others involved? At the rate Neil ran through names of possible perpetrators, it seemed like he had a mental database jam-packed with names of unscrupulous operators and competing archaeologists, any of whom might be poised to snatch, from under his very nose, the next tasty morsel of history that he uncovered.

Did they want the glass dolphin for its value as an antiquity or was there some other motive? Knowing what Cecilia Wardley had revealed in her diary made me wonder just how many others knew of the legend besides us.

The other question that kept darting through my mind was: If we didn't hand over the glass dolphin, would they follow through with their threat to kill Marco?

No, no, no, the voice in my head replied. We couldn't let that happen. I refused to entertain that thought because it opened the door to fear. If I allowed that to happen I could end up so afraid that I wouldn't be able to think straight.

In my room upstairs in the manor house, I straightened up the clothes in my suitcase after I changed into the requisite skirt and blouse. In spite of the recent storm and chill, it was too hot out now for pantyhose and frankly, I didn't even know why I had brought them along. I balled them up and stuffed them in a corner of my suitcase then threw my camera and miniature binoculars into my tote bag. If all went according to plan, Marco and I might be on a flight home by tonight. That was my fervent hope but every time I tried to picture that happening, it seemed like God took out his eraser and rubbed that image out.

An uneasy feeling settled around my shoulders, tightening the muscles up the back of my neck again. I prayed as I gathered up my things – for Marco's safety, that this mission would go well and that God's purpose would be served in everything that happened.

We left shortly after breakfast. Cardy and Kev agreed that the traffic could be horrendous going into London and we needed to leave lots of extra time, just in case. Much better to arrive early and have to wait than end up stuck in traffic and miss the rendezvous. The prospect of arriving late didn't bear thinking about.

Kev's white trade van sat in front of the manor and Burton had brought Lord Wardley's Jaguar from the garages. It sat idling quietly, waiting for our departure. Neil drew me aside, out of earshot of the others. "I don't want you to worry," he said, holding my arms and staring into my eyes. "Everything is going to be fine."

"I'm not worried," I replied, forcing a little smile. "I just want this over so I can get Marco back and we can go get married."

"Good for you. One way or another, we'll get that guy for you." He slung an arm around my shoulders as we walked back toward the Jaguar. I didn't like the sound of that 'one way or another' comment.

I wanted it one way, and no other.

CHAPTER ELEVEN

Even though Kev had promised that he knew the fastest routes into London, the streets still resembled a four-year-old's bedroom after all the cousins had been for a visit. I glanced at my watch from time to time to see the minutes ticking away. On some roads the car had barely moved. Cardy travelled with Kev in his swaying van and Bobby drove Cardy's car since he had more experience driving on the left side of the road than either Neil or I had.

Thankfully, Kev led the way and we managed to keep his van in sight in spite of the hair-raising traffic snarls. As it turned out, we reached the park entrance at 2:15. The Italianate pavilion stood too far into the park to see from the gate, so even though we slowed down we couldn't glimpse so much as a flash of marble through the trees. We parked on the roadside and got out, did a quick review of our plans and proceeded.

Neil set off first toward the Italian Gardens, stopping periodically to snap photos of trees and flowers. A wide-open grassy area ran alongside the road where we had parked and he did a good job of looking like an enthralled tourist bent on recording every possible blossom, view and angle.

Bobby crossed the road alone and loped toward the pavilion, glancing at his surroundings with surreptitious intensity. I knew he worked out regularly to stay fit but as he ran I couldn't help but marvel at how light he seemed on his feet, as though it took no effort at all. I shook my head and promised myself that I would join a gym when I got home – if I got through this ordeal alive.

Kev and Cardy had driven off, making a U-turn in the road

and heading back toward the gate where, hopefully, Kevin would dazzle the park authorities, should he encounter any, with his cool plumbing aplomb.

I pulled my tote bag up on my shoulder and walked down the sidewalk toward the Italian garden. Behind my sunglasses my eyes dodged around, examining every face, every head of hair, every movement that seemed out of place. As a portrait artist, I tend to notice and remember faces and visual details and I knew that if I laid eyes on any one of the men I had seen take Marco away I would recognize him instantly. I didn't know exactly what I would *do* if that happened but trusted that the Holy Spirit would alert me and show me what I needed to know.

My pulse drummed in my ears as I walked and my heels clicked along the pavement. Through the trees, I could see the water gardens with their spraying fountains so I took a shortcut on a well-worn path across the lawns, now crisp and brown from the late summer heat. As I approached the nearest pond, I could see Neil with his camera zooming in on a geranium in one of the flower boxes that stood within a glossy iron railing that ran around the perimeter of the compact park. Most of the benches sat empty in the shimmering heat.

I strolled up the path alongside the gardens until I reached an opening. I couldn't see Cardy or Kev anywhere but Bobby had taken up a position on the opposite side of the pools. At the far end of the garden, a lush, moss-festooned fountain, flanked by scantily-draped maidens holding dribbling urns, rained water into the crescent-shaped body of water with the descriptive name of Long Water. Evidently, it became the Serpentine farther on, something I remembered from years before when my first husband, Roger, and I had backpacked through Europe early in our marriage.

Pushing those memories out of my mind, I forced my concentration back to the task at hand. Ambling to a nearby bench, I sat down, blistering the backs of my legs on the hot slats before scooting forward so my knee-length skirt could provide a barrier. Clipping up my hair made my neck only slightly cooler and I could feel the sun beating it red already. I reached into my tote and pulled out a paperback romance novel that I'd found on the plane and flipped it open. By now it was a quarter to three. Neil still pottered around, snapping photos of flowers and who knew what else. Bobby looked bored, so bored in fact, that he appeared to be dozing off. Knowing Bobby as I did though, this would not be the case.

The minutes crept by with agonizing indolence. The sun searing my dark head made me dizzy as I tried to fake concentration on the words crawling across the newsprint pages of the book in my hands. Neil wandered past me without acknowledgement but I heard him whisper, "Won't be long now. Hang in there," as he turned to photograph the fountain in the centre of the nearest pond.

Even with a few children running around, it was too quiet. The air felt like it was about to explode, as though every living thing in the park held its breath. Tension tugged my nerves into violin strings that seemed to resonate at a pitch only a dog would hear.

Breathe, I reminded myself again and again. My skin ran with sweat and my thighs stuck together like they had been pasted with contact cement.

Something had to happen soon. I glanced at my watch.

It was two minutes to three.

From the far side of the park I saw Cardy come into view carrying the box containing the fake glass dolphin. A little farther back, Kev appeared with a bag of tools, swinging a big wrench in one hand. He headed off toward a fountain situated behind the pavilion. For a moment he was out of my line of sight but then he re-appeared and hopped the low fence that ran along the pavilion's rear. Within the little fence I could see pipes sticking out of the ground and some other waterworks that he proceeded to examine like he belonged there.

My gaze slid to my watch again. So far there was no sign of the kidnappers or Marco. My heart pounded and all my muscles had gone taut, ready to run or swing my tote as a weapon, or something. I tried to preview how the events of the next few minutes would roll out. In my mind's eye, I had envisioned a perfect transfer. The kidnappers would accept the box without looking in it and relinquish Marco then disappear. Naïve, I know, but that was my fervent wish and I had imagined that God would make it all work out just like that for me. Once the kidnappers had turned their backs to flee I would throw myself into Marco's waiting arms and kiss his beloved face.

I glanced over at Bobby who still looked as lethargic as a lizard on a rock. I knew he wouldn't be, of course, but he did a great impression of a lazy tourist. One hand rested next to a pocket and the other behind his back where I knew he had concealed a weapon under his loose-fitting shirt. He gave me the faintest nod, almost imperceptible, but it calmed me ever so slightly. Just knowing he was there and could be counted on to leap into action in a fraction of a second assured me that even if things didn't pan out as I'd dreamed, he would still be able to make something work in our favour.

Neil believed that the kidnappers might know him and if the glass dolphin ploy didn't work out he was willing to step in and offer himself. I was dead set against that. How could I want to trade my uncle for my fiancé? Neil assured me that it wouldn't come to that. I prayed he was right.

From the far side of the pavilion two men appeared through the trees wearing dark two-button suits and sunglasses. Sunlight glistened off their oiled hair. One man, almost as tall as Neil's six feet in height towered over the other man who, though short and slight, had a menacing air that seemed calculated to instil instant fear, like an unsheathed stiletto – the dagger, not the shoe. I shuddered then drew in a long, slow breath. Marco was nowhere to be seen. I glanced toward the trees that bordered the street outside the park but could see nothing. The two men wasted no time striding to where Lord Wardley stood holding the box. They walked right up to him and said something. Cardy shook his head and replied. They were too far away for me to discern their conversation and I nearly jumped up right then to get nearer. Instead, I glanced toward Neil who looked directly at me and shook his head. *For crying out loud, he must be reading my mind,* I thought. I wanted to run past those two villains and find Marco. He had to be in the vicinity somewhere. I could find him; I knew it but Neil's gesture kept me glued to that sticky bench.

The conversation seemed to grow more heated. I saw Cardy step back, angling the box away from the kidnappers. He had drawn himself up as only a British peer could do and looked down his imperious nose at the scoundrels in front of him. Stiletto-man stood erect, looking as cold as an icicle. He barely turned his head and said something to his companion before the other guy made a lunge for the box in Cardy's arms. Out of the corner of my eye I saw Bobby stiffen then re-arrange his body into a sprinter's stance so swiftly that I nearly missed the movement. He was ready to spring.

Neil, too, had changed his position, at once both nonchalant and wary. With one word, Stiletto-man called off his dog, the other man who was clearly his muscle. I couldn't take it any more.

Gulping a lungful of air, I peeled my legs off that grill of a bench and stood to my feet. I could see Neil's look of alarm. Bobby's quick glance in my direction nearly nailed my feet to the hot concrete but the nervous energy coursing through my body was too much. I wasn't born yesterday, though, so I wasn't about to do anything really stupid. My intention was to stroll past where this scene played out, as slowly as I could, so I could get the drift of the conversation. Tugging down my skirt, I used the book in my hand to fan my neck as I walked away from the bench toward the pavilion. As I drew closer, the interchange registered on my hearing.

"Unless I see Mr. Jimenez, there is no deal," Cardy declared. "I shall not be handing over a priceless artifact until you produce him."

"Mr. Wardley," Stiletto-man said, his voice barely above a whisper. "You will see your friend when we see what you have in the box." The slight to Lord Wardley's position did not go unnoticed I saw his back stiffen and his nostrils flare.

"Bring him here and we'll make the exchange simultaneously," Cardy said.

The thin man shrugged and jerked his head toward his cohort who turned and strode off toward the street. By this time I was nearly even with where Cardy stood facing our enemy. I wanted to stop but didn't dare. Instead, I followed the other man at a relaxed pace as though I was in no hurry to get back to work. I sensed Bobby's eyes following me and could see Neil over my right shoulder as I passed. He didn't say or do anything but I knew he had to be questioning my sanity. I was too, but everything in me ached to see Marco, to be the first to get near him.

Before I reached the edge of the grass, Kev intercepted me. He must have been lurking behind the pavilion because before I knew it he was beside me. While he stayed a couple of arms' lengths away, still he matched my steps, wrench in hand. I scanned the park and the passing faces for the one that I would instantly recognize, yet when Marco appeared I nearly missed him. His usually impeccable appearance had vanished. His ragged jacket hung off one shoulder, one shirttail dangled over his belt and there was a deep purple bruise across his right cheekbone His eye, nearly swollen shut, squinted at the brightness of the day as though he'd been in darkness until moments before. The other eye, though undamaged, looked puffy and red. A trickle of dried blood ran from the corner of his mouth and a raw, red line on his neck indicated he'd been beaten.

I gasped and covered my mouth with my hand. He appeared not to notice me even though in his line of sight he could not have missed me. Two men accompanied him and the park visitors, what few there were, got out of the way. The tall man had a vise-like grip on his arm and the other walked about two steps behind him with a hand in his bulging jacket pocket. They passed within a few feet of me and I stopped – trying, and probably failing, to look like a curious passer-by.

As his captors thrust him forward, Marco trudged along, feet dragging. When he passed me his eyes slid sideways and for a half second they locked with mine. I expected acknowledgement, some sign that he saw me, knew me, or that he was all right but I saw none of these.

He looked like the walking dead.

CHAPTER TWELVE

I stood at a tall, multi-paned window and looked down on a tiny square. Like most public areas in France it hadn't a blade of grass. Below me, two iron benches sat under a couple of scabby, ancient plane trees, looking like they were making an effort to create a park.

Across the courtyard, a tall narrow house with ivy crawling up its façade stood dozing in the morning sun, the windows shuttered like sleepy eyelids. I could visualize the door opening and a troupe of little French girls appearing in their identical navy uniforms complete with beribboned caps, descending the steep flight of worn stairs and perambulating off down the street behind an aging Mademoiselle.

I glanced at my watch, not sure if it was on the correct time zone for Paris then remembered that I had changed it at Heathrow in England. A young woman wearing rolled-up yellow pants and pink plaid flats appeared from around the corner, walking a ratty terrier on a leash. She stopped and allowed the animal to sniff the base of a tree before it lifted its leg and marked a spot as its own. They continued on, past the benches and the other tall, narrow houses that lined the street as the dog studiously examined all things of dog interest.

It hadn't worked. The ruse with the fake glass dolphin had gone so awry, so suddenly, it still seemed impossible.

The encounter in the Italian Gardens had been a fiasco. When I looked into Marco's expressionless eyes, I knew that something was terribly wrong. Either he'd been beaten into senselessness or he'd been drugged. A third option bashed away at my heart but I rejected it. I had to reject it.

71

The men dragging Marco into the park had not given me so much as a sideways glance. I realized, in retrospect, that was probably a good thing. If they thought I was a curious passer-by, it might help protect me should we meet again which, I was pretty sure, would happen sooner or later.

At the command of the kidnappers' spokesman, Cardy opened the box containing the glass vase, trying his best to conceal as much as possible. The other two thugs had held Marco a good way back from the transaction. Bobby had risen from the bench where he'd been lounging and wandered around behind where they held Marco, blending effortlessly with the other inquisitive onlookers. Kev stood on the other side, near the pavilion tinkering with a pipefitting. I glanced past Marco to where Neil stood leaning against one of the pavilion's pillars holding a newspaper, ready to jump into action.

What happened next still remains a blur. The kidnapper, Stiletto-man, demanded that Lord Wardley hand over the box before Marco would be released. Cardy refused, insisting instead that Marco be allowed to join them before he relinquished the box. The kidnapper lunged at Cardy, wrenching the box from his grasp and slashing the packing material away from the contents. The moment he saw that we'd been trying to dupe them, the three acted as though their actions had been scripted. The glass vase, ripped from the box, crashed to the stone steps of the pavilion sending splinters of crystal skittering across the paving stones in a sparkling spray. At the same moment, the other two men began hauling Marco back the way they had come and as Bobby and Kev sprinted after them, the kidnappers drew guns and pointed one at Marco's head and the other at Kev's chest. The thin man, with a gun in his hands, barked orders at Cardy who stood motionless, stunned by the sudden turn of events, before running after the others as they dragged Marco from the park.

In seconds it was all over. I had watched in horror as

Marco's head disappeared without a backward glance. Then I took off after his retreating form. Before I'd gone three strides, Bobby's big arms encircled me, lifted me from my feet and spun me around. I fought like a wet cat against him but it made no difference. I was no match for his colossal strength.

"No," he whispered into my right ear. "Not a good idea."

I whimpered in reply, craning my neck over his shoulder to see Marco but it was too late. They had disappeared, taking him, once more, away from me. Bobby set me back on my feet but kept a hard grip around my waist. There was no point trying to elude him; he was bigger, stronger and faster than I. He marched me over to where Neil stood with an arm around Cardy's sagging shoulders. Only then did Bobby release me and I ran to Neil. He opened his arms and folded me in a hug as I sobbed on his shoulder, blubbering about losing Marco and soaking his shirt with tears and makeup smears. "Look," Neil murmured as I gained control of myself, "this is not the end of the world. Cardy," he said as he glanced at his stricken friend, "buck up. It's not over yet."

"But I don't even know what he said," Cardy lamented. "The bloke was screaming at me in some foreign language."

"It's okay," Neil said, patting him on the back. "I know what he said." By this time Kev had joined us and stood with his thumbs hitched in his belt, shoulders bunched like he wanted to punch someone.

"They still have Marco," I said, sniffing and dabbing my eyes with a tissue this time.

"Not for long," Neil replied. "What they said in Spanish was that we'd see Marco when we handed over the glass dolphin. That means that they're going to continue to hold him. He's the only leverage they've got and they don't know where the dolphin is. So that gives us the upper hand because they believe that we do know where it is." He grinned and looked from face to face.

"Didn't you see Marco?" I cried. "They've beaten him ragged and he looked like he'd been drugged or something. He didn't even know me when he stared right at me."

At that moment, a pair of uniformed park security officers ran up and Neil and Cardy took them aside to smooth over the situation. When they had both nodded and retreated to shoo away the crowd, another park employee showed up with a broom and garbage bin, glowering at us and muttering, "Bloody tourists, bloody Americans...what a bleedin' mess!"

His comments struck me as a final insult and the final assault on my raw emotions. "We're not 'bloody tourists'," I snapped. "We're here on international business. And we're not Americans either. We're Canadians and British, and, okay, one American, who is one of the finest people I know." I could feel Neil tugging me away from the scene of the debacle but I wasn't finished. "Now, we apologize for the broken glass but it was an accident. So, why don't you just do your job and clean it up, you snivelling little wiener of a man?"

By this time, Neil had his arm around my middle and was hauling me away from the pavilion toward where we had parked the car. I half expected Bobby to pick me up and throw me over his shoulder but instead I saw him biting the inside of his lips and studiously surveying the treetops.

Once we'd gone out of sight of the Italian Gardens and were back on the sidewalk bordering the road Neil released his grip on my arm.

"What was that all about?" He tilted his head and looked at me.

"Oh, oh. He didn't deserve that, did he?" I pressed the heels of my hands into my eye sockets. "It's just that I'm...I'm so... Now what are we going to do?"

Neil took my arm and continued walking. "We're going to go back to Wardley Hall right now and figure that out."

"Jill." Standing by the window, my mind registered the voice on one level but was pre-occupied with something much more momentous. *How, after all we'd been through, could Marco still not be with me? How could he not even have recognized me?*

"Jill. Talk to me." Neil's voice broke through my stumbling thoughts. I turned my head away from the window, dragging my eyes from the vine-covered house, and looked at him.

"What?" Irritation and fatigue tinged my voice. I didn't have the energy, or even the want, to feel apologetic.

"Have you been listening at all?"

"Yes," I replied, casting about in my mind for fragments that had penetrated. "You said we're going to have to go to Peru. I already guessed that."

Neil glanced across the room at his colleague, Dr. Jay Sharp. There was something written in that glance, I knew, but I didn't bother trying to interpret it. Instead, I sighed and crossed the room, sitting down on the edge of a red leather sofa. Dr. Sharp, I had learned only hours before, happened to be an Andean expert, one of the foremost explorers and anthropologists studying the various tribal cultures, past and present, from the Pacific coast of Peru through to the Amazon Basin. He specialized in the Inca culture and others that had existed prior to the rise of the Inca Empire, through its ultimate demise, and up to the present.

While Neil knew a lot about the archaeological ruins, he felt that we needed to consult with a specialist of a different ilk. We had to know if anyone since Cecilia Wardley had heard of the glass dolphin and where we might have a hope of finding the thing.

CHAPTER THIRTEEN

Dr. Jay Sharp's apartment, situated in an elegant, Napoleonic-era building, had been decorated in sleek, minimalist stainless steel and leather décor. Massive non-representational paintings hung on the apartment's walls, sporting swaths of vibrant colours, mainly red and orange. Three plain, red leather sofas formed a U around a glass and steel table upon which sat a Moche ceramic jug in the shape of a warrior's head, complete with staring eyes and a fancy headdress. The Moche, I knew from reading some of Neil's reports, pre-dated the Inca in Peru and had built advanced and complicated societies on what is now a desert west of the Andes. I wondered how he came by this priceless artifact or if it was just a good copy.

After leaving the garden in Hyde Park, we had returned to Wardley Hall just as Neil had said. At the dinner table, with Cardy, Neil, Bobby and me present – Kev had said his good-byes and gone home – we tried to figure out what went wrong and what our next move should be. Neil's translation of the kidnapper's tirade went something like: "You'll get him back when you hand over the glass dolphin and not until. You find it and we'll find you."

Neil decided that the best course of action meant hopping over to Paris to consult with Dr. Sharp to find out if he had any ideas. Since by this time it was already late, we booked a commuter flight for early the next morning. I spent a fitful night, alternately dreaming that my alarm clock didn't ring and that I missed the flight, and images of Marco enduring unbearable torture. More than once, I woke in a dripping sweat with my bedcovers in a messy tangle around me.

Now we sat here with Dr. Jay Sharp, who in his early forties had already begun balding. He had a blonde walrus moustache and a cast on his left leg clear up to his hip. He explained that he had recently been in a car accident on a rural Andean road when the vehicle, driven by a "madman," fishtailed in loose gravel and slid off a cliff. The driver had been severely injured and Sharp had suffered multiple compound fractures and spent several days in a hospital in Cusco before being flown home to recover. He explained that he kept this apartment in Paris for when he was not tramping through the jungles in the upper Amazon. Though American by birth, his mother was French and lived one floor up. He had no wife, nor any children – "No time for that yet," being his terse explanation.

As I stood at the window, lost in my thoughts, the discussion between the two men had swirled around me.

"I think what you may be looking for is the area farther north," I heard Sharp say, hitching his body up on the sofa and wincing when his cast twisted. "There is a town called Chachapoyas, east of Chiclaya, which is on the coast. It's not easy to get to because the roads are pretty treacherous but south and east of there rivers run down the valleys through some pretty rough country, dense jungle and mountain terrain. There's not much in the way of population. If you like poisonous snakes and jaguars, you'll love that part of the world." He grinned and winked at me. I was not charmed.

"I've been through a few of those valleys," Neil said, "but it has been a while. What were you doing there?"

Sharp smirked. "I was poking around, hoping to find some evidence of lost civilizations. You know the drill."

"And did you?" I hadn't said much until now but I needed to know if this guy had anything to offer us.

"Yeah, I found some things. Nothing I didn't already know was there though." He looked at Neil again. "So tell me some more about this lady explorer you mentioned. Did you say you had a map?"

Neither of us had said anything about a map. "No," Neil said, not elaborating. "We have some information about a location where she had travelled but it is pretty vague, somewhere in the highlands or foothills on the east side of the Andes in Peru. I'm wondering what you know about ancient tribes that may have existed there. That's not my main area of expertise but I know that you have the reputation of being the guy to talk to."

"True," Sharp answered. "You know where Tres Cruces is, at the edge of the Manu Cloud Forest?" Neil nodded. I didn't. "Up north of there is a lot of uncharted wilderness, jungle, forest, call it what you want, all along the eastern flank of the mountains. There are a few little outposts, some of which even have landing strips. From those, the only way to get in there is to go up the rivers and hack through the bush. The elevation is high. I've heard rumours that there are still small tribes that no one has studied living back up there in the mountains away from civilization. Some of them may come out for supplies but they disappear again and no one really knows where they go. It's like they evaporate into the forest where they don't want to be found."

"Do you have any names? Is there more than one tribe?"

Jay Sharp shrugged. "Your guess is as good as mine. I've never been that far back up there in the mountains. I was following a tip about a small group of families living back in the forest farther to the east and that's when this happened." He tapped the cast on his leg. "Roads are bad at the best of times – narrow, dirt tracks carved out of the sides of mountains – but when it rains, you can get washed down the valley before you know what hit you. And it rains a lot. You're getting into the Amazon Basin rainforest, after all."

"Do you know anything about the origins of those people?" Neil asked.

"Well, I've heard rumours that when the Inca overran the area and supposedly conquered the Chachapoya, some of them ran off and hid in the hills rather than getting their heads split open. I suppose it's not inconceivable that there are descendants of those people still tucked away in the jungle. After all, they had to have come from somewhere, at some time, don't they?"

"Who were the Chacha...?" I enquired.

"The Chachapoya," Sharp said, looking my way. "Their civilization pre-dates the Inca but little is known about them. The Inca apparently conquered them prior to the Spaniards showing up so most of what we know comes from archaeological evidence, as Neil could tell you. The Chachapoya liked to bury their dead in tombs up on the sides of cliffs. No one knows how they got them up there. Everything else was second hand, recorded by a Spaniard by the name of Pedro Cieza de Leon and another guy named El Inca Garcilaso de la Vega. I've studied their work, what little there is of it. The archaeological finds are farther north, closer to the town of Chachapoyas but that's not to say they stayed around there. If my enemies were looking to slaughter me, I think I'd also want to get as far away as I possibly could."

He stroked his moustache and seemed to be considering something for a moment. I noticed a large, ornate ring on his left hand that displayed an intricate insignia that I didn't recognize. I glanced at Neil but he didn't react.

"The odd thing about the Chachapoya, according to de Leon," Sharp continued, "is that they were light-skinned, fair-haired and tall, quite unlike the indigenous Indians that you find throughout the country today and presumably in the days when the Spanish first arrived on the scene. There was even some conjecture that they had European ancestry but of course that's impossible. We know that Europeans never arrived in South America prior to the Spaniards in the 1500s."

Earlier in the year when Neil had sent me on a quest to collect a ring of stones he had unearthed in a dig in Mexico, it had been clear from the inscriptions on them that peoples from across the Atlantic had touched the shores of the Americas long before most of the scientific establishment believed. Neil had never publicized his find and it had ultimately proved to hold the secrets of great scientific and technological knowledge from the ancient world. Neither Neil nor I mentioned this to Jay Sharp.

"Do you believe that there are remnants of these light-skinned people still in Peru? If so, why would they not have assimilated?" Neil asked casually. I could tell there was a lot more going on in his head than he was letting on.

"Your guess is as good as mine," Sharp replied with a shrug. "It is thought that there are still undiscovered tribes living in the Amazon. Getting through the jungle is still enormously difficult. What we're talking about here is roughly the same. The eastern slopes of the Andes are practically jungle and, like your Rocky Mountains, have pockets where no man, or woman," he added, nodding at me, "has set foot in known history. The other possibility is that similar to when World War II ended, years later Japanese soldiers were found still hiding on Pacific Islands with no idea that the conflict was over. It is certainly possible that these people fled deep into the mountains, set up their villages or settlements and just never came out. They may even have drifted around. Who knows where they ended up? In any case, the world could have gone on without them."

"Surely there would have been some sign of such people by now," I suggested. "Wouldn't their villages show up on satellite imagery, for example?"

"Not necessarily," Sharp answered. "A lot of that country is nearly impenetrable. If they didn't want to be found, I'm pretty sure they could stay hidden. Besides, to find something you actually have to be looking for it."

Half an hour later, Neil and I stood on the sidewalk outside Jay Sharp's apartment. "That was puzzling," I said as we started walking. "I got the distinct impression that he knows something he wasn't telling us. How do you know him anyway?" During the course of the conversation, Neil had not said much about our mission, only that a friend was in trouble and we thought he might have gone into the area that we discussed. Even though Dr. Sharp had asked some probing questions, Neil had sidestepped answering them with the same dexterity that Sharp had avoided some of our inquiries. Neither of us mentioned the glass dolphin.

"I ran into him a couple of years ago in Oaxaca, Mexico, when I was attending a conference on the plight of indigenous peoples and how the archaeological community has helped or hindered. Jay was one of the speakers and I must say, he acquitted himself well. I can't say I agree with everything he proposed but he seems to know what he's talking about with regard to improving the lot of distinct communities in the poorer regions." We walked a little farther in silence.

"He was hiding something, wasn't he? I mean, I don't know him at all but that was the impression I kept getting. He kept skittering away from answering direct questions."

Neil nodded slightly as he walked, his eyes on the sidewalk. "I'm not sure what's going on there but I have a few theories. Why don't you pray about it and let me know if the Lord tells you something."

We turned a corner and headed toward the Metro station. As we waited on the platform, Neil pulled out his cell phone and called Bobby. After a brief conversation he turned to me. "How would you like to go for a nice dinner tonight then fly out in the morning? There is a little shopping I think you need to do this afternoon."

I looked sideways at him. "You want me to go shopping?"

"Well, yes but not for Parisian fashions, exactly."

"Did Bobby have something to tell you?"

"Yes, and no. You'll see."

CHAPTER FOURTEEN

With a groan I rolled into bed and pulled a sheet up over my legs. My stomach felt like it would groan too, given the opportunity. Neil and I had gone for a lovely dinner at a perfectly French sidewalk café on a tiny square, and spent three glorious hours sitting under a green umbrella and watching Parisians stroll by as the sun sank below the rooftops.

Prior to that he had dropped me off at an outdoor outfitter store with a list of items to purchase for trekking through jungles – and enduring both heat and cold, depending on the altitudes we might have to encounter in the Andes. Being a gifted and dedicated indoors-woman, I have to admit that the prospect of trekking farther than the nearest museum did not entice me in the least but I dutifully presented Neil's list to an English-speaking clerk, a wiry young guy with sun-browned skin and boundless enthusiasm for the job of outfitting me. By the time we'd gone through the entire store I left weighed-down with bags containing boots, socks, pants with legs that zipped off but that also tied at the ankles should I need to keep out uninvited insect or reptilian guests. Repellent, sunscreen, mosquito netting, a backpack, a sleeping bag and a sun hat had also been tossed into the shopping basket. Neil's expense account from the corporation in Israel had paid for the lot.

Now the bags lay strewn about the hotel room. Exhausted as I felt, I had two more tasks to attend to before I rolled over and turned out the light. My tote bag lay on a chair by the window and I pulled Cecilia Wardley's diary out from the sealed plastic bag. Lord Wardley had allowed us, with some reluctance, to keep the journal for the time being so we could study it.

Plumping the pillows against the headboard, I leaned back and gently opened the aged volume. We hadn't had time to go through it thoroughly since I'd found it, what with all the excitement going on. Tilting the bedside lamp to shine on the pages I began to peruse the cramped script. Why had Cecilia Wardley gone off to the far side of the world all alone? She was intrepid and seemed almost fearless, though from time to time she did admit to trepidation in the descriptions of her travels.

Initially, she had taken a ship around the tip of South America accompanied only by a maid named Josephine Adams. Miss Adams fell madly in love with a young man on board ship and as soon as the ship docked in Lima she left her employer and sailed on toward San Francisco. After disembarking, Miss Wardley continued inland toward Cusco in order to explore Inca ruins and study the indigenous cultures. She made mention of attempting to gain entrance into the membership of the Royal Geographical Society in London shortly after its inception in 1830, which was prior to her departure, but was soundly rebuffed as women were not allowed.

Figures. I thought. Here was a woman willing to go half way around the world to study and explore and she got no help or support whatever from her peers. According to her writings, however, the family had the means to underwrite her endeavours so off she went, evidently to the horror of her parents and the jealousy of some poorer members of the Geographical Society. I had the impression that she felt justified in thumbing her aristocratic nose at them all.

From Cusco, Cecilia headed east into the mountains. Machu Picchu was still hidden in the clouds at this time, since Hiram Bingham did not discover it until 1911. She claimed to be driven by nothing more than boundless enthusiasm and insatiable curiosity.

My mother was right, she wrote on one particular page, *when she said I would never be satisfied with society life. Nothing sounds more stifling to me now than having to dress in lace and ribbons, standing around making polite conversation with boring men inflated with their own importance. I swear, I'm surprised they do not lift off the floor like so many gas balloons. How much more satisfied I am here, with the sun on my face and my boots following a twisting river!*

As the pages turned I got a clearer picture of this woman who forsook all to learn new languages, see new sights and experience new things. She travelled with guides and porters, though her entourage (with a few notable exceptions) remained small, usually no more than ten people. She packed a machete and a rifle as well as a couple of pistols tucked into her belt. Her descriptions of locations meant little to me since I had no reference points but I assumed that Neil would be able to verify where she had travelled.

By the time she met the tribe associated with the glass dolphin, she had been in Peru for nearly two years. She had learned Spanish to communicate with her hired guides and had also picked up several dialects of indigenous tribes. After a jaunt to the brink of the Amazon Basin, Cecilia had spent several months in a small village hidden in the forest on the Andes' eastern slopes. It was here that she learned of the custom involving the glass dolphin.

My eyes, which had been speeding across the pages, now slowed down to take in every detail of Miss Wardley's descriptions. However, the combination of fatigue and jet lag coupled with a cozy bed finally won. Even if I could keep my eyes open, I knew that it was unlikely I would retain anything I read anyway. Closing the book, I wrapped the worn thongs around it and placed it on the bedside table next to my travel alarm clock.

As I switched off the light and curled up on my side I could see the glow of the streetlamps through the drapes. *Lord*, I said silently, *I know that you know where Marco is tonight. Wherever that is, please keep him safe and unharmed. Give Neil and me wisdom and understanding in what we need to do to find him. Help us hear your voice and follow your leading. I know things could get a little crazy if we end up in the jungles of Peru or somewhere, so we're really going to have to rely on you to show us what to do. Please warn us of danger and keep us safe, and Bobby, too.*

A blanket of peace settled over me as I drifted into a deep sleep. My dreams rambled through vistas of jungle and city, down rivers and up mountains. Marco's face appeared and vanished, only to materialize again in some other bizarre location. I woke to the sound of a motorcycle revving its engine on the street below my window and sat up to squint at the clock. It read 7:08.

I can't say that I leapt out of bed but within forty-five minutes I had showered and dressed, packed my purchases into two smaller packages and had opened the curtains to greet the morning. The early autumn sun promised another warm day. When the telephone rang, Neil suggested we have breakfast at a small café down the street before checking out. Our flight back to London didn't leave until around 11:00 a.m. so that gave us time to eat and get to the airport without rushing. I dropped the diary into my tote bag and left the room.

"Am I really going to need all this stuff?" I asked Neil as I piled my shopping bags in the trunk of the taxi later on.

He grinned. "That and more."

"The only thing I'm missing is a machete," I joked.

Neil tossed his one small bag into the trunk. "We'll pick those up in Peru."

I stared at him for a moment then slid into the back seat. "What else do you have in mind that I should know about?"

"I've arranged for a stop at a tropical diseases clinic in London this afternoon. We'll need to get some anti-malaria meds. I don't expect that we'll be travelling very far into the jungle but just in case the situation calls for it, it's best to be prepared."

85

As we sped through the streets of Paris, I tried to see as many of the sights as I could. It had only been a few months since I had been in the city chasing down Neil's ancient stones the previous spring but even then I had only stayed overnight. After picking up the first stone from Neil's colleague, Dr. Bernaud, I had immediately headed off to the next location. *One of these day*, I thought, *I will come back here with Marco and we'll have a proper holiday*.

"I was reading Miss Cecilia's journal last night," I said as we careened around a corner.

"And?" Neil's voice, saturated with exaggerated patience, barely registered.

"And what?" My head swivelled towards him.

"Try to focus, Jill," he said, giving my arm a poke. "Did you find out anything worthwhile?"

"She was quite a woman," I replied, dragging my attention away from the sights and my thoughts of Marco. "I didn't get far enough last night to make sense of locations or get more details on the, um, object before I conked out." I glanced at the taxi driver, a young North African who hummed softly as he drove. While I doubted that he posed any kind of threat, I had learned from working with Neil that we could never be too careful.

"We'll have a closer look at it tonight back at Wardley Hall," Neil suggested. "There has to be something useful in it. After all, Cecilia Wardley effectively discovered the thing and was the first westerner to learn what it means."

"It's quite possible that she had no idea what it means," I answered. "Only God knows that."

CHAPTER FIFTEEN

Before the plane even landed, the heat and humidity seeped into the cabin, sticky and suffocating, making me feel trapped in my window seat. Below, I could see the outlines of barrier islands, swampy and uninhabited, crisscrossed by squiggly waterways. The "Fasten Seatbelts" sign came on overhead and the captain announced that within minutes the plane would land at Charleston International. The temperature hovered just below ninety degrees Fahrenheit at six o'clock in the evening.

We had been up since before dawn to get to Heathrow for the only available flight that would arrive this early and we still had to make two stops to change planes on the way. I could think of nothing I wanted more than a tepid shower and a tall, cold drink. Each leg of the trip was supposed to bring me closer to finding Marco yet it felt like each day that passed might be taking him farther away.

We had spent the previous night at Wardley Hall as planned but stayed up late examining Cecilia Wardley's travel journal for any scrap of information that might lead us to the glass dolphin. Who knew if the object even existed and if it did, where in a whole, vast country might it be found? For all we knew, it may have long since been removed from the country. If that were the case, it did not seem to have been removed by Miss Wardley herself. According to her writings, she seemed to want nothing to do with the artifact and once the pilgrimage to the sea had been completed, she became gravely ill. When she recovered to a degree that allowed her to get out of bed and travel, she set sail for England on the first ship out of Lima. The Panama Canal would not open for shipping passage until decades later so Cecilia had to endure the long and dangerous voyage around Cape Horn again. My guess was that, given the way she felt, she was willing to take any form of transportation so long as she could lie down. The glass dolphin or the people who revered it were not mentioned again.

Most of her writing had covered the difficulties of travelling in a foreign land and dealing with porters, animals, provisions and nature. Her route took her from Lima, where she had initially landed, overland to Cusco. With a goal of adventure and discovery rather than archaeology or anthropology – studies that were to develop later in the century – she set off in search of the unknown. She had learned a bit of Spanish prior to sailing from England but hired an interpreter to deal with that and other local dialects until she became fluent herself.

"I'm going to leave this investigation to the two of you," Lord Wardley had informed us, glancing at the ornate mantle clock now chiming 11:00 p.m. "I can no longer think straight," he said, unbending his long body from deep in a wing chair, "and I have no other information to offer the discussion. I'll bid you both goodnight."

After he had gone, Neil and I turned back to the journal. "Miss Wardley was in Peru for over two years," he said, "and only mentions getting ill after the processional with the glass dolphin."

"It could be coincidental. She was spending time on the east side of the Andes where at lower elevations, malaria can be a problem even today."

"True, but she didn't travel down into the Amazon Basin at all. In the higher elevations, mosquitos aren't so much of a problem."

"Do you think something else caused her illness?"

Neil shrugged. "Given the details of her malady, it's hard to guess what might have caused it. I find it interesting that according to family lore, she simply wasted away and ultimately died, once she returned home. You know as well as I do that a curse, when believed, can result in any number of dire situations. She might have been an intrepid traveller for her day and her gender, but does her journal reflect her spiritual beliefs? Did she have any protection against falling for the paganism she encountered on her explorations?"

I thought about what I had read in the journal, about travel conditions, social customs, food, scenery, even cities and villages that Cecilia Wardley had encountered but could not recall even one instance where she had mentioned her faith. Either she was extremely private about it, which seemed unlikely, since believing in God was pretty much a given in her era and this was her private diary, or she had thrown any of the teachings from her early years away in order to embrace new experiences or customs. Who could say which it was?

"Not that I could find," I answered. "She chronicled her day-to-day experiences, with descriptions and sketches of the places she visited but she didn't talk about herself much. She seemed to be intensely interested in ancient cultures and in the indigenous peoples. I got the sense that our Miss Cecilia was seduced by her own situation and was kind of a sitting duck for the cultural and spiritual practices she ran across. It's possible that she contracted some infection or even something like cancer. In those days, medicine would not have been much help."

"That's true." Neil seemed to mull that over for a few minutes then surprised me by saying, "We have to go to South Carolina tomorrow."

"What for? I thought we would be going to Peru right away."

He reached out and patted my hand. "I know you're anxious to go after Marco but if we dash headlong into the Andes mountains we could waste a lot of time and even risk our lives. We have to go about this with a plan in place."

I leaned my head against the old sofa back. "Why South Carolina? Who or what is there that is going to make a difference?"

"For one thing, we're going to rendezvous with your friend, Quentin McSweeney, because we need him in on this search. There is also someone else I need to talk with. Greg Tisdale has been my right-hand man on more than a few expeditions. I talked with him earlier today and he has agreed to be our American liaison. McSweeney is coming with us to Peru."

I ran my hands through my hair and let out a deep breath. I had so many questions but I felt so wrung out from the past couple of days that I could hardly line my thoughts up long enough to know where to begin.

Apparently Neil could see that. He continued, "Greg knows the Andes like his own back yard and far better than I do. As you know, my specialty has always been Central America, not South America. The trip I've been planning would be my first in years but I wasn't ready to go yet. Having Greg on the team at this point, even though he can't join us, will go a long way to getting a handle on what we'll be dealing with once we land. And you know McSweeney, he's just a good guy to have around in a crisis even if only because he throws a mean punch."

I looked at Neil and laughed. Quentin McSweeney had been an old pal of Neil's probably since before I had even been born. He had entered my life the previous spring when he took me out off the Florida Keys on his rust-bucket of a treasure-hunting boat called the "Angela," named for his wife. Not only had we found a couple of Spanish silver pieces in the shimmering, shallow turquoise waters but we had unearthed from the shifting sands of the Caribbean little gold blocks that were exact replicas of the carved stone blocks that Neil had sent me on that around-the-world chase to secure. To say that McSweeney was something of a character would be greatly understating the case.

"Well," I said, finally, "that should liven things up."

Now as the airplane taxied toward the terminal I wondered just what part McSweeney would play. While I didn't think he was much of an athlete, he was probably as fit as I when it came to trekking through the mountains. And like Neil had said, he was a good guy to have around in a fight. Not quite as good as Bobby but I'd still want to be on McSweeney's side, given the choice.

The tinny voice on the plane's sound system announced that we could now use "devices" so I switched on my cell phone. The chime announced incoming emails. Neil had already begun pulling items from the overhead bin as I flicked through the list of artist-related newsletters, junk mail about buying pharmaceuticals from Canada and a couple of Facebook comments. One subject line caught my eye. It read, *Read this now, Jill.* Curious, I opened it and my breath caught in my throat as my eyes scanned the tiny print.

The message read simply, *Jill, Don't bother trying to find me. It's over. I'm not coming back. Marco.*

CHAPTER SIXTEEN

The letters swam before my eyes and a moan of pain escaped from somewhere deep in my belly. Neil took one look at me, dropped my carry-on bag on the seat and grabbed the cell phone from my hand. He scanned the message and clicked the device off.

"Jill, look at me," he said, sitting down beside me. He took my face between his hands and forced me to face him. "This is a hoax. Do you hear me? Marco wouldn't send that."

I wiped at a tear that dripped off my jawline. "But what if it's not?"

"No," he said, giving my shoulders a shake. "He would not send this. It's designed to provoke you. Don't let it. Don't play into their hands. Do you understand me?"

I nodded. "Okay. But it might be easier to believe if I knew whose hands we're talking about." *Who would send that email?*

"We're getting to that, so just for now, forget it. Grab your bags and let's get off this plane. It's hotter than a pancake griddle in here."

I staggered up the crowded aisle of the plane, my thoughts in a whirl. As much as I had tried to deny it, since the moment I realized Marco would not be showing up to our wedding, a niggling thought would not leave me alone. *What if he hadn't wanted to marry me?* Seeing him in that London park had shaken me to the core. It was clear that he'd been kidnapped, or at least it looked that way. *Maybe he only made it look that way,* came the harassing thought. *No, that's not possible,* I argued. Though we hadn't known each other long, only a few months really, everything about his actions told me his feelings for me were real. Then why had he not acknowledged me when he had seen me? A blink of his eyes would have been enough. But there had been nothing.

I trudged up the ramp behind Neil and emerged into a blast of air conditioning so cold that it made me shiver.

"Come with me, Jill," Neil said, taking my elbow. "The exit is this way."

We passed through a set of sliding glass doors into the baggage claim area. Jostling bodies pressed in, making me feel claustrophobic, almost nauseated. I couldn't wait to get out of there even though I didn't know where we were going.

"Hey, there he is," Neil bellowed, striding ahead of me and waving. A second later, Quentin McSweeney grabbed me in a bear hug, nearly squeezing my chest back to Grade Five. The man stood over six feet tall and had a build like a bear. With a Hemingway-esque beard, a mop of grey curls usually squashed under a ball cap, and an accent that landed halfway between Glasgow and Galveston, McSweeney was one of a kind.

"Put me down," I gasped, "before you asphyxiate me."

McSweeney let out a booming laugh. "I thought y'all'd be happy to see me, Moss, and all you can do is hit me over the head with big words. Come on. I've got a car parked illegally at the curb and I don't think that parking Nazi'd take kindly to bein' punched out." He snatched my carry-on bag from my hands and took off. I had to jog just to keep him in sight.

With Neil in the front seat and McSweeney driving, I leaned my head against the edge of the window and watched the city glide past. First came the tangle of airport roads followed by freeways, bridges then finally a long causeway over marshy lowlands.

Fatigue sat on my chest like an overfed cat, hot and implacable. I couldn't remember when I'd last slept for more than an hour. It might have been on the last leg of our flight from England but it didn't matter. Somewhere along the way, despair had latched onto me, sucking like a leech on what little hope I had left. All the while, I told myself that I could not let my thoughts even go there. As a visual artist, my imagination could fill in the blanks with details far too graphic for my emotions to handle. When I had seen him, he looked so defeated that the man was almost unrecognizable.

I have to pull myself together. I couldn't be any help to Marco if I dissolved into a puddle of self-pitying tears. Neil had explained that this colleague of his, Greg Something-or-other, should be able to help us get into the part of Peru where Marco was most likely being held. Neil and I had deduced that since the captors already knew something about the glass dolphin, they would probably be heading to the area where Cecilia Wardley had last mentioned seeing it. I couldn't help wondering how on earth they had found out about it to begin with. Was it tribal lore? Had they found some relic that made mention of it? According to Neil, and from what little I had read about Peruvian archaeology, the entire country was awash in relics of ancient cultures. The Nazca, the Inca, the Moche and the Chachapoya were only a few of the people groups who had left their mark on the country in stone, pottery, burial sites and monuments. Once the Spaniards showed up, they not only destroyed a lot of the cultural heritage that preceded them but they too changed the country, this time into a replica of their own civilization, building quite literally on top of the architecture of their conquered peoples.

I saw a sign for Sullivan's Island flash past the window and I sat up straighter to observe the surroundings. Within minutes we turned onto a street that was not much more than a paved lane with old beach-style cottages interspersed among towering new homes. Low palm trees edged the scrub-grassed yards.

"Is this it?" I heard McSweeney ask.

Neil consulted the map on his phone. "Yes, it's this one on the right."

McSweeney spun the wheel and the rented SUV swung onto the concrete driveway of an older home that looked as though it had been subjected to a major upgrade both in style and in size.

A lazy Golden Retriever looked up from where it lay sprawled on the top step of a long veranda and gave a perfunctory woof before resting its chin on the step again. The screen door opened and a child of about five ran out, a little girl with messy pigtails, wearing a faded yellow swimsuit.

"Daddy," I heard her shout, "there's somebody here." She stood next to the dog and stared at us as we exited our vehicle. In another moment, a man emerged from the house and bounded down the steps, giving the child's head a rub on his way.

He wore a pair of shorts, the kind with pockets all over the legs, and a blue tank top that had "Go Bluejays" written in white across the chest. His hair, a mop of sun-streaked, sea-blown brown, needed cutting and he sported a white, untanned band across the bridge of his nose. He grabbed Neil and hauled him into a hug before pumping McSweeney's hand. Neil made introductions and when it was my turn, the man said, "Ma'am, I'm Greg Tisdale. So pleased to meet you. I've heard so much about you."

I blinked. "You have?"

"Why, shore. You're the one who picked up all those mysterious stones that made up that ring. Neil told me all about it. I think you're just amazing, ma'am."

Flattered, I thanked him for the compliment and as he led us up the steps to the veranda, I couldn't help wondering who else Neil had told about me and exactly what he had said.

Inside the spacious home, Greg poured cold drinks and offered us seats on the veranda on the ocean side of the house where we sat in the shade as the sun glinted off the waves. The little girl, who told us her name was Josie, perched next to me on the porch swing and watched every move I made, her brown eyes even following my hand as I lifted my drink to my lips. I remembered when my own daughter, Julia, had been the same age, the age where children are curious about everything and understand a lot but have zero judgment. They can be a great source of information about a family's life.

The men talked about archaeological digs they had worked on and other details of getting into the backcountry of Peru. I tried to concentrate but my mind kept wandering off the topic as I watched the waves rolling onto the beach. A trail cut through the scrub brush, connecting the stairs that led down from the deck with the white sand shoreline beyond.

"Go on." Neil pointed with his chin, his voice breaking through my drifting thoughts. I turned my eyes toward him, questioning. "Go on," he repeated. "Go down there and take a stroll along the beach. I know you; you need some peace and quiet. I'll fill you in on all this later." He tilted his head toward the other two men.

"Okay," I said, getting up from the swing seat.

"Josie, you stay here with me," Greg instructed. Josie looked disappointed and went into the house as I ambled down the stairs and set out on the beach path.

A gull wheeled overhead, kew-kewing at me before tilting a wing and soaring back out over the water. I slipped off my shoes and rolled the legs of my pants up to my knees as I headed for the line where water swooshed over the sand and slid back out to sea. Standing in the low surf I let it wash over my feet and ankles. *Neil knows me well*, I thought. He knew that I was what he called, "one of you introverted artist-types" and I needed time alone and time to talk with my Lord. Even though my conversation with the Holy Spirit was somewhat continuous, my days never quite seemed complete until I had spent real time alone with God.

I turned north with the sea on my right and strolled along the water's edge, slowing my thoughts as my bare feet skimmed through the lapping ripples. I waited for that voice, so familiar and so sweet, to comfort my heart and whisper into my thoughts. As I walked, the heaviness that had hung over me like a thundercloud since my so-called wedding day, began to lift and dissolve away, scattering in the rays of the slanting sun. I thought of Marco and sought for a sense of peace to surround my heart but it would not come. I felt as if I were chasing a beautiful, pastel butterfly with a net that was nothing but holes.

"Why did this happen, Lord?" I whispered. The beach, at this hour lay nearly deserted. I couldn't remember what day it was but I thought it must be Tuesday by now. Where was everyone? Did they all work in the city and arrive home late? Had they grown so bored or satiated with beach living that they no longer bothered to walk the piece of paradise that lay right outside their doors? I pulled my wayward thoughts back again.

"Why, Lord? Why did this have to happen? Why on my wedding day?" Questions tumbled out of me. I had had so little time to think since the day of the wedding – the wedding that wasn't – that now all those pent-up questions grappled to be asked. *Did Marco even love me? Was he really kidnapped or was it all a grand ruse of some kind? If so, what could he possibly be up to? Who were those horrible men who held him captive, the ones we had seen in the Italian Gardens in London? When was that? Yesterday? The day before? Had he been with them by consent or was he really their prisoner? Why did he not seem to know me?*

I shook my head. I knew Marco to be a man of integrity, a man Neil trusted. If Neil trusted him, how could he be anything but upstanding and honest? Neil had always been a good judge of character, though I had to admit that he lacked the spiritual sensitivity that I treasured. It was not that he was not a man after God's own heart; he was. He just practiced his faith in more practical ways.

I thought of the events of the past spring when Neil had sent me to pick up the stones and how we had ended up at the hidden compound in Israel. There was so much I didn't know. To be honest, I wasn't sure I wanted to know it all. Sometimes, it just made more sense to me to follow the leading of the Spirit day by day and trust that he would make everything turn out right.

A bigger wave rolled in and splashed up my ankles. The husk of a sand dollar tumbled past my toes, flipping end over end through the surf. When the sea drew the water back out, the sand dollar went with it, riding through the sea foam and letting the tide take it.

I stood and watched as it disappeared and felt I was like that little empty urchin, tumbled and swept along by the tides of change in my life.

On the other hand, sometimes awful things happened anyway. Things like Marco being kidnapped the very day he was to marry me. Sometimes nothing made sense, or perhaps there is no sense to be made of what happens. It seemed some things would not be fully comprehended until we got to heaven. That didn't stop me from asking for answers.

I turned away from the water and found a smooth hollow in the sand, up against a small clump of bushes, and sat down facing the sea. Another gull wheeled overhead, screeching at me, and a squadron of seven or eight pelicans soared over the glimmering surface farther out, nearly touching the wave tips. A cool breeze had come up but I could feel the day's heat still in the sand, warming me. I wrapped my arms around my knees and gazed toward where the horizon curved into the sky.

"Father," I prayed softly, "only you can know how much my heart aches from losing Marco and how terrified I am for his safety. You know where he is and what's going on even if I don't and Neil doesn't. Please keep him safe wherever he is tonight." I stopped and put my head down on my knees, fighting back the tears. I was tired of crying, tired of the terror and just plain tired. "God," I continued, "please give me rest. I can't do this if I'm exhausted."

I had no idea exactly what Neil had in mind for the rest of the evening. We had talked about taking the next available flight out to South America but I did not know when it flew and I didn't even want to check. Lying back in the warm sand, I gazed up at the amethyst-streaked sky. "Lord, I am asking you to handle all these details for me. I will do whatever you ask me to do but for tonight, I just ask for a good rest."

For a long while, I lay there, feeling the soft heat of the sand and listening to the shush-shush of the waves. I must have drifted off because I opened my eyes with a start when the keening of a gull just overhead startled me. I looked at my watch and decided it was probably time I headed back to Greg's house and find out what the men had planned in my absence. Sitting up, I glanced down the beach and saw a figure running toward me. It was Neil. I hopped to my feet and started toward him. In a moment, we met.

Out of breath, Neil stopped running and bent over, panting heavily, his hands braced on his knees. When he stood again, his face glowed.

"What?" I said. "What is it?"

"We think we've found him," he said, gasping for breath.

"What do you mean?" I grabbed Neil's arm.

"Bobby went on to Peru before we left Wardley Hall, remember?"

"Yes?"

"He's seen Marco."

CHAPTER SEVENTEEN

Alejandro Velasco Astete International Airport swam into view through the rounded window next to my seat as the airplane banked for approach. Neil still slept beside me, breathing heavily. Over the wing I could see patches of forest green slanting up the slopes of rounded, velvet brown mountains and below, the outskirts of the city of Cusco straggled across the wide valley floor.

I had been asleep myself until a few minutes before when the announcements woke me. We had been fortunate to find flights the following day with only two stops – Miami and Lima – and now as the morning sun tossed its first rays over the mountaintops, here we were in Cusco. I prayed that Marco's kidnappers held him somewhere in this city, that we could find him, rescue him, go home, get married. The prayer repeated itself like a tape in my head: Find him, rescue him, go home, get married. Find him, rescue him, go home, get married. It had taken on a desperate tone even to me.

I pulled my gaze away from the approaching city and shook Neil's arm. His eyelids fluttered as he hauled himself upright.

"We're about to land."

"Already. Wow! I was so sound asleep."

"I know. I was too until a few minutes ago. It has been a long night."

After meeting Greg Tisdale at his seaside home, Neil and McSweeney and I found a hotel nearby, checked in, showered and rested for a while then went for dinner in the hotel restaurant. The place was quiet, the tables occupied by single business people eating alone. Thankful about that, I suggested we take a booth as far from the rest of the diners as possible, both for privacy and quiet.

As the flight we found didn't depart until after 5:00 p.m. the next day, we decided to call it an early night then meet with Greg over breakfast in the morning. If we had time to spare, he would take us on a quick tour of his historic city. The three of us were so jet-lagged that Neil and McSweeney merely summarized the content of their conversation with Greg, leaving out the details. I couldn't concentrate anyway. The combination of emotional mangling, high anxiety and travelling across the ocean twice in three days had left me as wrung out as a dry disk rag. Immediately after dinner I took the elevator to my room and went directly to bed. Sleep knocked me out like a steamroller and I barely moved until nine hours later. Blessed sleep, bless God.

Greg had already secured a booth at the hotel coffee shop by the time I straggled in for breakfast. Neil and McSweeney looked like they had already been out jogging or something. I could read the excitement in their eyes; the thrill of another adventure. I wished I could share their anticipation.

I smiled as I sat down beside Neil and ordered coffee from a grey-haired server with a nametag that read, "Esther."

"Sorry I'm late," I apologized.

"Just got here myself," McSweeney said. "Man, I slept like a hibernating bear."

"That's because you are one," Neil teased, picking up a menu.

"And ye're like an otter. You think risking your neck over an old pile of rocks is what passes for fun."

"Play nicely, you two. We have work to do," I said with a giggle as the others laughed. It felt good to laugh, if only for a moment.

"I agree," Neil said, taking on a more serious tone. "We've got some ground to cover this morning while we're together.

Jill, we have to bring you up to speed on some of our discussions from yesterday."

"Good. Tell me about Bobby. Have you heard anything more from him?

Neil shook his head. "I've tried numerous times but am not getting an answer." I saw a shadow cross his face and my heart lurched.

"Do you know something you're not telling me?"

"No. I'm just a little concerned. It's not like Bobby to be unresponsive."

"Anything could have happened," McSweeney offered. "He could have dropped his phone and had it run over in the street. Bingo! No response."

I let out a deep sigh.

"Well, since we don't know anything at the moment," Neil suggested, "how about we not worry about him right now and plan our next move." The others nodded in agreement.

I tapped a fingernail on the polished wood table as an outlet for the fidgets. "What I want to know is, who is this group that wants the glass dolphin so much anyway? What do we know about them? That guy we encountered in the park, the little skinny one, is one scary character. Do we know anything about these guys and what they're after?"

Greg spoke up. "I've been doing a little research and might have some answers. Sometimes I can't sleep, so last night I thought I might as well use the time I was awake to do something constructive."

Our breakfasts arrived and Esther poured more coffee all around. After she left, Neil said, "Tell us what you've found."

"While I was lying in bed, hoping to sleep, this name kept coming to mind. As you know, I've spent a lot of time in Peru and know a lot of people there. My wife is part Peruvian," he added, nodding toward me, "and she has some relatives in pretty high places. For example, her uncle was a high-ranking police officer in Cusco at the height of his career. He has retired now but over the years I've learned a lot about some of the criminal activity there – more than I want to know, actually."

I took a sip of coffee and wondered silently if God was taking us somewhere with this. I sensed that he had a hand in this meeting and more than a passing influence on Greg's insomnia.

Greg continued, "Anyway, this name kept coming up. Goncalvez; Goncalvez. I couldn't place it; don't think I've ever met anyone by that name. So I got up and did a little Internet searching. It took me a while to find anything interesting but then I happened upon a reference to this guy named Luis Estrada Goncalvez. He was a troublemaker in the eighties and early nineties, involved in drug trafficking and prostitution – the usual organized crime stuff. They managed to catch up with him and put him away but he was released several months ago. Since then his name hasn't been in the news but that doesn't mean that he's not up to his old tricks."

"Do you think he has something to do with Marco's kidnapping?" I asked.

Greg frowned. "Don't know. All I can say is that his name kept coming up in my head and he's a possibility."

"I've heard of that guy," Neil said. "He was involved in some kidnapping case years ago. If I remember correctly, he weaselled out of it somehow. They couldn't get enough evidence to nail him."

"That's the guy," Greg agreed, cutting into a fried egg.

"What does he look like? Is he the skinny guy we saw in London?" I pulled out my cell phone. "Did you find any images online?" Greg gave me a couple of search terms, which I tapped into my phone and flicked my finger across the screen to find a picture. Sure enough, a grainy black and white photo appeared. I shook my head. "It's not the same person we encountered in London." This man had a heavy face with thick jowls and no neck. A pair of dark, intelligent eyes squinted out from beneath heavy brows. I turned the phone and showed the picture to Neil and McSweeney.

"I guess we might as well follow it up," McSweeney remarked. "We don't have too many other options at the moment."

For the remainder of the meal we discussed different strategies for either finding the glass dolphin or rescuing Marco. We agreed that rescuing Marco would be our first priority with or without the figurine. Then the conversation turned toward the dolphin itself.

"I can't help thinking," Neil said, "that there is something about the crystalline structure of the dolphin shape that we haven't noticed, or can't until we actually see it. I'm sure you know that crystals have been used for things like optical components, avionics and satellites, sound systems and electronics for some time. It is possible that there is some…" he stopped and rubbed his chin, a habit he had when deep in thought, "…some feature of that crystal that has properties important enough for someone to commit a crime to obtain. This area of science is beyond my scope but I know someone who might be able to help with it, even without the object in hand."

McSweeney nodded and Greg gave us a quizzical look. Neil smiled back at him. "I have friend with a technology company," he explained. "He should be able to enlighten us a little."

Not long after, Neil tapped on the door of my hotel room while I tucked the last of my toiletries into my carry-on bag.

"Please let me see Cecilia Wardley's journal," he said. "I want to send a few photos to our friend, Dr. Ben Shalev in Israel, and see what he has to say."

CHAPTER EIGHTEEN

Neil snapped the photos with his phone and emailed them off. Fifteen minutes later, we had checked out of the hotel and joined Greg in his car for a quick city tour before heading off to the airport. While our flight would not leave until after 5:00, Greg had to get back home so we decided just to arrive early at the airport and take the extra time to relax, have a meal and, in my case at least, poke around the bookstore. A nap was not out of the question either, though after the previous night's gift of a great sleep, I felt like a new person. After a bit of convincing, McSweeney agreed to come along for the ride around the city.

"I have to get home today," he complained. "We're putting Angela's ninety-seven-year-old mother into a care home and Angie will wring my neck if I bail."

I had a hard time picturing McSweeney's wife tackling a man of his size and told him so.

"I know she's only as big as a sparrow," he explained, "but you don't want to cross her. She can be one pushy sparrow."

His plan was to catch the first commuter flight he could find, help get his mother-in-law settled then grab the next flight to Cusco. The information that Greg had provided led us to believe even more strongly that the part of the country where we would most likely be able to find Marco had to be east of Cusco in the mountains past the Urubamba River, and not where Jay Sharp had steered us. Apparently, Luis Goncalvez had originally come from a little village tucked up in the mountains and still spent time in that area from occasionally. We surmised that if we could not locate him anywhere else we could always go to his hometown where we might be able to pick up a trail. It wasn't much but it was something. The thought still nagged that we were grasping at straws but since straws and the nudging of the Holy Spirit were the only things we had to go on, it made sense to move forward with what we had and rely on God to direct our movement.

While driving through the old, picturesque streets of Charleston, past the elegant historic mansions with airy balconies and painted shutters to keep out the tropical heat was interesting, I couldn't keep my mind on what I saw. Thoughts of Marco crowded out everything else. I slipped into daydreams, remembering our summer together. He had travelled back to Spain a couple of times to take care of business in his restaurant supply company then hopped the first possible flights back to me. We shared romantic dinners, went canoeing on nearby lakes, travelled to islands in the Northwest Pacific coastline, and talked. I discovered that he loved seafood, couldn't spell very well, at least in English, and liked to collect knives, especially medieval ones. I fell in love with his laugh and that he liked to cook. That last one was particularly endearing since cooking has always been low on my list of fun things to do.

A deep sigh escaped. "I wish we could have found an earlier flight," I muttered.

Neil looked across the back seat at me. "If we had as much money as Quentin McSweeney," he said, reaching to squeeze my hand, "we could have hired a private jet and flown all night."

"Ha!" McSweeney barked from the front passenger seat. "If I had that kind of money, I'd buy a new boat instead of trying to hunt for treasure in that decomposing bucket I run now." I had been on McSweeney's boat and knew that his description of it was not far off.

"If you found more treasure instead of just loafing on deck eating your wife's baking," Neil quipped, "we could do both."

After we taxied into the airport in Cusco and found a nearby hotel to get our bearings, Neil and I sat in the shade on a small terrace, finishing up our morning coffee. I felt as though I had spent the night clinging to the airplane's wing, not crumpled into a seat in the cabin. I even had the hair to go with it.

McSweeney had not yet arrived in the country and wouldn't until early evening. He had texted us that his mother-in-law had been moved without incident and that he would be driving from his home in Key West up to Miami in the wee hours of the morning to catch a 5:00 a.m. flight.

Our job now would be to find out what happened to Bobby. We located the hotel where he had stayed without difficulty but found out that he had not checked out. However, when we quizzed the housekeeping staff we discovered that his room had not been cleaned for two days. The "Do Not Disturb" tag hanging from the door handle made sure that no one bothered him. With a bit of cajoling and communicating our fears that something had happened to our friend, we managed to gain entrance to his room.

Inside, we found his things, what few there were, as Bobby travelled lightly. His backpack lay on the floor, its contents strewn around as though it had been unzipped and dumped. His shaving paraphernalia littered the bathroom counter. It was evident from everything we saw that he had not planned to leave. So where was he? The bed remained unmade and his wallet and gun were gone. It appeared that he had left his belongings in the room on purpose and, taking only the essentials, had gone out for a meal. We decided simply to clean up a little then leave the room as occupied in case he returned. I jotted a note on the pad by the telephone and left it in plain view, telling him we had arrived and where we had booked in. I tried his cell number again but got no answer.

"I guess that's about all we can do," I said, turning to Neil. Then my eye caught a tiny flash of white beneath the hem of the bedspread. Reaching down, I pulled out a scrap of notepaper. A few figures had been penned diagonally across it, followed by a telephone number.

"Look at this." I handed the note to Neil.

"This looks like what an investigator would call 'a clue.'" He read it quickly and stuffed the note in his pocket. "So let's go follow it up."

Back at our own hotel, Neil called the number. It turned out to belong to a mountain guiding outfit, a local father and son team, that offered private guiding through the mountains to places that most people want to avoid. Neil had a short conversation in his fluent Spanish with the father of the team, one Juan Carlos Gutierrez, who explained that his son was off in the mountains right now but he might be able to help us. No, he had not spoken to Bobby but his son, Daniel, had left on his trek the previous day so it was possible that he had spoken with him. Unfortunately, Daniel would not be reachable due to the terrain and the mountains, but he would be back in a week.

Forty-five minutes later, we had visited Gutierrez in person and, assured of his credentials after a couple of well-placed calls to Neil's colleagues in the Incan archaeology trade, hired him to lead us through the back country to Luis Goncalvez' village in the event that we didn't find Marco first.

After that, we began our search for Bobby and for any news of Marco having been through the city. Our visit to the police proved pointless but on Greg's recommendation and because of his family connection, we managed to secure a meeting with his wife's uncle, Antonio Huamani.

The taxi pulled up in front of a modern looking yellow home with clay tiled roofing, situated on the side of a hill overlooking the city and surrounded by a well-tended garden. Señor Huamani invited us in as we apologized for interrupting his day. He was of short stature with a head of wavy grey hair swept back from his forehead. Serious dark eyes greeted us from behind wire-framed glasses. A maid fetched cold drinks from somewhere in the house as we settled onto contemporary black furniture in the living room that looked out on a back garden and a swimming pool. Obviously, being a high-ranking police officer had many perks.

"How may I help you, my friends?" Señor Huamani asked in smooth, slightly accented English after the maid had left the room. "I just had a telephone call from my niece's husband in South Carolina and understand that you are in some difficulty."

Neil briefly explained about Marco's kidnapping and Bobby's disappearance. He also enquired about the man called Goncalvez.

"Ah, yes. He was released from prison not long ago. A very objectionable individual is Luis Goncalvez. I haven't heard anything about him lately but it would not surprise me if he has gone straight back into his old ways. In fact, he likely never stopped in spite of his incarceration. He can be a ruthless man but I'm sure he knows that if he wants something from you, it is in his best interest to keep his prisoner, your friend, unharmed. However, the moment he has what he wants, your friend is in grave danger."

He must have seen the shiver that ran through my body as he gave me a gentle smile. "If you can give me a detailed description of your friend, I will be happy to make some inquiries for you with regard to your Señor Jimenez and also see if the police have tabs, as you would say, on what Goncalvez might be up to."

While I produced my photos of Marco, he gave us a few tips on searching for missing persons, starting with checking the hospitals, which was the next item on our list anyway. While we waited, he placed a call to the main police station and spoke softly with someone for several minutes. After posing a couple of questions, he spent the remainder of the call nodding and responding with, "*Sí.*"

I glanced around the elegant room. It too had examples of Moche art, either copies or the real thing. I had heard that the Moche burial grounds, scattered all over the desert, were frequently looted for artifacts that found their way into basement shops, back door dealers and the black market. Poor farmers often used this activity during the off-season as a way to supplement their meagre farming income. One could hardly blame them but it still made me wince to think of these exquisite pieces of art created by hands during the first century after Christ's birth being treated so cavalierly. I could only imagine how Neil felt when he saw such blatant looting of a nation's treasures.

I remembered the man with the antique shop in England, with his shifty eyes and vague answers. Had he acquired his pieces through unsavoury means? I studied the jars, jugs and figurines prominently displayed on teak shelving in Antonio Huamani's living room. *Perhaps they are merely copies*, I thought, mainly to mollify myself.

Neil appeared to be listening to the telephone conversation and watched our host surreptitiously. Neil's fluent and adept use of Spanish definitely made things easier for us. He spoke it well, though with a slight Mexican accent owing to his years in the Yucatan jungles.

After a few minutes, Señor Huamani put down the telephone. "The news is not good," he reported. "The police know nothing about your friend, Bobby Buckingham, but will keep their ears open for any reports." Bobby would be hard to miss on a Peruvian street as he stood a half a head taller than even Neil and had skin the colour of dark chocolate. In this country where the indigenous people tended to come to my shoulder, Bobby would look like a giant, a detail that we had explained to Huamani.

"What about Marco Jimenez?" I asked, suppressing my anxiety by sheer force of will. "Has anyone heard from him or seen him? Bobby called us a couple of days ago to say that he had seen Marco but that's the last we have heard of either man."

Huamani sat down on the edge of the striped sofa and brushed non-existent lint from his pant leg. "The police heard a rumour about this man's appearance in the city but he disappeared just as fast. It was only a chance encounter. A street officer happened to be walking his beat when a man fitting the description you gave them of your Señor Jimenez exited a car and was ushered into a hotel. Since no crime appeared to be in progress, the officer did nothing. However, he had the foresight to stroll past the hotel and watch what was happening inside. I spoke with an officer on the telephone just now who was good enough to check around his office. That is how this information came to light. It is not much but perhaps it will be of use to you."

I nodded, blinking back tears.

"I assure you, Señora, that now that the police have been alerted, they will be on the lookout for both men. In the meantime, I suggest that you check the hospitals and clinics to see if either man has been admitted. Unfortunately, our police force does not have the capability to do this for you. I'm sure that with persistence, you will find your friends. Now, if you will excuse me, I have work to do. My maid will show you out."

CHAPTER NINETEEN

Neil and I showed up together at the airport to meet McSweeney's plane. For some reason, just knowing that he would be here with us gave me a measure of comfort. The man, besides being big, tough and smart, had a keen strategic sense that enabled him to cut to the heart of any matter without getting hung up in useless details. While Neil treated me almost as his own daughter, McSweeney made me feel safe, even when doing crazy things like diving for treasure in shark-infested Caribbean waters.

He strode out of the customs area and threw us a wave.

"Well, we got Granny settled and I hopped on the first plane they'd let me on," he announced as we headed for the taxi stand. "I got here as soon as I could. Angela was a bit steamed but she'll get over it. What have you guys found out?"

We told him that after we left Antonio Huamani's house we went straight to the nearest hospital and enquired about Bobby and Marco. Neither had been there. We checked with the other two hospitals in the city then headed back to our hotel where Neil spent an unproductive hour calling every clinic he could from a list obtained at the front desk. Nothing. No one had heard of or seen either man.

"Maybe Bobby took off after Marco when he saw him," I said, after Neil put down the phone. "I can't see him coming back to his room to collect his things if he happened to spot Marco being hauled out of town, can you?"

"It's possible that Marco is still in Cusco, you know," Neil answered, stretching out on the bed and closing his eyes. Within seconds the soft rumble of a snore escaped his throat.

112

McSweeney went off to his own room to settle in.

Pretty multi-paned glass doors opened out onto a tiny balcony with filigree wrought-iron railings. I had just stepped out into the still afternoon air to have a look around when I heard a soft knock on the door. Scurrying across the room in bare feet, I peered through the peephole in the door then yanked it open. Bobby stood in the hallway, his hands in the pockets of his jeans.

"Bobby!" I squealed, throwing my arms around his neck. He hugged me lightly then stepped away.

"Mind if I come in, ma'am?"

"Come, come," I said, beckoning him. "Quiet though; Neil's asleep." Bobby followed me past the sleeping body of my uncle and out to the balcony. I pulled the glass doors closed behind us.

"What on earth happened to you?" I asked in horror as I got a good look at Bobby's face in the sunlight. A dark red gash ran across the side of his forehead surrounded by a purplish lump. One eye was so bloodshot that I could see no white at all and the side of his left forearm sported a long bandage held in place by strips of surgical tape.

"I guess you could say I was mugged," he answered. "I'm fine, really, though my arm is a little banged up. I had to have stitches."

"But where did you get that done? We called every hospital and clinic in the entire city. No one had heard of you."

"The infirmary at my hotel had a nurse on duty and she fixed me up."

"I'm so relieved, Bobby, but what happened? Neil said you called, that you'd seen Marco then you disappeared and didn't answer any of our calls."

"I did see Marco but only briefly. Shortly after I arrived, I checked into my hotel and then decided to have a look around, ask a few questions, since I had a photo of Marco I could show people. No one had seen him but as I walked down the street a few blocks from here, who should appear but the man himself? Four thugs had him surrounded and hustled him from a building, shoved him into the waiting car and took off. I ran down the street to see which way they went. Just as they turned a corner, three other guys jumped me."

"Did he see you?"

Bobby hesitated, looking down into the street below the balcony. "I thought he did," he said, finally. "I could swear that he recognized me for a second but just as quickly looked away. If I'm right, the only reason I can think of is he was trying to protect me. It was no time to pick a fight. Even together we were outnumbered seven to two."

"Were they the same guys we saw in London?"

"Yes, and then some."

"Did they knock you out? That looks like a nasty bump on your head."

Bobby reached up and gingerly touched the wound. "Thankfully, no. They were mean and fast but not nearly as strong or as well trained in combat as I am so they got the worst end of it. I managed to get away from them after cracking a few skulls and staggered back to my hotel. By then I felt pretty woozy and when I reeled into the lobby, the front desk attendant took one look at me and called the in-house medic. I didn't call Neil or you again because my cell phone got smashed in the fight. I was kind of out of it for a while, too. I don't know what she gave me but I slept like the dead for I don't know how long."

"I am so glad you're here and you're all right," I said, rubbing Bobby's uninjured arm. "But what do you know of Marco? What happened to him?"

"I'm sorry, Mrs. Moss, I don't know. But we've got to find him and that glass dolphin. I'm just not sure in what order."

CHAPTER TWENTY

After the sun sank beyond the purple mountains surrounding the city, the air took on a chill that reminded me of autumn in the Canadian Rockies – dry, crisp and biting. I pulled my only sweater up under my chin and wrapped my hands around a mug of hot herbal tea. The four of us had gathered over dinner on a terrace to compare notes and plan our strategy.

Bobby and I had roused Neil from his deep slumber to let him know that Bobby was back safe, if not quite sound. The moment Neil opened his eyes he catapulted from the bed and threw his arms around Bobby.

"I was afraid we'd lost you, son," he said, grinning widely. "I'm so glad you're all right."

The cool night air swirled around my bare ankles. I pushed the remains of my irresistible Torta De Chocolate, a rich cocoa cake with fudgy topping, around with my fork. I didn't usually leave chocolate this delectable on a plate but my appetite had vanished.

"The way I see it, we're going to have to split up," I said. "We have two objectives; rescue Marco, and find the glass dolphin. Frankly, if we only accomplish the first of the two, that would be fine by me."

Neil turned his head slowly toward me. "I can understand your concern for your fiancé," he said, gently, "but there is something else at stake. The glass dolphin has to have enormous significance if these people are willing to go to such lengths to obtain it."

"What do you know that the rest of us don't?" McSweeney growled through a mouthful of lime pie. "You're the archaeological brains of this operation."

Neil glanced over his shoulder at the surrounding restaurant. We had decided to eat on the outdoor patio for more privacy since, with the evening rapidly cooling, most diners wanted to be inside. Our table was the only alfresco one occupied now that the hour had grown late. "I have made a few calls to some of my trusted colleagues," Neil said, "and have found out some interesting bits of information."

"Yeah? Like what?" McSweeney wanted to know. The lime pie demolished, he mopped his mouth with a crumpled napkin before taking a swig of coffee.

"As you all know, the operation in Israel has been studying ancient technologies that are largely believed to be lost in time, or not believed to have existed at all. We have a different view of that since we know that God has set things up in certain ways and just because modern science has not figured those things out does not make them null or void. When the technologies revealed by the sixteen stones that we gathered last spring were revealed, with all your help, the organization was able to use our computers and equipment to affect gravitational fields in ways that no one else in the world is doing right now. We're ahead of a lot of mainstream science on that since we've been building on the Word of God, prayer, and the study of ancient civilizations for decades now."

A cool breeze drifted down the street, lifting my hair and sending a shiver down my back muscles. It was past time to call it a night but I couldn't leave yet.

"There is more than one reason that we have to get to the glass dolphin before our Mr. Goncalvez, or whoever is ultimately behind this. If he believes, as Cecilia Wardley suggested in her diary, there is some magical or spiritual power associated with the artifact, then he is a dangerous man indeed. I am guessing that a spiritual power not his own is behind this. As you know, the Bible warned us that our enemy, Satan, goes around like a roaring lion seeking to devour whomever he can.

Unfortunately, lots of people rush headlong into his hands in an effort to further their own greedy ends."

"The world seems to be crawling with those kind of crackpots," McSweeney observed. "Why do I always have to be the one to roust them out?"

Neil laughed. "Because you'd go bonkers sitting at home weeding your flowerbeds, that's why – and tinkering with your old boat."

"Hey, don't knock my boat," McSweeney protested.

"He doesn't have to," I replied, reaching across the table and patting McSweeney's arm. "It knocks all by itself."

"Do you believe that the artifact has significance for the work of the organization?" asked Bobby, the serious one. He had been with us when we had delivered the ring of stones to the compound hewn out of the centre of a mountain in the middle of a forest in Israel. As Neil's trusted security man, it was vital that he be kept in the loop of everything regarding not only Neil's safety on his travels and archaeological digs but also anything pertaining to the whole organization when the need arose.

"As a matter of fact, I do," Neil replied. "Like I said, I've made a few calls and am pretty convinced that my hunch is correct about this glass dolphin." A chair scraped against the tiled terrace floor nearby and Neil stopped talking.

"*Disculpe*, Señor." Turning to determine the source of the woman's soft voice, I saw the figure of a tiny nun wearing a plain grey habit with a white head covering materialize out of the shadows. "Excuse me, Señor," she repeated, this time in clear English.

"*Sí*," Neil turned to face her.

"May I join you for a moment? Please forgive me. I don't mean to interrupt your conversation. I just came now, up the street."

"Please, sit down," Neil answered, pulling a chair over from a nearby table and placed it between him and me. "How may I help you?"

The nun smiled and winked at him. Yes, winked at him. "It's not how you can help me so much as how I can help you," she said in a hushed voice. "My name is Laura Weaver. I'm American but I'm working with a mission here in Cusco. You could say I'm its liaison and logistics." She appeared to be about thirty years old and had light brown hair and blue-grey eyes. Her fingers danced when she talked as though she had too much energy and didn't know what to do with it. "I was sent to speak to you."

"How'd you find us?" McSweeney asked, scowling from beneath his woolly eyebrows.

"I was sitting at home reading tonight when the Lord spoke to me to put on this habit and come down to this restaurant, that there is a man here who needs me." She grinned. "I'm not actually a nun but I have this habit as a disguise because here nobody suspects a nun of anything but good. You become somewhat invisible in garments like these."

By this time she had our attention. "What did God tell you to do here?" I asked, leaning forward with my elbows on the arms of my chair.

"Do you need horses?"

The four of us glanced at each other. The purpose of our meeting was to discuss strategy both to find Marco and to discover the glass dolphin. We had not yet got to the discussion of how we would get where we had to go.

"We might," Neil answered but offered nothing more.

"I can get you as many as you need whenever you're ready."

"From where?"

"You're going up into the remote valleys past the Urubamba, aren't you?"

Neil hesitated. "I believe so."

"That's what I thought. I live in a village out there in the mountains. I can arrange for your horses, or burros. Unless you want llamas," she added, her eyes crinkling at the corners.

I shuddered at the thought of having to deal with llamas. They had a reputation for being nasty and intractable.

"I have this sense that you'll need to go far into the jungle," Laura continued. "The horses can only take you so far but you can leave them at another village and continue on foot. It will save you lots of time."

"How do you know where we're going?" Bobby asked, frowning suspiciously. We both knew that we had not yet discussed where we would go or what we would need to get there.

Laura tilted her head. "The Holy Spirit told me, of course. You're looking for something, or someone; I don't know which. Or, maybe both, someone and something. Am I right?" Heads nodded. "It's okay. You don't have to tell me. That's not why I'm here. Do you have a guide for the mountains? It's easy to get lost out there."

"I talked with a guide earlier today," Neil said. "A quick call will secure his services whenever we're ready to go."

"What's his name?" Laura asked, directing her question at Neil.

"It's Juan Carlos Gutierrez. Do you know him?"

She nodded. "I've heard of him and even met him once. He's good. In fact, he's supposed to be the best. Get the dad, though, not his son. He's the one who really knows the passes and the trails."

We made plans to meet with Laura Weaver the following morning and she got up to leave. "One more thing," she added, turning back towards us and looking at me. "This isn't going to turn out like you think it will," she said, "but God has something unexpected for you."

"What is it?" I asked.

She shrugged. "I couldn't say. That's all he told me." With that, she turned and walked away, disappearing into the night.

119

CHAPTER TWENTY-ONE

The first rays of morning sun tripped over the jagged line of mountains outside my hotel room window and slanted across my journal page, casting a long shadow from the pen in my hand. We had arranged a time to meet this morning to eat and gather our provisions for the trip up into the high country. Neil had agreed to engage the services of Juan Carlos Gutierrez as our guide and insisted that he, and not his son, accompany us. Since Neil spoke the best Spanish among us from his years working with Mayan and Aztec archaeology in Mexico and Central America, and because he had already been planning a trip to investigate ruins in Peru, he was the natural choice for official spokesperson and logistical captain. McSweeney and Bobby spoke rudimentary Spanish from living, and having learned some in school, in the southern U.S. while I, when forced to communicate in any foreign language always defaulted to my high school French, which frequently was not the language required. I discovered, however, that if I could drag up the French vocabulary and put a Spanish sounding accent on it, sometimes it worked but not often enough to give me any confidence.

I had no doubt that Neil had already contacted the guide, in spite of the early hour, and that my job, besides listening for the guidance of the Holy Spirit and sending prayers up pretty much without a break, was to show up in my new trekking attire and with all the gear that I had purchased in Paris from Neil's must-have list.

I had awakened earlier than I had planned and rolled over with a groan, knowing that my brain, whirling with thoughts, would never allow me to drift back to sleep. Instead of trying to recapture the elusive delusion of a full night's sleep, I pushed back the covers and got up, did the morning bathroom trip then grabbed my journal and Bible and took a chair by the window, leaned back on a cushion and propped my feet up on the opposite chair.

Anxiety had seemed to be my constant companion from the moment I realized that Marco was not going to show up for our wedding and that something terrible must have happened. Normally, I handled most anything that came my way quite well, having survived one of life's great traumas, the unexpected and untimely death of my husband, Roger.

My marriage to Roger had never been easy and as time went on, he had become more morose and bad tempered. Unpredictable outbursts of anger and vituperation spattered his poison around our home and into my heart. He was never intentionally abusive, just miserable and belligerent to live with. I began to wonder if he even loved me, or indeed, if he ever had. I examined myself relentlessly. What had I done to cause his wrath? Was I a bad wife? Was I so unlovable?

Even after he had died, those questions plagued me and woke me at night in a cold sweat from dreams that made me not want to sleep again. I knew in my head that God loved me but something in my heart still questioned whether I was fit to be loved by a man. My self-confidence drained away and I sank into a lethargic depression, barely managing to keep myself pulled together for the sake of my children who had their own emotional trauma to deal with. It was only after I had a dream in which I met Jesus on a mountain meadow and Roger was with him that I turned a corner. The peace of God flooded my weary soul and miraculously lifted my spirit, and equally astonishingly, the spirits of my children, too.

Now as I sat in the golden rays of the Andean sunrise that streamed through the glass balcony doors, with my sweater

121

tucked around my middle and my pen in hand, I reflected on all that had happened since that fateful day. Only five months before, Marco Jimenez had collided with my life. I had not been looking for another man; in fact, I didn't even want one. I had pretty much had my fill.

My children had grown up enough to leave the house. My daughter had her dream job in fashion in the city and my son had gone travelling. The house and my life were my own. My career as a fine artist, with gallery showings and commissions flowing in, was in full swing, making my dreams of artistic success finally come true after years of rejection and struggle.

That's when Neil contacted me about picking up the pieces of the rare and extremely valuable artifact that he had unearthed at a Mayan dig in Mexico. His desperation and the imminent danger that drove him into hiding had sent me off on a wild chase all over the world to gather up the pieces and safeguard their delivery to the organizational headquarters in Israel. This organization and Neil's association with its mandate had been a complete surprise to me, both because my beloved uncle had such a deep involvement with it and because its purpose – to discover and utilize ancient and lost technologies for the benefit of the world – had as its main customer, the Government of Israel. The scope of the organization was nothing short of eye-popping.

The stone artifact proved to have value far beyond its archaeological worth. Knowing Neil, I suspected that the glass dolphin would be in the same class. He knew his stuff and wouldn't likely pursue such a quest if it did not have far-reaching and perhaps even prophetic consequences. The nature of his work in digging up the past usually meant finding artifacts that filled in the blanks of technological history.

"Father," I prayed out loud in my empty room, turning my thoughts back to the problems at hand, "help us make the right decisions. Help me to remember to seek your direction." I rested my forehead on my hand. "Oh, Lord, I hardly even know how to pray right now. You know what we have to do, where we have to go today. Please send the right people to help us. Thank-you for sending Laura to help us find horses. Watch over us and maybe give us extra angels to go with us as we hit the road today, or when there is no road. We must find Marco. We must find this glass dolphin too, even if I don't exactly know why."

I stopped and took a long, deep breath then released it. In that moment, I sensed that God had something specific to tell me. Picking up my pen again, I wrote the date at the top of a clean page in my journal then began to write the words that flowed from his spirit into mine, into my mind and out through my hand.

"My child, fear not. I see that you are troubled with anxiety and fear. Have I not said in my word, over and over, 'Fear not'? Fear will cloud your mind so that you can neither think clearly nor hear my voice saying, 'Go this way' or 'Turn that way.' It is imperative that you listen for my leading, for the way ahead is perilous and there are many dangers. Concentrate on listening for my voice throughout your day. Quiet the noise and confusion in your mind and open your mind to my Spirit."

The riot of confusing emotions and turmoil-filled thoughts stilled like a pool, as the drops of peace again settled into my heart. It wasn't much but as the trickle of peace stole into my soul, the anxiety edged out, displaced. I raised my hands in the morning sun and began to praise the name of the Lord. I knew that fear and anxiety couldn't stay in the presence of praise to God and somehow in the disappointment, confusion, jetlag and fatigue I had forgotten that. I closed my eyes and the sun's rays turned the inside of my lids a brilliant, glowing red and still I praised my Saviour. With each minute of praise and adoration, my own spirit seemed to lift as though buoyed on a helium balloon and as it lifted, the fear fled. I knew that somehow, something would work out. I didn't know what nor how but by trusting in God's grace, I knew that if I listened to him, he would tell me what to do. He loved me. No matter what else happened, God loved and never condemned me, regardless of my own emotional hopelessness or moments of skepticism.

After a while, I opened my eyes and glanced at the clock.

"Oh, my goodness," I said, dropping my hands and leaping up. I had only fifteen minutes to shower, get dressed, pack my bags and be downstairs for an early breakfast with the rest of those I had come to think of as our rescue team. Laura Weaver had decided not to accompany us. I knew that between McSweeney and Bobby, a full background check would have already been completed. Whether or not she was who she said she was, was not my problem.

Twenty minutes later I appeared in the dining room of the hotel for breakfast and was relieved to find that I was not the only one who was late. Neil wasn't there either. I eased myself into a booth next to Bobby who was busy stuffing big bites of cheesy omelette into his mouth.

"He's outside talking to that guide," McSweeney explained. So much for not being the last to get going in the morning. "That Weaver girl is out there, too. Seems to think she needs to be in on the conversation."

CHAPTER TWENTY-TWO

My head thumped against the windowpane and woke me. Wincing from the impact, I sat up.

"Where are we?"

"It shouldn't be much farther now," Neil called over his shoulder from the driver's seat. The little Peruvian guide, Gutierrez sat in the front passenger seat so he could give directions along the way. Neil's original plans for archaeological excavation had taken this same route, east from Cusco, rather than north toward the famous ruins of Machu Picchu. He believed that there was something of interest in these mountains where drier alpine heights gave way to wet eastern slopes. While he had not elaborated on his suspicions, I knew from his past record that between his research and his meticulous preparations he almost always found precisely what he expected.

We had left Cusco in the early hours in a rented van, five of us. Laura Weaver had made her calls and provided the information we would need should horses be required but had stayed behind in Cusco, stating that she had done her part. Now, as evening loomed, we approached our destination for the day. With only a couple of stops for food and toilet breaks, the trip had taken nearly nine hours, first on a paved road then as it wound up and over mountains in heart-stopping hairpin turns, finally on a rutted, potholed dirt road. The swaying of the van had made me so nauseated that my only hope of not throwing up had been to sink into a semi-slumber, opening my eyes only occasionally to view the surrounding countryside.

Twenty minutes after I had last asked how long it would

take to get there, we drove onto the wide central street of a town called Pillcopata. Hardly more than an outpost in the jungle and on the banks of the Alto Madre de Dios River, in the fading light we could see scarred buildings with corrugated tin roofs and ramshackle businesses lining the main drag. A couple of small boys kicked a soccer ball in the street then jumped out of the way to stare as we drove past.

Gutierrez had arranged for a hotel for the night and we all gladly extricated ourselves from the confines of the van, McSweeney grumbling about never being able to stand up straight again and Bobby stretching and twisting his body to loosen the stiffness. I groaned as I straightened my legs and exited the seat, my feet landing with a puff of dust.

"Come on, you feeble lot," Neil chided, grabbing a couple of bags from the rear of the van. "If a little drive does you in, what're you going be like after a day slashing through the jungle with your bright new machetes?"

I scowled at him, pulled my backpack and tote bag from the vehicle and followed Juan Carlos into the modest hotel. Once rooms had been parcelled out, I dragged myself down the hallway to find my own. Inside, the furnishings had the look of a youth hostel – simple but neat and clean. A single window looked out on the street.

An hour and a half later, after meeting for something to eat, we sat around a table in the dusky evening light sipping cups of strong coffee, or in my case, a bottle of water. I didn't need anything that might interfere with my night's sleep.

"What's your rationale for that?" McSweeney wanted to know.

"We don't know exactly what we're after or where to find it," Neil explained. "Juan Carlos has indicated that Goncalvez is rumoured to have some kind of compound out in the jungle overlooking the Alto Madre de Dios River." He twisted a thumb in the direction of the river that ran past one side of the town. Guttierrez had explained that the Rio Pillcopata angled toward it on the north side, and the two rivers met just to the east, and farther on, the Rio Pini Pini also flowed into the Madre de Dios on its way to the Amazon Basin. "I think you and Bobby should hire a boat and go down the river for a look. You know boats and water better than the rest of us. It makes the most sense."

McSweeney shrugged. "Okay, you're the boss on this one. Bobby, it looks like you're stuck with me."

Bobby grinned. "Well," he said, rubbing his ear, "this will be a new experience for me. I've never navigated an Amazonian river before."

"That makes two of us," McSweeney muttered.

"Juan Carlos and I have already made arrangements for you to leave first thing in the morning."

"What about you and me?" I asked. Neil's reputation for charging off into uncharted jungles was legendary and I had a sudden horrific vision of myself running after him swinging a machete through some snake-infested wilderness.

Neil clapped a hand on Juan Carlos' rounded shoulder. "Our trusty guide here is going to lead us by a different route in the off-chance that we can get information from the forest people to aid in our search. He knows the ways of the jungle. Besides, I've heard tell of a site of ruins back in there somewhere that might lead us to that glass dolphin."

I pressed two fingers into my right temple. "All right. I'm willing if you are," I answered gamely.

Gutierrez muttered something in Spanish and Neil replied briefly.

"What? What did he say?" I asked.

"He says it's no place for a lady."

I snorted. "You can say that again."

"I told him you're no lady; you're my niece."

"You did not!" I reached over and smacked his arm. "I

127

guess I have to take that as a challenge," I said then took another sip of water. "Just remember, my main goal is to find Marco. Whatever that's going to take, that's what I'll do. The sooner we can find and free him, the better." Thankfully, I received no argument.

That night, in spite of having shunned the coffee, I slept fitfully. The hotel, with its thin walls, echoed with banging wooden doors and bathroom visits all night, not to mention the mob of rainforest trekkers who arrived after midnight directly from celebrating their prowess over multiple beers. I found myself hot then cold then hot again, sweaty then shivering, then at 3:00 a.m. wide-awake and staring at the ceiling. Rather than flipping from my right side to my left side and back again for the next two hours hoping for sleep to return, I clicked on the dim bedside lamp and dug my Bible out of my bag.

For a while I tried reading something soporific like the laws in Leviticus but I found that I needed a text that would capture my attention more than that. The thought of venturing off into the Amazonian jungle didn't exactly put me at ease. I remembered having read, years before, about the early Amazonian explorers in the beginning of the last century, the so-called Age of Exploration, when intrepid travellers like Lt. Colonel Percival Fawcett set off into the jungles of Brazil in order to find what he called the Lost City of Z, and was never seen again. I would be lying if I said that the prospect of wandering around in circles in the jungle and never emerging again hadn't crossed my mind. It had – about four hundred times.

As I flipped idly through the Bible's thin pages, the book seemed suddenly to drop open in the book of Judges, at the story of Gideon. As stories always have had the power to draw me in, I began to read, hoping that focusing on Gideon's predicament would take my mind off my own. My tired eyes drifted over the lines of the story, all about how God called

Gideon to go out against the enemies of his people. Poor Gideon didn't know what befell him and tried his best to persuade God to choose someone else, someone stronger and far better suited to the demands of war. But the angel had already promised him that the Lord was with him.

Suddenly, a verse seemed to glow before my eyes, as though the surrounding text had grown blurry and this verse stood out clearly and alone. "And the LORD looked upon him, and said, Go in this thy might, and thou shalt save Israel from the hand of the Midianites: have not I sent thee?"

Oh, my goodness, I thought. The reminder that I didn't have to do this trip alone struck me. I'd never had to. God had always been with me and even though trekking into the jungle to look for Marco was no job for a "lady," I knew that it would not be my own strength that would carry me through. Thanking God for delivering his comfort to me, I closed the book, turned off the lamp and dropped into a deep, restful sleep for a full three hours.

I was wakened by the simultaneous banging on my room door and the insistent crowing of a rooster outside my window.

"Hold on, I'm coming," I muttered through my night-dry mouth. Throwing a shirt on over my pyjama tank top, I unlocked the door.

"Time to hit the road," McSweeney chortled, leaning against the doorjamb and grinning at me.

"Who put you on wake-up call?" I crabbed, glaring at him.

He grinned and said, "Breakfast is on. Neil's ready to head out." Then he pulled the door closed and I heard the sound of his boots receding along the wooden floor of the hotel hallway.

"He would be," I grumbled, flicking the lock and heading for the bathroom. "Has that man never heard of the concept of sleeping past 6:00 in the morning?"

As I hastily got ready I realized that the great thing about trekking through the jungle is that you don't have to spiff yourself up for the journey. Ten minutes later, having my teeth brushed and my wet hair pulled back into a tight bun and stabbed with a handful of bobby pins, I had my bags re-stuffed and ready to go.

By the time I had gulped down a quick breakfast and burned the roof of my mouth on a scalding coffee, Neil, Bobby, McSweeney and Juan Carlos had all gathered outside. As I stepped out into the street, a sudden chill quivered up my spine. We were being watched; I knew it. I lowered my head to glance sideways up the street, first in one direction then in the other. At this early hour, not much was moving. A yellow dog lay sprawled smack in the middle of the road and a round woman with a sack over her shoulder scuttled down an alley. It seemed peaceful enough and I was about to shrug it off when something caught my eye. A shadow, or a movement down to my right, slinked past a doorway and disappeared. In an upstairs window of another building I saw a curtain twitch ever so slightly before hanging still again.

CHAPTER TWENTY-THREE

In his early thirties, tall, blonde and with a distinct Dutch accent, Henry Van Hoogendoorn sauntered up to join our group.

"Just call me Henry, the boatman," he said, politely shaking hands with each of us. "I'll get you where you want to go. I've lived here about five years and I take visitors up and down the rivers to the Manu Cloud Forest Reserve regularly. I also go to missions and the towns downriver for trade. When it comes to these rivers, I'm your man."

The previous evening we had agreed that if everything went perfectly we would meet up with McSweeney and Bobby downriver at a little place called Salvacion. Failing that, since river travel could be unpredictable at best, even farther downriver was a place called Shintuya where we would try to get in touch with each other should we miss connecting sooner. Our plan was that whoever found either Marco or the glass dolphin first would get word to the other party by any means possible. Neil had handed out encrypted satellite phones, which we hoped would work if we needed them.

Neil and I would follow Gutierrez through the jungle, passing through villages hidden in the forest and seeking information. Juan Carlos assured us that he knew where these settlements were and could take us there without any problem. The horses that Laura Weaver had engaged for us now waited at some post in the forest where we would drive until the road petered out. Horses were kept in Pillcopata for tourists to ride into the jungle and we would be taking the same route for a while, looking like any other small group of jungle tourists. At some point, we would leave the horses and continue on foot. Nevertheless, I had to remind myself it would not be my strength that carried me through this but the strength of the Lord.

McSweeney and Bobby gathered up their packs, a raft of bottled water and enough insect-repellent to take a swim in and prepared to join Henry, the boatman. They would drive down river on the only road through the jungle for a while before boarding his boat.

"The road is so bad in some places that the river is faster and safer," Henry explained. Bobby and McSweeney's task was to find out whatever they could about Goncalvez and his whereabouts as well as fishing for information about the ancient stories involving a relic like the glass dolphin.

Neil and I stood with our guide in front of the hotel and watched as the other three crossed the dusty street and threw their packs in the back of Henry's pick-up truck. About to pull himself into the cab of the vehicle, McSweeney turned around and loped back across the wide street.

"Moss, I've got a message for you. Gee, this never happens to me," he said, turning red and looking off down the street, his hands jammed into his pants pockets. "This might be completely off the wall but I'm pretty sure you'll know what it means."

I looked at him quizzically. "What is it?"

"Proverbs three, twenty-five and six." With that he turned away, ran across the road and hopped into the pick-up. With a wave, they drove out of sight.

"Interesting," Neil said.

"Do you know what those verses say? I can't remember and my Bible is tucked away in my pack."

Neil smiled, squinting at me in the morning sun. "Be not afraid of sudden fear, neither of the desolation of the wicked, when it cometh. For the Lord shall be they confidence, and shall keep they foot from being taken."

"Oh, dear. That sounds a bit like a warning."

"You could take it that way. Sounds more like a promise to me."

We tossed our bags into the van and Neil pulled himself into the driver's seat.

"We go now?" Gutierrez inquired, nodding.

With the Manu National Park on our left, we headed out of town, crossing over the Alto Madre de Dios River on the east side of town and following Henry's cloud of dust for the next half hour. The road wound through forest, curving and looping and making any kind of speed impossible. The rutted dirt surface, pitted with potholes and protruding rocks could take the breath away from even the most daring off-road enthusiast. Every now and then the forest opened up to reveal small cleared patches where bananas or corn grew. After bouncing along for a while the guide said something and Neil jammed on the brakes. Without warning, he cranked the wheel hard, turning off the main road onto a narrow two-lane track almost completely obscured by vegetation.

The van bumped and swayed as it crept up a slope and around several tight corners and switchbacks. Low-hanging vegetation slapped at the vehicle. After a half hour, a clearing appeared up ahead. Juan Carlos chattered in rapid-fire Spanish, pointing out the windshield. In the clearing, a dozen grass-roofed buildings circled a central open area. Neil parked next to one of the homes, in the shade of a broad-leafed tree.

"This is where we switch modes of transport," Neil let me know. "Juan Carlos says that Laura's horses are here."

"How did he know?"

"She arranged it with her friend, the local pastor, and made sure that Juan Carlos had the details."

We alighted from the vehicle and grabbed our packs, following the guide across the open expanse to the tallest house on the far side of the clearing. There didn't appear to be anyone about except for a wrinkled woman with chopped grey hair, holding a naked baby and sitting in a doorway. I smiled and gave her a little wave but got no response.

When we reached the big house, a man wearing baggy shorts and a dirty T-shirt advertising a cruise line appeared and came out to meet us. Juan Carlos began speaking with him in a language I didn't recognize. I glanced at Neil to see if he was following the conversation and though he appeared to be concentrating hard, I don't think he understood it either.

"Horses ready," Gutierrez said abruptly, waving a hand to follow him as the other man took off toward the back of the house. Down a short trail we came upon a small fenced area and sure enough, three sleepy-looking horses awaited us, already saddled, with reins looped over a fence rail.

The trail into the jungle started out fairly wide, grassy and in places cleared enough for a small vehicle to travel but it didn't stay that way for long. Soon the forest began encroaching on the trace so closely that we had to be careful not to be smacked in the heads by the shrubbery.

"How long until we leave the horses?" I asked Neil who had already talked this over with the guide.

"About two hours."

Sweat trickled down the middle of my back under my pack and it wasn't even nine o'clock yet. I wished I had thought to tie it on the back of the saddle rather than hang it off the back of the rider. My mount, a scrawny plug with a laconic air about her, didn't take kindly to extra work, like walking. Digging in my heels, I managed to catch up with the others, only to be straggling behind again within minutes.

As we plodded through the jungle, swiping ferns and vines from our path, I reviewed a conversation I'd had with Neil at one of our airport stopovers between Europe and Charleston. Finding the diary at Wardley Hall had been a thrill beyond measure for him; the archaeologists version of catnip. Since his main field of interest lay in the discovery of ancient technologies, those discovered in cultures and ruins around the world and those alluded to in the Bible, this one had more than piqued his interest.

"What do you think it means?" I had asked.

"Of course, I can't be sure of anything until I see it but from the drawings, the dolphin shape appears to house a massive crystal, and from what Miss Wardley describes, its clarity and shape are phenomenal. Unique, perhaps one of a kind in the world," Neil continued.

"And used for?" I tilted my head and eyed him. "You're thinking this holds another key to ancient technological knowledge, aren't you?"

He could barely conceal his excitement. "Maybe. In the same way that the ring of stones led us to such an amazing discovery when the message was deciphered and the jar with the Urim and Thummim was found in the cave, I can't help thinking that this artifact may have similar importance. God is leading us, and the world, toward his conclusion and those who understand the meaning of the times can also understand the prophecies, the ones in the Bible and those that we're hearing today. The times as we know them are winding down and I believe that God has brought you and me into this race for knowledge for a reason. Me, because of my training and experience with ancient cultures and ancient and modern technologies, and you, because of your ability to clearly hear his voice."

Neil's excitement was always infectious and I found myself anticipating finding the artifact so I could be part of unlocking its secrets, too. There are few things more thrilling than discovering ancient keys to modern problems and watching how the results impact the world.

However, finding the glass dolphin still took a back seat to my heart's real desire – holding my fiancé in my arms again. I only hoped that was something he still wanted, too.

CHAPTER TWENTY-FOUR

My head snapped around. I scanned the greenery but could see no one. Still, it felt like the jungle was full of eyes. Watching, ever watching. The silent guide led us along a winding trail through dripping vegetation, shrouding fronds, biting insects and sticky heat. Was I imagining it or were we being observed? More than once, I thought I caught a flicker of movement. Had a figure just slipped behind the root flange of a massive kapok tree? Was that a pair of unblinking eyes regarding us silently from between the drooping fronds of palm? I kicked my lazy horse into a trot to catch up with Neil.

"Do you get the feeling we're being watched?" I asked quietly as I drew alongside him.

"I hadn't noticed but if you have then we probably are."

"What makes you say that?"

"There are still tribes in the area that want to keep out of sight of Westerners. They keep a sharp eye out for what is going on in their territory but like to avoid contact. That's why it's important that we have a guide."

"I thought that was so we wouldn't get lost."

Neil laughed. "That too," he said, "but he not only knows the jungle, he knows the people of the jungle. He's from one of the tribes, the Murunahua, which is also known as Chitonahua. Others include Cacataibo, Isconahua, Matsigenka, Mashco-Piro, Mastanahua, Nanti and Yora. He's deliberately leading us on a path where we don't directly encounter anyone."

"Are they dangerous?"

"Could be. But we're probably more of a danger to them than they are to us. While many of these peoples are unreached by the gospel, many others have been wiped out, or nearly so, by disease brought on by exposure to mahogany loggers, oil workers and even foreign missionaries. Without government protection, they are losing their lands to the encroachment of foreign and domestic business interests."

For a few minutes I said nothing. The trail had widened enough so we could see the sky and the sun beat upon our shoulders, making me long for the cover of the forest again. "Do you know where we're going today?"

"Juan Carlos is taking us to his village. He thinks that they'll have information about any compound that might be tucked away in the jungle. With the help of his people we should be able to get some direction."

"I can't shake the feeling of impending...something. What do you think is going to happen?"

Neil reached over and patted my arm. "I think that the Lord is leading us to some amazing find, something that will put another chink in whatever evil plans our adversaries may have. Whoever they are."

"How can you be so nonchalant about all this?" I asked, frowning at him.

"According to the Bible, God always causes us to triumph. I just consider that it's a foregone conclusion."

"Aren't you even nervous?"

"No. It's like the Apostle Paul said about his 'light afflictions,' you know – the shipwrecks, the beatings, and the imprisonment. None of that compared with 'the eternal weight of glory' waiting for him when he met Jesus again face to face. I believe that I have a job to do, one that will somehow further the Kingdom of God on the earth. I made the decision a long time ago just to do what God tells me to do and be happy."

"I hope we don't have to go through anything like the Apostle Paul did. I'd like to skip all that other stuff and go straight to the glory part."

"Sometimes the fear of something bad happening is far worse than the event itself. Just trust God, Jill. No matter what happens, things will work out. You'll see."

We rode on in silence after that as the jungle closed in around us again. The heat had risen several degrees as the sun climbed higher in the sky and the skin under my pant legs chafed against the rough saddle leather. I pulled a long drink from my water bottle and recapped it. The ice had kept it cold in spite of the steam bath we rode through and I longed to pour the contents over my throbbing head. Sweat ran in rivulets down my sides and even tugging my cotton shirt away from my skin made no difference. I was tempted to tie it up to allow air to reach my damp body but dared not. The flying insects would only seize the opportunity to torment me even further.

I drifted into a kind of heat-drunk stupor as I let the horse have her head. Cecilia Wardley's diary had been zipped into a pocket of my pack and, since I had nothing else to do but keep up with Neil and our mute guide, I tugged at memories of the illustrations she had drawn. Miss Cecilia had clearly shown a six-sided crystal within the shape of the dolphin. Actually, construing the glass object as a dolphin was a bit of a leap, too, since it was pretty rough. A convoluted lump of glass formed the base, like a pool of water rising in a splash around the tail of the dolphin, and had been ground off flat so it would stand.

According to the diary, the figure measured about the length of her forearm, including her hand. I had no idea how large a person Miss Wardley was but if her height bore any resemblance to mine then her arm would likely be similar in length too. The body of the artifact curved like a dolphin leaping from the crystal sea. While it wouldn't be too difficult to imagine the shape of the artifact as a dolphin flinging itself from the water, people believe what they want to believe. All you had to do was ask for a few eyewitness reports of a traffic accident to find that out. Maybe Cecilia Wardley wanted to believe the legend.

The journal had gone on to say that the tribe believed the artifact denoted a level of spiritual elevation or stature to whoever possessed it. The original discoverer of the item had evidently been standing on the seashore during a storm when lightning had struck the sand nearby and melted it into the dolphin's shape. It crossed my mind to wonder what kind of idiot stands alone out on the seashore during a thunder and lightning storm, being the tallest thing around, but again, people will believe a lot of strange things in the pursuit of spiritual enlightenment.

Legend had it that since the original priest had survived his experience on the beach and lived to tell about it, he must therefore be some kind of demi-god. Thus began the story that captured the hearts of this unknown forest tribe. Why were they on the beach in the first place? It would have taken many days to walk from the eastern slopes of the Andes, over the mountains, past other unfriendly tribes and through untold danger to reach the Pacific coast. Whenever the ruling or reigning high priest died, his successor, usually his son, according to Wardley, would take the entire tribe, or perhaps just a select number, on the same trek across the mountains to the sea to renew or commemorate the original lightning strike event. Wardley didn't say whether a storm was required to bestow supernatural powers upon the new priest. My guess was that they might lose the new guy before he had a chance to put on his royal vestments if a lightning storm were a prerequisite.

Somewhere along the way since Cecilia Wardley had travelled these paths, the legend lost its power or the artifact became lost or stolen. Or, perhaps the tribe had just disappeared deeper into the jungle, beyond the reach of logging and big oil companies or even the eco-tourist. It was entirely possible that the artifact still existed and was still revered by the people who believed in its powers. If that were the case, Gutierrez might not even know anything about their whereabouts. According to Neil, almost all the uncontacted people were somewhat nomadic, living in extended family groups and moving into the forest when the rivers were high and onto beaches to fish during the dry seasons. How then had Luis Goncalvez got wind of this artifact? Did he actually know of its existence or was he simply guessing? Did he crave the power he believed it held? If so, what did he expect it to do for him? There had to be something we missed from Cecilia's writings, something that indicated what power the dolphin was supposed to bestow.

I swatted at a stinging insect that landed on the back of my hand. "Get away from me, you beast," I growled.

"Are you okay back there?" Neil called, twisting in the saddle.

"I'm coming." I booted my horse's ribs and for a few seconds she picked up the pace from a dragging slog to a semi-brisk stride. As I drew closer to Neil, the animal lapsed back into trudging along the path and seemed to be half asleep.

As we ambled on, I found myself wondering about the crystal formation that had supposedly formed within the dolphin at the time of the lightning strike. I knew that crystals had many uses in science and industry and some people even attributed supernatural powers to them, such as the ability to heal. I didn't ascribe to those beliefs much myself but I couldn't rule out the possibility that crystals might have vibrational powers beyond powering wristwatches.

Up ahead I could see a clearing where the forest gave way to open sky. Gutierrez said something to Neil, which I didn't understand, as the two of them rode into the sunshine. In another second, I caught up. Before us lay a tribal village with thatch-roofed dwellings arranged in a circle. The place looked deserted.

Something was not right.

CHAPTER TWENTY-FIVE

It felt like a snake had just slithered up my back. I wiped at a trickle of sweat that had crawled down the side of my face.

The air above the clearing suddenly filled with smoke – thick and black – obscuring the sky. *How can that be?* I stared as a sense of dread crept over me. A moment before, the sky had been as high and blue as a glass bowl.

I glanced to where Neil had stopped at the edge of the clearing. His horse stood stock-still, ears laid back, eyes wide. My own nag suddenly came to life, stomping her hooves and prancing backward into the forest. I yanked on the reins as I dragged the back of my hand across my eyes again. When I opened them, the pall had disappeared. The horse went still.

"What just happened?" I asked so that only Neil could hear.

"I don't know." He glanced over his shoulder at me.

"Did you see that cloud of black smoke?"

He shook his head but a frown creased his brow. "Something is wrong here." He turned and said something in Spanish to Gutierrez who looked frozen.

"Where is everyone? This place is too still," I said. The only sign of life was a dog that lay in the shadows beneath a raised dwelling. When I took a closer look, I realized that it didn't count as a sign of life. The dog was dead.

Gutierrez dug the heels of his boots into his horse's sides and urged the animal forward. Reluctantly it moved, snorting and flinging its head from side to side, eyes wild. He motioned for us to follow.

The settlement was not large, consisting of only eight small huts and one larger one, all with high, steep roofs made of palm thatch. The dwellings stood on stilts about hip height and each had a single door. Neil dismounted and took a firm grasp of the side of his mount's bridle, leading the horse toward one of the houses. He peered through the door then shook his head.

"No one in here," he said, both in English and Spanish. I slid off my horse and checked in another home. Cooking pots and the remains of a meal still littered the centre of the floor as though everyone had dropped everything before finishing.

Suddenly, Gutierrez halted in his tracks. I glanced across the clearing and even from that distance I could see that the blood had drained from his face. The man looked ill. In a moment, Neil stood beside him. Both men studied the ground at their feet.

"What is it?" I asked, drawing up beside where they stood staring at the ground. For a moment I couldn't take in what I was looking at.

At our feet were the biggest human footprints I had ever seen. And they each had six toes.

Neil crouched down to examine the nearest print. Beside it, his own foot looked miniature by comparison. He looked up at an ashen Gutierrez who appeared ready to vomit or faint, or both, and was backing away from the footprints. His eyes, round with fear, darted around the clearing. He jabbered something at Neil in his native language.

Neil stood to his feet and gripped the guide's arm, giving it a firm shake as he spoke to him firmly in Spanish. Gutierrez's head wagged from side to side as Neil continued softly. Finally, the guide calmed down a bit.

"What did he say?" I wanted to know.

"He lapsed into his mother tongue," Neil explained, "before he got a grip on himself. He says the giant men were here."

My eyes narrowed. "What 'giant men'?"

Neil lifted a shoulder. "He's not very coherent. He insists that we get out of here. Now."

"That sounds like a good plan to me." I glanced over my shoulder, unable to shake the sense of menace.

An hour later we emerged from the jungle into another small clearing and sat down in the shade at the edge of the little meadow. It had been impossible to continue by horseback from the village and we had originally planned to leave the horses there to be returned by someone whom the guide had engaged for that purpose. Since the village was deserted, we instead removed their bridles, tied them to the saddles then sent the horses back down the path the way we had come with a couple of firm whacks to their backsides. Gutierrez assured us that they would end up back where they belonged.

From there we changed our plans and instead of travelling on a well-worn trail into the jungle, the guide led us in a different direction, explaining that going with our original plan might land us in the middle of the "giant men." He feared nothing more than encountering these mythical creatures. He set off through the jungle, slashing with his machete at such a speed that Neil and I were hard-pressed to keep up. By the time we reached this open patch we simply collapsed, out of breath and pouring sweat in the steamy afternoon heat.

Now, with a little prodding, Neil managed to extract more information from the terrified little man.

"He says that there are still tribes in the jungles and the slopes of the Andes that have never encountered anyone from the outside world," Neil said, paraphrasing Juan Carlos' explanation. "The locals know of these people but are so afraid of them for their violent and evil natures that no one wants to investigate whether the stories are true."

"What about these 'giant men'?" I asked. "Why does he call them that?"

A Spanish conversation ensued, which I assumed from Gutierrez's gestures and expressions, included some horrific descriptions of these tribes people and their habits.

After a bit, Neil translated. "You've heard of the Sasquatch, haven't you?"

"Of course," I replied. "A few decades ago there were reported to have been sightings in the mountains not far from where I live. No one ever verified anything, though. Why? Is he talking about the same thing?"

Neil hauled a hand across his brow. "Well, yes, and no. What he's describing sounds a lot more organized, like a real tribal culture, and a lot more sinister, as in, people of a cannibalistic nature."

"Yikes! Are you serious?"

He nodded. I glanced at Juan Carlos who couldn't seem to stop checking over his shoulders. He looked like he was ready to cut and run if we didn't tie his leg to a stake. I took a drink from my bottle of lukewarm water then mopped my face and neck with a small towel from my pack. Images of old photographs of the so-called Sasquatch, also known by such monikers as Yeti and Bigfoot, swam across my mind. The idea that such a creature existed, or in this case, a whole tribe of them, seemed preposterous and I said so.

Neil gave me a look. "Jill, you know your Bible. Jesus himself said that in the last days it would be as in the days of Noah. Most people take that to mean that sin would abound to such a degree that God would want to destroy his creation, right?" I nodded. "What most people don't grasp, or don't want to, is that the source of the immense evil in the land mostly centred around the creatures known as the Nephilim or the Rephaim. Remember the passage that says, 'There were giants in the earth in those days; and also after that, when the sons of God came in unto the daughters of men?' They had children who became known as mighty men or men of renown. Wickedness was a big problem for God because these people did whatever they could imagine, no matter how evil.

"Yes, I know they were giants who were birthed as a result

of fallen angels having sexual relations with earthly women. But didn't the flood wipe them all out? Wasn't that the whole purpose of it? Or, wait a minute. I remember now, they were still around when Joshua and Caleb were ready to enter the Promised Land, weren't they?"

Gutierrez eyed us closely as though trying to understand the conversation. Perhaps he did grasp some if it; I didn't know.

"Yes, and David killed Goliath, don't forget."

"Are you saying that there still may be that kind of giant roaming around, in this jungle?" Now it was my turn to look over my shoulders. "What does Juan Carlos say?"

At the mention of his name, the guide leapt to his feet and began talking rapidly to Neil in a low voice, tugging at his arm and gesticulating wildly.

"What's he saying?" I demanded.

Neil held up a finger, taking it all in and nodding. After a couple of minutes he stopped Gutierrez and pulled him back down to a sitting position. "Okay," he began after wiping a hand across the back of his neck. "He says that legend has it that these so-called giants have been living in the mountains and the jungle here for centuries. Early explorers came across others on the continent down in southern Argentina and documented them. There have also been recorded sightings from aircraft but when anyone flies anywhere close enough to get photos the giants start firing arrows at them and then vanish back into the forest. Jill, this is not a surprise to me. I've been hearing for years that other archaeologists have dug up enormous elongated skulls with a non-human type of bone structure. Other bones also point to the existence, at least in the past, of humanoid beings reaching the height of two or three of me. They often have six toes and six fingers just like the giants in the Bible."

I suddenly felt faint. "Oh my. Do you think they know we're here?"

"I doubt it. By the time we reached that village, they had

already gone. I imagine that the villagers who managed to flee were hiding in the forest watching our every move. That's probably why you felt like we were being watched."

"That's not all I felt, Neil. I sensed an overwhelming cloud of evil in that place. I even saw some of it. I guess you could say that the Lord somehow allowed me to see into the spirit realm. There was a dense black cloud of smoke hanging over the entire clearing. I saw it for a moment and then it was gone."

"Well, no doubt you were right. The giants were known to be intensely evil, so evil that there was no good in them at all."

"And you believe that they are still alive."

"Remember when I said that I had been mounting an expedition into Peru already, before Marco went missing?"

"Yes." I nodded, not really wanting to hear what might come next.

"Part of my mission was looking for evidence of these giants. Reports of bones and skulls being found in burial crypts have been surfacing for some time and I felt God leading me to come down here and see what I could find out for myself. As you know, before I could pull the expedition together all this happened with Marco and the whole glass dolphin thing."

The sky had clouded over and the first splats of rain pattered on my back. In spite of that, the heat never abated one degree. Juan Carlos sat between us like a coiled spring, ready to bound into the forest at the first rustle of leaves.

"Do you think that the glass dolphin has anything to do with these giant people with all the toes?"

Neil spread his hands. "Your guess is as good as mine. What's your sense in this?"

I pressed the heels of my hands into my eye sockets. If the giants had any connection to the glass dolphin or to this Goncalvez character whom we believed held Marco, we were up against a bigger adversary than we had anticipated. What was my sense of it? The truth was, I was filled with such an all-consuming dread that just like Juan Carlos, I wanted to pick up and sprint from that wretched jungle, run until my legs and my lungs would not allow me to go any farther. If not for the danger that Marco must be enduring this very minute, I would have quit right then, left the heat and the rain and the bugs, the poisonous snakes and the venomous plants. And now, there was the threat of giant cannibals somewhere out there lurking in the forest, perhaps even hunting us at this moment.

I lifted my head and glanced at Gutierrez then looked Neil in the eyes. "The first thing we have to do is pray for safety, for God to give us extra angels to accompany us and for the grace of God for our quest. Then we have to get up and go find Marco. God will go before us and his glory will protect us from behind. If we listen for his voice, he will lead us where we should go. We have no other choice."

Neil reached over and patted my knee. "Good girl," he said with a smile. "I knew you wouldn't give up."

CHAPTER TWENTY-SIX

In the middle of the afternoon it started to rain in earnest. Not one of those light rains where the drops hit you one by one. No, the sky opened up and dumped such a drenching on us that we finally had to take cover under some plants with giant, umbrella-like leaves. They merely lessened the pounding on our heads and when it eventually tapered off, the three of us were soaked to the skin, right down through our socks. If I had thought it was steamy before, nothing compared to how it felt after the rain fell.

In spite of that, we set off again anyway, knowing that time was still of the essence and any progress we made would hopefully take us closer to Marco and farther from the tribe of so-called giants. That was fine with me. Our guide indicated that within a couple of hours of walking, we should encounter another tiny settlement where we could eat our evening meal and spend the night. Because of our change of direction, we would not be visiting his village after all.

We battled our way through the undergrowth, slashing at vines and branches, beating off the attacking insects and keeping a sharp eye out for snakes both at our feet and above our heads. Nothing horrified me more than the thought of a snake dropping around my neck like a string of beads and twisting itself into a choker. My arm ached from hacking with the machete that Neil had made me buy. *Like I will ever use this thing again,* I thought sourly.

By the time we reached the river gorge the afternoon had passed. This close to the equator, night falls suddenly and we didn't want to be caught out in the middle of nowhere when it did. The latitude at my home delivered a long twilight, so the sudden plunge from daylight into blackest night always caught me by surprise. One minute it was daylight and the next, dark. The unrelenting rain had accompanied us for hours and the blisters on my feet made every step torture. I felt certain that my blood mingled with the rainwater running down my legs and into my boots. Neil was in the lead and now Gutierrez had taken the rear.

We could hear the roar of the torrent before we saw it. Suddenly, we emerged on the cliff overlooking the wild river below. By this time, physical fatigue tainted my thinking. All I wanted was to get out of this festering rainforest, away from the danger, the bugs, the pain and the fear. My hope of finding Marco had even dwindled to a frayed thread.

The forest opened out to a jagged line cut through the greenery, carved by the force of the water crashing down from the mountains. How the guide managed to find this string bikini of a bridge, I will never know. He was earning his pay, at least.

When I looked at that bridge, a mere set of ragged ropes strung across the chasm, my heart failed me. My muscles, my courage, my determination – they all failed me. I could not go on, couldn't risk my own life crossing that river where one slip would send me plummeting down into the torrent to my death upon the serrated boulders. I turned back.

Neil caught my arm and stopped me. Then he said the only words that could give me the will to go on, to take the chance on my life, come what may. He said, "There is no other way, Jill. If we don't cross here you may never see Marco again."

So with tears streaming down my cheeks, I tugged off my boots and placed my mangled feet on that rope, gripped the two hand riggings and step by agonizing step moved out over the river after Gutierrez. The swaying of the bridge in the rush of wind that blasted down the canyon was nearly my undoing. My head swam. My stomach lurched and even closing my eyes did not still the dizziness. That's when I cried out to God and he stilled the wind. Within minutes the three of us had crossed the abyss and scrambled up the opposite bank. The trail was more defined on this side of the river and in a half hour or so I learned why. We emerged from the dense forest into a clearing just at dusk and found a small settlement of native people.

Oddly enough, some of them seemed to be waiting for us and had prepared a meal and places for us to sleep. They spoke a language that neither Neil nor I knew but that Juan Carlos spoke with ease. He explained that they had expected us to arrive.

Shy children dressed in nothing more than a string under their rounded bellies or a scrap of skirt, gathered around to touch us, giggling behind their hands. The adults of the village, who numbered only about twenty people, seemed equally friendly and curious. We graciously accepted the meal they had prepared, some unknown meat cooked over a fire and accompanied by roasted tubers that tasted like sweet potatoes, followed by bananas.

Juan Carlos translated for us as we asked how these people had known we would arrive. They said that they heard us coming through the jungle grapevine, as it were. Aghast, we wanted to know more. The leader of the group, a man who appeared to be in his late forties, wearing a bright red loin cloth, red paint on his face and his black hair cut in a straight line around his head, told us that their ancestors had taught them to read the signs such as the movement of animals and birds and sometimes even scents on the prevailing breeze.

Night fell, and after an evening of uneasy conversation we were shown to our sleeping quarters, a small, raised hut with a steep palm-thatched roof and a plank floor. The dwelling had signs of spirit-worship hung inside and out which, not knowing their beliefs, made me edgy. However, exhaustion won in the end and I fell asleep with a full stomach not long after the sun had set as the jungle was once again plunged into the black of night. Some time later all traces of slumber fled. I sat straight up out of sleep, grasping my throat with both my hands. My breath came in short, sharp wheezes through constricted airways as though someone else's hands were wrapped around my neck, squeezing. The pressure made me nearly pass out. Letting go of my throat, I swung my arms to beat off the attacker but there was no one there. No living person. My hands connected only with the mosquito netting draped around my bed on the floor.

Eyes wide, I stared into the darkness, my head swinging from side to side. Someone, or something, had entered the hut where I slept. Its presence was palpable, dripping with malice.

"In the name of Jesus," I choked out, coughing. "Leave. Now." I hacked again, nearly retching. Suddenly, it disappeared. I dragged in a lungful of sticky night air and ran my hands over my bruised neck.

"What is it?" Neil's concerned voice came out of the darkness. He switched on a tiny flashlight and the piercing blue beam ricocheted across the expanse between us and shone in my eyes.

"There was an attack."

"Of what? Who was here?" The beam flashed around the hut. Gutierrez rolled over in his sleep and continued to snore.

"It was demonic, I'm sure of it," I replied in a harsh whisper. "I woke up choking like I was being strangled."

"And it's gone now?"

I nodded. "When I spoke the name of Jesus, it vanished. Thank God."

"That does it," Neil said, leaping to his feet and flinging off his own mosquito netting. He strode to the low door of the dwelling and reached up. Yanking a fetish from a string over the door he flung the offending jumble of animal bones, feathers and twigs out into the jungle. "I was going to do that last night but I didn't want to upset the locals. I know it's not responsible for the attack but I can't stand those things."

I reached for a bottle of water and downed several swallows. My throat ached.

"Are you going to be okay?" Neil asked.

"I think so."

As I lay back down with my head on my pack, Neil also went back to his blanket and within minutes his heavy breathing matched Gutierrez's.

Even with my eyes closed, sleep had fled. Adrenalin still coursed through my body and my heart rate was nowhere near calm enough for sleep to return. I purposefully slowed my breathing and concentrated on the peace of God.

As I relaxed, my fatigued mind began wandering randomly from scene to scene over the events of the past several days: Flying to England, finding Cecilia Wardley's travel journal, the wedding and our lovely plans, which never materialized. Would they ever? As I lay in the darkness and my nerves settled down, my thoughts drifted to Marco and the life we had planned together.

He still ran his restaurant supply business in Spain and thankfully, my life and career as a fine artist was portable so we had agreed to spend part of our time in Canada and part of the year in Spain, as the need to be there arose. He had been considering selling his business but we felt that there was no real hurry to do that and had decided just to wait and see what the Lord had in mind for us. We also knew that Neil's dealings, both with his archaeological work and with his work at the compound in Israel, had far-reaching impact and, given that events on the world stage pointed to the fulfilment of certain ancient prophecies, perhaps in our lifetimes, we wanted to be available to work with him, should that be God's plan for us.

Surely Marco was still alive somewhere, I thought. He might

even be nearby but how could I know? Perhaps the ruthless Goncalvez, or whoever was behind Marco's abduction, had killed him. His use as a hostage relied upon us simply *believing* that he was still alive. I shivered, even though the air hung warm and heavy like a damp blanket. I couldn't allow myself to wonder if Marco was dead. I had to believe that he was alive and was out there in this jungle somewhere, waiting for us to find him.

A fly buzzed somewhere in the space above me and I checked the mosquito netting for bug-tightness. This was only the second village we had encountered in the jungle. While malaria was not common at this elevation, I was told, it made sense to take every precaution. I rolled onto my side and pulled my knees up, tucked a sheet up over my shoulder, absent-mindedly stroking my aching throat, as the muted sounds of the jungle acted as accompaniment to my jumbled thoughts.

Imagination can be a great thing or a dangerous one, depending on the time of day. The blackness hung heavily on me and I sensed every flicker of an insect's wing and even imagined the slither of venomous snakes sliding across the floor. My mind replayed the awful strain of the day in vivid detail.

The image of those six-toed, gigantic footprints haunted me. I remembered the verses in the Bible describing various giants and overlaid that knowledge with discussions that I had had with Neil regarding these humanoid creatures in various books of the Bible. In our modern culture, the existence of such creatures had all but been relegated to the land of myths and legends, yet I couldn't help but surmise that if Christians the world over believed the other parts of the Bible, how could we simply pick and choose what we supposed to be true about the rest? *In for a penny, in for a pound*, I thought. Either it's true or it's not.

My mind roamed from one thought to another. What if

these giants already roamed the earth, perhaps hidden for centuries in pockets of civilization, tucked away in inaccessible regions of the globe? The very idea made me shudder. I recalled reading news reports from diverse locations in the past century recording the discovery of huge skeletons, many three or four times the size of modern man. What had happened to those findings? Where had those remains gone? Had they been hidden from public view by well-intentioned, or even, not-so-well-meaning, people in positions of power? People who had their own agendas? Around and around my thoughts spun.

I sighed. I didn't want to be lying awake listening to men snoring. My limbs ached for relief yet, even as I repeatedly forced my muscles to relax, breathing slowly and concentrating hard, as soon as my mind wandered back to our quest my whole body tensed up again.

During discussions with Neil, McSweeney and Bobby, and armed with information that had been gleaned from research, conversation and general sniffing around, we'd concluded that the hideout of Goncalvez might be as close as a half day's walk away. Juan Carlos' discussions with the villagers led him to believe that he would find this place in the jungle. Apparently, it was near enough to a river to be able to make quick manoeuvres in and out of the property. Both Neil and the guide also held the belief that the ruins of an ancient civilization, pre-dating the Inca incursion by some one thousand or more years, lay hidden somewhere in this almost impenetrable jungle. This was no Eldorado, Colonel Fawcett's fabled city of gold, but something much older and more mysterious. What we didn't know was if Luis Goncalvez had found it already.

While Neil had never explored in the region himself before, he assured me that for the past several months he had been conducting extensive research on the possibility of a set of hidden ruins much farther east from the mountain valleys where the Inca, and before them, the Chachapoya, had left the remains of their civilizations. No, what Neil sought was antediluvian in nature, so old that it pre-dated the flood of Noah. Given his work in other areas of the world and his findings regarding pre-flood history, I didn't doubt for a moment that he knew exactly what he was talking about.

CHAPTER TWENTY-SEVEN

The midnight choking incident finally driven from my consciousness, I had fallen back to sleep and dreamed about Marco. Scenes from our sun-drenched summer of falling more deeply in love filled my sleeping mind. Well, okay, some of those days were rain-filled. I do live in the Pacific Northwest. But my dreams were of the days when he had visited from Spain, or the couple of times I had gone back to Madrid with him while he worked. I stayed with his sister Mariana, and visited his sweet, elegant mother who lived across the street. The family had welcomed me with warmth and open arms. I looked forward to Marco's and my life together, alternating between my little artist's home and, when the need arose, his place in Spain.

I woke to find eleven pairs of eyes staring at me through the mosquito netting. Most of the children of the tiny village had congregated to study me, sitting silently on their haunches and watching me breathe. When I recovered from the shock of finding myself a study specimen, I looked back at each small face and smiled. With that, they rose as one, like a flock of starlings, and fled out the door of the hut.

Throwing back the thin sheet that covered me I crept out of my netting tent still wearing a tank top and my shorts with the zip-off legs. After checking my sandals for deadly insect squatters, I stuck my feet in them and peered out the door into a steaming morning, desperate for a bathroom. A young girl of perhaps thirteen jumped to her feet from the steps and said something to me, reaching for my hand. She led me off into the jungle.

When I returned, I found Neil talking on the phone at the edge of a clearing. Juan Carlos sat next to a small fire eating a piece of fruit, as did several other members of the community. Some villagers lounged in hammocks or busied themselves with daily chores. Two women came to me and motioned for me to follow them, offering me fruit and some kind of bread. Neil was still on the satellite phone.

After eating, I gathered up my things and sat in the doorway of the hut where we had slept, pulled my journal out of my pack and began to make sketches of the village. It didn't take long before I had an audience of children again, crowding around me and watching every stroke of my pen. They clambered up beside me, leaning against my arms and draping themselves over my shoulders as though this kind of affection was the most natural thing in the world. For them, I'm sure it was.

"Bobby and McSweeney have news," Neil said when he finally rang off and joined me. "They've been asking around and have discovered that this Goncalvez appears to have a place not far from here though no one they talked to seems to know exactly where it is. Everyone is afraid of him so no one wants to go poking around." At the mention of Goncalvez's name, I saw Juan Carlos flinch like a thorn had pricked him, and turn his right ear ever so slightly toward us.

Neil casually picked up a four-year-old and sat down beside me, placing the child on his lap. "Apparently, he runs his criminal operations from a compound up ahead in a small valley. McSweeney talked to a pilot who flies over the area regularly and swears that 'sometimes it's there and sometimes it's not.'"

"What does that mean?"

Neil shrugged. "It could mean that the pilot isn't very good at reading the jungle terrain from the air, which isn't too likely, or it may mean that Goncalvez has some method of camouflaging his camp. Army camo netting, perhaps?"

"How big a place are we talking about?"

"By the sound of it, at least five times the size of this area." He swung his arm around to indicate the clearing. "There are two large buildings, probably sheds or maybe his headquarters, plus a house, other smaller outbuildings and a swimming pool. It's close enough to the river to house a floatplane and have a dock but those appear and disappear, too. Even Henry, the boatman, insisted that he had seen a dock in the water one time but the next time he went down river it was gone."

I tried to imagine how someone could have temporary camouflage for such a large area and came up blank. "It's possible that the dock disappears in flood season, isn't it?" I said, thinking out loud. "But docks are usually high enough out of the water to accommodate rising water levels, or they're made so they float up and down with the water." I knew that on the Pacific coast near where I lived that concrete docks, big enough for loaded semi-trailers to drive onto, floated with the aid of massive blocks of plastic foam fitted underneath. "Even if you pulled your dock on shore when you're not using it…well, I suppose you could hide it in the jungle but how do you hide an entire compound?"

"I guess that is what we have to find out."

Our guide had obtained instructions from the tribe's leader on the best paths to take. They seemed to know about the jungle compound of Goncalvez though they made every effort to avoid it. When we inquired about any knowledge they might have about the existence of the glass dolphin they shook their heads, faces blank. I watched closely for any sign of subterfuge but could not detect any. It seemed that these people knew nothing about the legend or the culture connected with the glass dolphin ceremony or else they were extremely good at hiding it.

This made me wonder again how Goncalvez had learned of the glass dolphin. If these local people didn't know about it then who did? I glanced around the circle of faces and saw dark-eyed gazes slip sideways. Perhaps they weren't so innocent after all. Even so, it was unlikely we would learn anything more from them.

Neil and I had spent little time alone since we had arrived in Peru so I divested myself of the layer of children covering most of my body and motioned to Neil that we should take a little walk together. We let the children know that we did not want to be followed and endured their sad and perplexed looks as we casually walked a short way into the jungle.

"What is our plan today?" I wanted to know.

Neil ran a fingertip over his right eyebrow, another habit he had when he was considering what to say. He glanced back toward the camp where the guide still sat by the dying fire. I followed his gaze.

"What?"

"I'm not sure we can trust Gutierrez," he said finally.

I gasped. "I've been feeling the very same thing! Something about him makes me uneasy. I didn't sense it at first but I do now."

"He's getting nervous."

"That's it, and watchful," I added. "What is that about?"

Neil shrugged one shoulder slightly and shook his head.

"What do you suggest we do? We can't really go anywhere without his guidance. It's not like we can turn around and go back the way we've come. We wouldn't have a hope of finding our way."

"I don't know about you but I suggest we carry on as though nothing is different. After all, he is our only hope for finding the compound."

"He's not our only hope, Neil. God is our hope. No matter what happens with Juan Carlos or Goncalvez or any of these desperados, our hope is still in God."

Neil smiled. "You amaze me, Jill. It's like nothing ever

makes your trust waver."

"Ha!" I sniffed. "It wavers all the time. I just keep making the decision to bring the needle back to straight up. What other choice is there?"

Neil grinned at me. "Anyway, I think we need to have some kind of plan and be especially watchful. According to McSweeney, this hideout is close enough that we're likely to find it today. We have no idea if they're holding Marco there but I have a hunch that's where we'll find him. Exactly how we'll find him, I don't know."

"What about Bobby and McSweeney?"

"They're coming in from the river side. If our sat phones keep working we should be able to coordinate a rendezvous when we get nearer. It's possible that Goncalvez will have guards around but they won't be expecting us at any particular time unless Juan Carlos is somehow tipping them off. Hopefully, the element of surprise will be on our side."

"How are we going to free Marco?"

Neil smiled and squeezed my hand. "I'll tell you what," he said. "I'll work on a few possible scenarios while we walk today and you work on praying and hearing what God has to say. Together I'm sure we'll come up with something that will free your sweetheart."

I threw my arms around my uncle and gave him a hug. "You get me into the biggest messes," I said affectionately, "but life is never dull around you." We broke apart and headed back to gather our gear. "I don't care who this Goncalvez is but as far as I'm concerned it's just like, 'Who *is* this uncircumcised Philistine, that he should defy the armies of the living God?'"

"Okay, David," Neil said, laughing, "grab your slingshot. Let's go get Goliath."

CHAPTER TWENTY-EIGHT

Before we had walked twenty minutes I was drenched in sweat. The blisters on my feet, though they had received copious first aid ministrations, still burned with every step. My arm ached from slashing at vegetation all the previous day and with each stride, I grew more and more apprehensive. Anxiety lurked at the doorway of my mind but I could not afford to let it in. With no idea what lay ahead, I needed every ounce of vigour and determination I could muster. Giving way to fear would most certainly undermine that. Still, the prowling spectre of apprehension would not leave. I could only assume that God was trying to warn me. It certainly wouldn't be the first time.

Before we had left the village, Neil had taken me into the hut where we had slept and passed me a handgun.

"Put that in your pack for now," he said, giving me a quick refresher on how to use it.

"Oh, Neil," I moaned. "You know how I feel about handling guns."

"That doesn't matter now, Jill. I'm sure you'd rather use a gun than be shot by one. We don't know what is up ahead so it's best to be prepared. I doubt that Goncalvez will want to settle this over a game of checkers and a milkshake so you'll probably have to protect yourself. This is no time to be squeamish."

"In other words, 'Buck up, kiddo'?"

"Yep," he replied, giving me a soft punch in the shoulder.

Now I concentrated on Neil's back and prayed under my breath, switching between English, as thoughts came to mind, to my prayer language to give myself courage and build myself up in the Holy Spirit. The two or three hours of sleep I had lost the previous night had left me in somewhat of a fog before we had even set off, and now the weariness of trudging was making me drag.

After trying unsuccessfully to go back to sleep in the middle of the night, I had dug my bright little LED flashlight out of my pack along with Cecilia Wardley's journal. Something bothered me and I couldn't recall what it was until I thumbed through the aged book. There was a line of scratchy writing that we had glossed over previously because it had been difficult to make out. Now, alone in the dark of night, I examined the fragment of text more closely. It seemed to say, "A cave appears then disappears....can walk past with no awareness...whereabouts. Mouth under rocky outcropping east of brown-water stream...tree...lightning, points..." The page had been folded numerous times across the corner so that wear and the fibres of the paper obscured the cursive script.

I couldn't help thinking that there was something significant about that passage in Wardley's diary, and I mulled it over as I fell farther and farther behind the men, hardly aware of the gap that had widened between us. More than once, I saw Neil look back and call for me to hurry and catch up. Finally, he insisted that I walk in front of him, explaining that it would be easy to get lost in the jungle within minutes of losing track of each other. That prospect made me pick up my pace and keep Gutierrez in sight.

Around noon, we stopped for something to eat, packaged food that tasted as much like the packaging as the food, followed by mangos that we had received from the villagers. We ate them whole, like apples, and they tasted like the nectar of heaven.

We had sloshed across a couple of small, clear streams and climbed steadily for the last hour before stopping. Cecilia Wardley's diary had mentioned a stream with brown water. At least, that's what I thought it had said. Now, in the light of day, my investigations from the night before seemed blurry.

"Are we moving away from the river?" I asked. Neil answered that he wasn't sure himself and translated my question to Juan Carlos.

"*Si,*" he answered, explaining that he had heard that Goncalvez's property was around a bend in the river and that actually it was the river that was moving away from us in a sweeping loop and we were taking a shorter route, he emphasized with hand signals.

"How long until we reach the compound?" I asked. When Neil translated the question, Gutierrez stiffened slightly, his black eyes refusing to meet either Neil's or mine. Neil's translation of his answer confirmed my suspicions.

"He says he's not sure," Neil explained, turning his head away from the guide and raising an eyebrow in my direction. It wasn't difficult to see that he shared my appraisal of Gutierrez's response. The sudden shiftiness did nothing to alleviate my unease.

After we had finished eating and before setting off again, I indicated that I needed a little privacy break and headed back into the forest by the way we had come. Not far from where we stopped to eat, the trail had taken a right angle turn and there was enough vegetation to give me concealment. I stepped off the trail to take care of business, had just pulled up my pants when I felt something plop onto my shoulder. I froze and slid my gaze downward and sideways. Staring me in the face was a lime green snake as slim as my finger. It looked to be about the length of my arm. I didn't wait to say hello. Leaping sideways, I flung the thing off then tore back down the path howling like a north wind and tugging on my pants.

"What? What is it?" Neil grabbed me when I reached him.

For a moment I just wailed. When I managed to catch my breath and calm myself by sheer determination, I gasped out,

"A snake It jumped out of the trees and landed right on me."

Concern darkened Neil's eyes. "What did it look like?" he demanded. "Did it bite you?"

I shock my head. "Flung it off and ran," I answered, gulping for air. "Bright green, yellow, long, skinny and shiny. Big round eyes." I shuddered and brushed my hands over my shoulder again to make sure that it really wasn't there.

"Sounds like a Parrot Snake," Neil decided. "It's not poisonous, luckily for you." He conferred with Juan Carlos who nodded in agreement.

"I think I hate the jungle," I said, as I picked up my backpack. "Where was that gun when I needed it?"

I'd had no idea that snakes liked to leap from the trees onto unsuspecting, half-dressed women. Now I knew better. I would have to be more vigilant.

An hour later, after tramping and slashing our way through more endless jungle, amongst piercing birdcalls and distant monkey hooting, we crossed another rivulet tumbling down from the high rocky outcroppings on our right toward the lower regions and the river. This stream, unlike the other crystal clear ones we had sloshed through earlier, ran with murky water the colour of tea. From a rock in the middle of the flow I crouched and searched upstream but could see nothing but overgrown vegetation. Within a stone's throw from my position, the ground rose sharply. I could hear the water splash and gurgle as it tumbled over rocks higher up. *This must be the stream that Miss Cecilia was talking about,* I thought, hoping I was right. *Or not.* This was a pretty big forest after all. There could be a thousand streams with brown water flowing from the mountain heights down toward the river valleys. All the same, it was one of the few clues we had for finding the glass dolphin. If it was the right place then up ahead somewhere there should be a rocky outcropping and the mouth of a cave. Given the heavy vegetation, I wondered if there was even a hope of seeing an opening. How far east of the stream this cave opening might be, she hadn't recorded.

The other reference had said something about a tree and lightning. Was there a tree that had been struck by lightning that pointed toward something? Possibly. But what? The cave opening? Could such a tree still be standing after almost two hundred years? Not likely.

My boots squelched along the mucky path. If I hadn't slowed down to navigate over a tangle of tree roots I probably would have missed the sound of Neil's satellite phone buzzing on his hip. Gutierrez was up ahead and as the path curved to the right, he disappeared from view. Neil and I stopped walking.

Thirty seconds later, Neil flicked the phone off. I looked at him.

"It won't be long now, will it?" I said.

He shook his head. "You'd better take that gun out of your pack and stick it in the back of your belt. You might need it sooner than you think."

CHAPTER TWENTY-NINE

From the time we had left the village we had climbed almost steadily. Not steeply, for sometimes it was hard to tell that we were even climbing at all but when I looked back down the track I could see the slope of the land. The guide kept up a steady pace, unaffected by the terrain. Neil and I had a little more difficulty with it so it wasn't until it finally happened that we realized Juan Carlos had marched ahead on purpose.

Our first inkling that something had changed came with only a soft metallic clink, somewhere off to our left in the forest. I froze and so did Neil. As I was ahead of him, he crept up beside me and simply tilted his head in the direction of the sound. We waited and listened. Through the thickness of the vegetation, we could see no one. Neil bent and picked up a stone from the path near his feet and turning silently, hurled it behind us.

The shot cracked open the thick air, scattering birds and sending ground creatures scurrying through the underbrush. In unison, our hands gripped our pistols under our packs and we crouched, hardly breathing. I shrugged my pack off one shoulder, and holding it against my body to muffle the sound, unzipped the outside pocket and yanked Cecilia Wardley's diary out. Stuffing it inside my shirt I threw my arm back through the pack's strap. A second later, Gutierrez appeared on the path ahead followed by a man holding a machine gun to the small of his back. Hands clutched behind his head he trod toward us. His face wore no look of fear, only what? Resignation?

That look said it all. I knew that we'd been set up. The man with the gun, a dead ringer for a desperado from an old Clint

Eastwood western, said something to us. Gutierrez nodded.

"What did he say?" I asked Neil.

"The usual. Come with us or we'll kill your friend." Another man stepped out of the jungle behind the two, his weapon trained on us. The sound of thrashing in the greenery off to our right told us a third had appeared on the trail behind us.

"*Vamonos!*" said the man at our backs, relieving us of our machetes and prodding me in the shoulder with the barrel of his gun. We raised our hands, leaving our own pistols concealed beneath our backpacks. It was a faint hope but maybe these brigands would assume that we weren't carrying any.

As we rounded a bend in the path, a fourth man joined our little greeting party. I glanced at Neil who kept in stride with me. He looked remarkably calm for a man with a gun at his back.

The fourth man walked right up to us and barked a command. Neil slipped his pack off and handed it over and motioned for me to do the same. He rummaged through them and tossed them back to us. Once the packs came off our backs, the man behind us wrenched the pistols from our waistbands.

The quartet of creeps ushered us along the path, which rose sharply over a ridge of rock before falling diagonally down the other side. In a few minutes we emerged into an open patch along the slope and could see for miles across the top of the verdant jungle canopy, veiled in ragged strands of cloud and mist. The view was breathtaking and I paused for no more than two seconds before being jabbed in the backside with a gun barrel and having another order snarled at me. I turned and glared at the man behind me. That's when I saw his face for the first time.

With a jolt, I recognized one of the thugs that we had seen in the park in London – not the skinny, nasty one but one of the hulking goons that had dragged Marco away. I gasped but before I could say anything, Neil yanked my arm.

"Come on, Jill. Don't stop and don't make trouble," he said under his breath. As I swung around to carry on, my gaze took a last sweep of the panorama before me. Up and to the right, on a high rocky outcrop, stood a lone dead tree, split in two by lightning. A single limb still jutted from the ravaged grey trunk and pointed toward the low, flatlands of Amazonia, what appeared to me to be straight east. I surreptitiously scanned as far around me as I could without moving my head, memorizing my whereabouts. Then we plunged back into the jungle.

The trail had now become so precipitous that we had to skid sideways down the decline. I briefly considered leaping off the track and into the deep ravine that fell away on our right, hiding myself in the foliage. Just as quickly I abandoned that notion. A leaf was no match for an automatic weapon and chances were good that even if I weren't immediately shot I could easily break a leg on the way down.

We continued down the steep grade for maybe fifteen or twenty minutes. I noticed that Gutierrez had been allowed to drop his hands and from time to time I could hear him conversing softly with his so-called captor. The sight of them made me furious. My earlier suspicions had proven correct. We had been led straight into a trap.

At the bottom of the slope the land flattened out and up ahead I could see a high wall made out of cut rocks. Some of the stones resembled the style of the Inca civilizations, precisely cut with bevelled edges, and I couldn't help but wonder if this structure was part of an ancient habitation or these stones had simply been pillaged from some nearby antiquities site.

Our captors marched us at gunpoint through double, iron gates that opened to the touch of a keypad mounted on the stone gatepost. The heavy gates swung open just widely enough for us to enter, then closed silently behind us. The sun, by this time perched on the horizon behind us, was spilling its last rays between the high Andean peaks. Inside the compound, the path leading forward had been paved. *That must have cost a fortune out here in the middle of the jungle*, I thought.

Off to the right stood a couple of Quonset-type outbuildings made from corrugated metal and to the left another building that looked like it might be a shop. The grounds had been meticulously designed and maintained, with plantings of beautiful tropical flowers, shrubs and palms artistically arranged. Within minutes, we were herded off the road onto a brick-tiled walkway and up to a massive patio next to a free-form, in-ground swimming pool that shimmered a deep turquoise blue in the dying rays of the sun. A sprawling one-level home stood next to it, its walls of windows reflecting the golden glow. The place was lovely but, given our circumstances, it was difficult to appreciate it. For the moment, at least, I felt thankful that we hadn't been tossed into a dungeon crawling with spiders and snakes.

Our captors steered us to a lavish arrangement of patio furniture, complete with tufted cushions in subdued shades of aqua and sand and indicated that we were to sit and wait while one of their members rang a bell attached to the side of the house. Neil and I sat side-by-side staring up the barrels of two guns while another one guarded us from the rear. The fourth guard had led Gutierrez away around the side of the house, presumably to pay him off and send him home, if he was that fortunate. If he was not, I hated to imagine what might happen to him. I had no illusions about the kindness of these people.

A few minutes later, a glass door slid open and a man strolled out, not bothering to close it behind him. He flicked a hand at his henchmen and they lowered their weapons and backed away toward the edges of the terrace. Dressed in a tropical-print shirt, worn loosely, and white trousers, Luis Goncalvez bore no marks of having suffered during his recent incarceration. The belly ballooning his shirt out spoke of rich food and leisure. A short man with wavy, black hair slicked away from his forehead, he dropped into a chair opposite us and kicked off his sandals. Two Dobermans, their ears trained up in sharp points, accompanied him, and flopping down at his feet, glared at us.

"Dr. Bryant, I presume," the man said in slightly accented English. "We meet at last. I have heard a great deal about you."

"I'm sorry I can't say the same about you," Neil answered evenly.

"Forgive me. My name is Luis Estrada Goncalvez. This must be your charming niece, Señora Moss." He gave me a greasy grin. "I have heard much about her, too."

"What have you done with Marco Jimenez?" I blurted out.

"My dear, you must be patient," he replied. The setting sun over his left shoulder cast his face in deep shadows, giving him an advantage over us. I felt sure it had been planned that way. "You will find your Señor Jimenez when the time is right but first, I believe that you possess something that I want."

Neil took over now. "What would that be, Goncalvez?"

"Please, Dr. Bryant, call me Luis. I would like to think that we want some of the same things, *si*? We are both interested in antiquities. Granted, perhaps not for the same reasons but" – he fluttered a dismissive hand again – "no matter. We both want a particular artifact with equal fervency, is that not so?"

Neil leaned toward Goncalvez, his elbows on his knees. "Why don't you tell me what it is you want and why you want it and I will tell you if I can give it to you."

Goncalvez laughed mirthlessly. "We both know that we seek the glass dolphin. I am sure you want it to place in some stuffy museum where it will be locked in a vault for the next century but will make a name for you amongst your colleagues."

I glanced at Neil. We both knew that he had no interest whatsoever in climbing the hierarchical ladder of the archaeological world. Clearly, Goncalvez knew nothing about

Neil's works with the corporation in Israel, or if he did, he wasn't letting on. Then again, almost no one knew.

"Perhaps you can tell me what you want with this glass dolphin," Neil suggested then waited for a response while Goncalvez snapped his fingers toward the open sliding door. A moment later, a small, old woman emerged carrying a tray with a pitcher of iced coffee and three frosted glasses that dripped with condensation. Setting it on the low table between us, she poured and we accepted the glasses, as did our so-called host. How had he known that I would have killed for an iced coffee after the day we'd had?

After a long draw on the icy drink, Goncalvez spoke. "My interest in the glass dolphin is no concern of yours. You will turn it over to me or I will kill your friend and," he nodded at me, "your fiancé, Señora Moss. There is no room for negotiation."

Neil smiled. I didn't think I had ever seen him look more relaxed and confident. "Mr. Goncalvez," he began. "– Luis, you'll have to forgive us if we can't fulfill your request. You see, we don't have the glass dolphin."

The sun had set behind the mountains by now and I could get a better look at Goncalvez's bloated face. It may have just been the light but it seemed to me that it went a little purple at Neil's statement.

"Then you will find it for me," he ordered through clenched teeth.

"I think not," Neil replied, still cool and calm. "We will be leaving here with Mr. Jimenez, unharmed, and you will not have the glass dolphin."

Goncalvez gestured with his hand and the henchmen moved in. "Dr. Bryant, I think you will find that I am a man who always gets what he wants. I want the glass dolphin and I will get it."

"Señor Goncalvez," replied Neil, leaning forward, "you may

have been able to force others to do your will by intimidation and other lawless tactics but I believe that this time you are up against a foe you can neither intimidate nor beat. You will see."

CHAPTER THIRTY

Before the last glow of evening light had vanished I had one good look at Goncalvez's face when Neil delivered his proclamation. It practically contorted with fury, suppressed only through sheer will.

"Take them away," he snarled with an apathetic wave of his jewelled fingers. "I will deal with them in the morning." A gun barrel jabbed me in the shoulder, forcing me to my feet. For reasons I still can't fathom, our packs had not been taken from us even though the pistols concealed beneath them in my waistband and Neil's had been confiscated. Goncalvez was evidently so assured of his position of power that he didn't see us as a threat. Perhaps in his mind, the prospect that we would receive help from any quarter was so remote that it didn't matter what we carried.

He rose ponderously from the patio chair and strode into the house, not even bothering to slide the screen closed behind him. Someone inside the house skated the glass door into position.

Lights sited around the perimeter of the terrace had come on automatically with the setting of the sun and illuminated the space in a soft glow that reflected off the surface of the pool. Barking orders in Spanish, the three guards prodded Neil and me with their guns, herding us toward the same walkway that led out to the paved lane.

"What now?" I whispered to Neil and was rewarded with a shove that nearly knocked me off my feet. Neil grabbed my arm and steadied me then let loose a stream of the fastest Spanish I had ever heard. The only word I understood was, *madre*, or mother. Was he insulting their mothers, I wondered, and would it work? I stole a glance over my shoulder and saw that our captors had backed off a pace. I guess whatever he said had an effect. I made a mental note to ask him later.

The door of the metal outbuilding screeched as it rolled open and once the lights came on we could see that it was a machine shed. A long workbench stood against one wall, littered with tools. In the centre of the floor space stood a forklift and a tractor with a scoop. The concrete floor, splotched with oily patches and sawdust, stretched back into the dark rear of the building, which is where the guards drove us. The pungent stench of oil and gas was nauseating.

A small room, not much bigger than a garden shed, had been built in the back corner of the hangar-like building. The leader of the pack yanked open a metal door and the other two shoved us into the room.

"Tell them we're hungry," I whispered to Neil. "Quick." He translated into Spanish, stopping in the doorway. For a moment the guards looked bewildered, glancing at each other before one of them answered Neil.

"What did he say?" I wanted to know.

"He said they'd bring us something from the kitchen in a while."

"No kidding!"

Pushing us into the depths of the small room, the guards slammed the door and I could hear a lock being clicked into place on the outside.

"Do you suppose this room was meant to be a cell?" I asked, feeling around the walls for a light switch. "If it was, that's pretty sick." My fingers touched the edge of a small box protruding from the wall near the door and I flicked on the light, a single bare bulb hanging from a wire in the centre of the room.

"Don't assign your values to someone like Goncalvez," Neil

said. "Some people just don't have that shred of goodness that you insist everyone has."

"Well, they did say they'd feed us," I answered in my defence, "so, they can't be all bad."

"They want something, Jill, and it's in their best interest to keep us in good shape. Goncalvez thinks we know where to find the glass dolphin and I'm sure he plans to set out soon on an expedition to do just that. With us in the lead."

The small room was empty and as hot as a kiln after having baked in the tropical sun all day. Far above, in the peak of the Quonset, a vent let in the sounds of the surrounding jungle. A monkey howled from somewhere up the mountain slope, its cry echoing out over the valley and a flock of birds scattered, squawking, from trees outside the compound. Not a breath of air came through the vent. I slipped the straps of my pack off my shoulders and let the bag drop to the floor. Pulling the back of my sweat-soaked shirt away from my skin felt almost cool and I lifted the diary out of my shirt and set it on my pack.

"I wouldn't do that if I were you," Neil said. "The last thing we want is for that journal to fall into these guys' hands."

I nodded and shoved it back under my sweaty shirt then lowered my aching body to the floor and leaned against my pack.

Half an hour later, supper arrived, along with the same three guards with their automatic weapons. The one carrying a tray of food had his weapon slung over his shoulder while the other two pointed theirs straight at us.

I pushed myself to my feet, careful to face the guards, and accepted the tray while Neil asked something in Spanish. A short conversation ensued, then the door slammed shut and was locked again from the outside.

"Okay, what?" I asked, setting the tray on the floor and sitting cross-legged beside it.

Neil sat down opposite me. "I just asked what their boss

intended to do with us. I was told to mind my own business."

"Marco has to be here somewhere. We have to get out of here and find him."

"Shooting off the lock is not an option. Even if we still had our guns, they'd be on us in a flash," Neil said, giving the door handle a shake. An answering shout from somewhere in the garage confirmed his words.

"Do you suppose all of them are out there? Or have they just left one guy on duty?"

"Do you want to find out?" Neil dug a spoon into a plate of beans.

"Yes, and no."

Over the remainder of the small meal of beans, rice and bread, with bottled water that I wanted to pour over my head, we discussed our few options for getting out of the cell and finding Marco. As soon as our stomachs were full, I had to go to the bathroom. I got up, banged on the door and hollered. In seconds I got a response – a blast of Spanish from the other side. Neil translated our predicament and a key scraped in the lock. The door swung open and two gunners stood outside. *That answers that question*, I thought. *They're taking shifts.*

They let us out one at a time, starting with me, and led me to a water closet in the opposite corner of the building's rear. Crossing the expanse from the cell to the toilet gave me a chance to look around the shop. An assortment of tools lay around on the benches, the usual wrenches, hammers, and power tools. Obviously, the maintenance of the compound and the vehicles happened here.

Once locked back into the corner cell, Neil switched off the light and we rolled onto the floor to sleep, our heads on our backpacks. Between the difficult past few days and the shortened night before, exhaustion had me out in seconds.

I woke sometime later to the sound of rain on the steel roof and the odd splash falling through the grate high above us.

Digging my little flashlight out of the side pocket of my pack, I checked my watch, which showed 3:45 a.m. Careful not to flash Neil in the face with my light, I checked him and found him sleeping on his side, snoring lightly. The air had cooled. Turning onto my back, I stared up at the ceiling. A faint glow from the yard lights shone through the lattice of the grate but it was too far away and at too steep an angle to illuminate the small enclosure.

I had just closed my eyes, preparing to drift back into sleep when I heard scratching at the door. Instantly alert, I stared into the gloom and listened. There it came again. The lock on the door jangled softly. I dared hardly breathe as my pulse quickened. I heard it again.

I reached over with my foot and nudged Neil's knee. He snuffled and shifted then breathed the sigh of the sound asleep. Sitting up, I jiggled his leg. That did it. He woke with a twitch and lay still.

"What is it?" he whispered, barely audibly.

"Listen."

The lock rattled again then it sounded like something snapped. Then all went silent. Five seconds later, the door creaked open a crack. I flicked on my flashlight and shone it straight into the black eyes of Bobby Buckingham.

Leaping to my feet, I pressed back on the door before he could swing it wide. "Wait," I said. "This door makes so much noise it will wake the whole jungle. Grab some oil from the bench over there if you can. Oh, and, it's great to see you. Where's McSweeney?"

"He's watching the door. Hold on, I'll be right back." True to his word, Bobby returned and began squirting oil over the door's hinges and gingerly manoeuvring it until it opened wide enough for us to exit without the infernal squeal that would crack open the night and wake every dog and guard in the compound. Neil grabbed his pack and slipped through the door. I followed suit.

At the door of the machine shop, which, thankfully, had been left open the previous night, Quentin McSweeney looked out into the darkness, holding an automatic weapon in his hands.

"What took you guys so long?" Neil asked, pumping McSweeney's hand and thumping Bobby's back.

"We had a tea party to go to," McSweeney retorted in a growling whisper. "Whaddya think?"

"What happened to the guards?" I whispered, squeezing Bobby's wrist.

"They've fallen into a deep sleep," he answered with his usual simple eloquence. I took that to mean that they had been clobbered over the heads with something blunt and efficient and would wake up with blinding headaches sometime later.

"We have to find Marco," I said.

"Any idea where he is?" Neil asked.

"We were kinda hoping you'd know," McSweeney answered, his eyes scanning the dark compound.

"Outbuildings first," Bobby suggested, "then if we don't find him, we tackle the house.

"Gutierrez finked us out," I said.

McSweeney looked at me. "He what?"

"You know, he led us into a trap. He was a fink."

McSweeney rolled his eyes, I didn't know whether at me or at my news.

"Okay," Bobby said, "Mrs. Moss, ma'am, you come with me, and Neil, you go with McSweeney. We'll take the shed over to the right and you guys check the one on the other side of the house. Are you armed?"

Both Neil and I shook our heads. "Confiscated," Neil said.

"I'll go get us some," Bobby said, slipping out into the darkness. He returned a minute later with one of the guns that our guards had carried and handed it to Neil. He pulled a pistol out of the back of this waistband and handed it to me. "Okay, we meet back here in ten minutes, tops. Let's go."

"Wait," I ordered in a harsh whisper. "Before we go anywhere and do anything, we're going to pray. Okay?" The men nodded and I began, "Lord it's no secret to you what kind of situation we're in so I'm asking you right now to help us find Marco and get him free. Please keep us safe and get us out of here unharmed, in Jesus' name. Thank-you." I looked up. Neil squeezed my hand. "Okay, let's go."

I followed Bobby out into the dark, around the corner of the machine shed and away from the house to the other Quonset. The big main door stood closed. Around the side of the building, we found a smaller door and when Bobby tried the knob it turned easily and opened. Thankfully, these hinges had been oiled and we slipped silently into the dark interior of the stifling building. Bobby held up a hand and we stood stock still for a moment, listening. Satisfied, he flicked on a tiny flashlight and directed the beam around the capacious interior. Huge machines stood idle, parked in tight formation, filling the entire building. Following Bobby's lead, I skirted the perimeter in case we might find another cell or enclosure tucked into a corner but this building clearly had other uses. The machines had wheels that towered over my head and after we'd had a good look around I asked, "What are these monster tractors and backhoe machines for? Any idea?"

"I'd just be guessing but I'd say they're for mining. McSweeney or Neil might have a better idea."

I considered for a moment what kind of business uses mining equipment in the jungle and the only thing I could come up with was gold.

"Marco is not being held here," Bobby said. "Let's head back."

We met up with Neil and McSweeney as planned and compared notes. "We checked both of the other sheds.

Excavation equipment in that shed," Neil submitted. "But not your usual stuff."

"Mining equipment in the other one, we think," I told them. "I guess that leaves the house."

"Okay, how are we going to do this?" Neil looked to Bobby for direction.

"Um, one thing," I said. "The dogs. Goncalvez has at least two Dobermans in there and they are not sociable."

A skiff of cloud that had been obscuring the moon slid away and bathed the compound in a silvery glow. McSweeney scratched his bearded chin. "That could be a problem," he said. "As soon as they sense something they're gonna start barkin' their fool heads off and wake up the whole countryside. How many people are in there?" He looked from Neil to me.

I shrugged. "At least two, probably more."

"How many guards did you knock off?" Neil asked.

McSweeney pursed his lips and squinted at Bobby. "Whaddya say, Bob? Six or seven?"

"Seven."

"In that case, you took care of every one that we know of. As for the house," Neil said, shaking his head, "there's the boss man, that little lady who brought us drinks, Gutierrez and hopefully, Marco." He glanced at me. "Sorry, Jill but we have to be prepared for the possibility that Marco is not even here."

I knew he wasn't saying what he really meant. Marco might have already been killed.

CHAPTER THIRTY-ONE

"So what about the dogs?" I wanted to know. "I'm not going in there with those monsters on the loose and if we start shooting, we'll wake up the whole house as fast as if the dogs barked their heads off."

For a moment we all just stood there, considering how we could dispatch the dogs without starting a full-scale war. A raft of cloud sailed through the sky blocking the moonlight again and casting the yard into blackness except where a light shed a pool of brightness onto the ground beneath it. Suddenly, I heard the crunch of gravel to my right. I tensed. Bobby swung around and drew his gun without making a sound as a figure crept around the corner of the machine shed.

"*No dispare, por favor,*" the voice whispered into the dark cavern of the shed. "Don't shoot, please." The figure slunk forward; then the man fell to his knees. In the faint light I could see his hands clasped before his chest as in prayer, pleading for his life. On his knees, he edged toward us. With a shock, I realized that it was Juan Carlos Gutierrez. Four guns immediately pointed straight at his quivering body.

Neil said something to him in Spanish and a short whispered conversation followed which he translated a moment later. "He tells me that Goncalvez forced him to lead us here or his son would be killed. He's very sorry but he had no choice. He managed to slip away from the house and wants to come with us. He's convinced that Goncalvez's men will kill him in the morning."

"What if he's leading us into another trap," I asked.

Neil shook his head. "I believe him," he said simply. He said

182

something else to Gutierrez. "He says Marco is in the house in a cell in the basement. He can take us there."

"Who else is in the house?" Bobby asked.

"Two guards, Goncalvez, the old lady and another man."

"And the dogs?" McSweeney prompted.

"*Los perros?*" Neil translated and waited for Juan Carlos's answer. "He's a jungle man," Neil said. "He has poisoned darts and a short blow pipe. It will only take a minute to put them out of commission." I didn't ask for more details. This was the only choice we had.

Ten minutes later, we followed Gutierrez through the kitchen, stepping over the inert forms of the two Dobermans. We had decided to stay together so we wouldn't accidently run into each other and, mistaking one another for a guard who might get up to use the bathroom, thump one of our own party on the head. Gutierrez had been in the house and knew the general layout. He had been treated like an unwelcome guest and been told he could sleep in a storage closet off the kitchen. Goncalvez had underestimated Juan Carlos's grasp of human nature, though, if he thought he would dispatch him in the morning and toss his body into the jungle for the bugs to devour.

Next to the pantry, Bobby opened another door. Inside, the elderly cook or server we had seen earlier, lay snoring in a narrow cot. Before she knew what had happened, Bobby had bound and gagged her while Neil explained that we wouldn't hurt her if she stayed silent. Eyes round with fear; she nodded and lay back onto her pillow.

Once out of the kitchen and in the main part of the house, we decided that McSweeney would stand guard at the top of the sweeping staircase that led downward to the basement and sound the alarm should anything happen on the main floor. The rest of us tiptoed down the thickly-carpeted stairway by the light of inset pot lights along the base of the steps. A wide hallway with several doors leading off it stretched what I assumed was the length of the house and led to a matching staircase at the far end. *Good to know*, I thought.

My heart banged against my ribs so hard and fast I felt sure it would burst. Marco could be right here, within steps.

Focus, I told myself. *Focus*.

The first room was empty. No furniture, nothing. The second door we tried squeaked slightly and Neil stopped instantly. He peered around the edge then left it open, shaking his head. Faint light from outside lit the rooms just enough. Neil reached for the knob on the third room and Bobby stopped him, pointing at himself. A master of martial arts and fifty pounds heavier than Neil, Bobby would be the one to subdue a guard if needed.

Twisting the knob in his fingertips, Bobby leaned in then stopped. He motioned for the other men to follow. Inside, two guards slept in single beds on opposite walls. A single swift chop to one man's neck produced a muffled grunt and he stayed still. In two steps Bobby dispatched the other man just as fast.

"They won't be getting up for a while," he whispered, motioning us out of the room.

Down the hall, one more door stood closed. Bobby tried the knob. Locked.

Gutierrez elbowed him aside and dug around in the pocket of his baggy army-style pants. A second later he produced a gadget that I couldn't make out and went to work on the lock. Making almost no sound, he tweaked it until I heard the soft "snick" and then he turned the handle and opened the door. Everything in me wanted to push all these men aside and tear into the room but Bobby went first then Gutierrez. Neil took up the rear.

The room was sparsely furnished with only a cot pushed up against a wall. The narrow window high under the ceiling sported thick iron bars, stark against the outside light of the now clear moon. For a moment I could see nothing and no one.

When my eyes adjusted to the pale moonlight, I could tell that the bed contained a pile of rumpled sheets, nothing more. Bobby swung his flashlight around the small enclosure then shook his head and turned to go. The rest of us followed. Back in the hallway Bobby whispered, "I'm going to go up these back stairs. You all go up the way we came down." He took off alone up the narrow staircase at the end of the hall.

I followed Neil up the stairs. At the top he stopped so abruptly that I ran into his back. Before us, McSweeney stood with both hands behind his head, his gun on the floor at his feet. With a gun to McSweeney's neck, stood Goncalvez.

"So," he said, "you were not happy with the accommodations I provided?"

"Put the gun down, Señor Goncalvez," Neil said, his voice so calm he might have been ordering sliced ham at a deli counter. Goncalvez chuckled.

Behind me, I felt rather than saw, Juan Carlos melt into the shadows below the floor level along the side of the staircase.

"You think you can just come into my home uninvited, whenever you like?" Goncalvez continued as though Neil had said nothing. "I believe that you have come to collect your friend, Señor Jimenez. I regret to inform you that you are in for a surprise, Dr. Bryant."

"What might that be?" Neil countered.

"There is no need for you to rescue Señor Jimenez. He has seen the error of his ways and has realized that there is much to be gained by joining my little, shall we say, business venture."

I gasped and clutched Neil's arm as Goncalvez laughed – a hollow, humourless sound.

"What do you mean, business venture?" Neil said, ignoring the comment about Marco. "Does this have something to do with the glass dolphin?"

"You really don't know, do you?"

"I have a hunch," Neil answered. "But perhaps you'd care to tell me your version."

"All right, I will," he answered, digging the tip of the gun barrel into the side of McSweeney's neck. McSweeney took no more notice than if a mosquito had landed on him. "My ancestors believed that the glass dolphin had special powers, as I'm sure you know. Whoever possessed it controlled many things and many people. Legend says that it controlled the passing of time, allowing the possessor to move backward or forward in time, almost at will and for whatever reason he pleased. My ancestors predate the Inca, you know. People believe that the Inca built the ruins at Sachsayhuaman, Machu Picchu, and the walls that still stand in Cusco but this is not true. The Inca built *on* these walls and they used these buildings and fortifications as their own but they did not have the understanding nor the strength to construct such perfect edifices."

"I didn't know that," Neil replied, playing along. "If the Inca didn't build them, who did?"

"I have already told you. My ancestors," Luis Goncalvez answered, irritated. "They were the same ancestors who discovered the glass dolphin by the sea when the great gods bestowed might, power and brilliance upon them."

"I don't understand," Neil said. "Are you telling me that these ancestors of yours actually had special powers? What kind of special powers?"

"I must have the glass dolphin," Goncalvez insisted, fury flaring in his eyes. "With the glass dolphin I will have the same powers as my ancestors, the power to manipulate time, to move backward and even forward, to change history. All that gold that the Spanish stole from the Inca, the Inca stole from my people. I will go back in time and get it. I will restore my people's wealth and dignity." Even in the semi-darkness, I could see his eyes gleam with fervid madness.

"I was not aware that the glass dolphin had such far-reaching powers," Neil said evenly. "But I can understand why acquiring it is important to you."

"Not just to me," Luis replied. "Your *friend*," he spat out the word with a curl of his lip, "Señor Sharp will pay millions for the artifact, which I have told him I will sell him once I have recovered my ancestors' riches. By then I will be the richest and most powerful man in South America."

At the mention of Sharp's name I stifled a gasp. I remembered being in his apartment in Paris and knew there was something about him, something that made me uneasy. Now I realized why.

"You would part with an article that possesses such great powers?" Neil asked, narrowing his eyes.

Goncalvez threw back his head and laughed. "Of course not, you fool. Sharp has no idea who he is dealing with. I told him I would sell it to him. That doesn't mean he will get it from me. He thinks because he has all those letters behind his name that he can outsmart me? He will find out, just as you have, that no one beats Luis Estrada Goncalvez."

For a moment we just watched as the man cackled his evil laugh. Tension sang through the night air like the twang of a taut guitar string. Suddenly, McSweeney jerked his raised arm downward. Goncalvez convulsed, his laughter replaced by a wrenching grunt. The gun at McSweeney's neck swung away and a wild shot rang out as Goncalvez doubled forward, gripping his chest, then lost his balance and stumbled sideways, his arm swinging for purchase. The next second he tumbled to his knees as his body collapsed to the floor. The gun dropped from his loose fingers and his head bounced on the carpeted surface before he lay still with a groan of pain.

McSweeney snatched up the gun and brought it down

behind Goncalvez's ear. Then all was quiet.

Suddenly, from a hallway off the palatial living room a chilling voice barked, "*No mueva*! No one move!"

Two commando-clad figures detached themselves from the walls and strode to where Goncalvez lay still before us. Faint light glinted off the cold steel of their poised weapons.

I froze and stared into the darkness, willing my eyes to adjust, to see their faces. Then my heart plunged and a cry escaped my lips.

The man leading with his gun pointed at Neil's head was Marco.

CHAPTER THIRTY-TWO

Marco stepped from the shadows and swung his weapon toward my head. With the flicker of a glance I saw that the man with him also carried a weapon but I couldn't make out his face in the dim light.

A strangled cry had escaped from somewhere in my middle. "Marco. It's me, Jill." I expected that would change everything, that he would drop the gun and gather me in his arms.

For an instant his eyes met mine, as cold and unyielding as obsidian. He barked something in Spanish. Neil threw up his hands. *What is happening?* the voice in my head screamed, unable to reconcile my rampant emotions with what I saw before me. I didn't know this man.

Marco shouted at me to kneel down. I didn't move.

"Do I have to tell you seventy times seven times?" he thundered

Suddenly everything happened. In the confusion I barely registered that from beneath the staircase leading to the second floor Bobby stealthily emerged from the darkness so fast that he looked like a black streak. He raised his arm and with a swift chop to the side of the neck, Marco dropped, first to his knees as his black eyes glazed, then face first onto the carpeting. The automatic weapon dropped from his limp hands. From the corner of my conscious mind I saw Bobby deal Marco's companion a karate kick to the back of the knees. The butt of a gun bashed the man's temple and he too fell like a toppled pillar.

"Marco!" I screamed, lunging over Goncalvez to reach his side. My hand just touched Marco's face when two strong arms encircled my middle and snatched me away from his limp body.

"No," I cried as Bobby hefted me and stepped over the pile of bodies.

"We're getting out of here. Now!" Neil ordered.

Bobby set me on my feet but kept a firm grip on my shoulder. Defiance was useless; I'd never win against his strength. On Neil's command, we grabbed the guns and fled back through the kitchen.

"Jill, you grab us some food and water while we tie this bunch up," Neil snapped, digging through a kitchen drawer and coming up with a roll of tape and some stretch wrap.

Snatching bottles of water from a pantry cupboard and raiding the fridge for food we might need for the next few days, I tossed whatever I could lay my hands on into my backpack and a plastic grocery bag I found in a drawer. A minute later, Neil, Bobby, McSweeney and Gutierrez charged back into the kitchen and Neil, honourable as ever, slapped a few bills for it on the kitchen counter, determined that no one would ever be able to accuse us of theft.

"Wait!" I cried as Neil grabbed my arm and headed for the door. "We can't leave Marco here. We have to take him with us."

"No," Neil replied, not slowing down. "You heard what Goncalvez said."

Neil dragged me past the dead dogs, through the door and out into the dimly lit yard. Darting back through the compound and keeping to the shadows, we headed for the exit. The place lay in silence. Once through the gates, Gutierrez closed and tied them with a length of vine as we headed off into the night. We ran, jogged and slogged through the jungle for what felt like more than an hour before stopping for a breath.

"I don't suppose it will be long until everyone in that compound comes to and lights out after us," Neil said after taking a swallow of water.

"There will be a few splitting headaches in the morning though," Bobby answered. I could hear a hint of glee in his voice.

"All the same, I don't think Goncalvez is a man to give up easily and he'll be looking for us this way," Neil added. He said something in Spanish to Gutierrez.

"*Sí*, Señor," Juan Carlos agreed. After a short discussion, it was decided that we take a different route away from the compound. Since Goncalvez's instructions had led us into the area, the way was not well known to the guide. Nonetheless, his native knowledge of the landscape made him the natural leader and we had to jog to keep up as he set off.

It didn't take long before exhaustion overtook me and I lagged behind, tripping over tree roots and slapping wildly at plants in the dark.

"Come on, Jill," Neil said, slowing to draw even with me. "You have to keep up or you'll be lost in no time." He gave a low whistle which someone up ahead returned. He put an arm around my back to urge me forward.

Suddenly, it all seemed too much. "How could he do that?" I sniffed, unable to fight back the sobs. "How could Marco promise he loved me then turn on me like he hates me? It's bad enough that he joined that evil man, Goncalvez, but he has betrayed me in the worst possible way." I trudged on at Neil's side with tears spilling down my cheeks.

"Wait a minute," Neil answered, drawing me to a halt and wrapping his arms around me. "Listen to me. Marco has not betrayed you."

"How can you say that? You saw what he did."

"I also heard what he said."

"Yeah. He was planning to shoot us."

"No, he wasn't. Do you remember him saying 'seventy times seven'?"

It took a moment but it came back to me. At the time it had

barely registered but I had recognized the words of Jesus, about how often a person should be willing to forgive.

"Was he asking me to forgive him?"

Neil laughed softly. "No. That phrase is our code for, 'I've got this.' He was telling me that he had to stay there. He has earned Goncalvez's trust somehow and is working it from the inside. He couldn't blow his cover in front of that other dude with the assault rifle but he had to let us know. Bobby had to take him down or when everyone comes to in the morning it would look pretty fishy."

I stared at him. "You mean that he hasn't defected to their camp?"

"You know Marco," Neil answered. "Do you really think that he would do that?"

"I didn't know what to think. Everything I've seen pointed to that conclusion. And after how he was in London, well..." I could barely think straight.

"He would have been trying to protect you, wouldn't he?"

I bit my lip. How had I got it so wrong? "That means if we find the glass dolphin, he can get out of there, right? He can come back to me." My heart lifted.

"He's highly trained and good at what he does, you know that. Don't expect him to give up until this whole thing is over. There are much bigger stakes here than your wedding, I'm sorry to say. If Jay Sharp is involved, I'd venture a guess that he has plans that Goncalvez doesn't even know about."

I hugged Neil's arm and couldn't keep from smiling.

We had been proceeding slowly along an animal path and could just make out the others now in the receding darkness.

Almost afraid to ask, I said, "Do you think Bobby killed him?"

"He'll have a sore neck when he wakes up but I'm sure he'll recover."

"I don't think I can run all night," I said, wiping my nose on a tissue from my pocket. By now we had drawn near to where the others waited. "Can we stop for a while and rest?"

"I don't think that's a good idea," Bobby said. "Even if they don't come around and start out after us for a few hours, we still need to get farther ahead."

"Wait a minute," I said. "There might be another way. If we could find a place to hide for a day, and they don't find us, they'll think that we've outrun them or got lost in the jungle somewhere."

"True," Neil replied, "but unless you know of a place to hide, we *would* just get lost in the jungle. People have died wandering around out here."

Even though it was dark, I gave him a look that told him I was no ninny. "Cecilia Wardley's journal talks about a cave near here. She mentioned it at the bottom of a page that had been damaged and is a little hard to read but I figured out what it says. There is a coffee-coloured stream near here that we waded through yesterday and just this side of it there is a dead tree on a rocky outcropping that has one craggy limb that points east. If we find that tree and follow the direction of the limb we should be able to find the cave."

Neil translated for Gutierrez who nodded slowly. After a short discussion, we agreed that it was worth a try. Gutierrez remembered the brown-water stream.

We pressed on. It didn't take long to come to the open stretch of the trail where I had seen the lightning-struck tree. From there we left the main trail and ventured through a small gulley, also running with a murky stream. To cover our tracks, Gutierrez led us up the stream, stepping on stones in the water until we could go no farther so we climbed up the bank and headed toward the split tree.

The rocks where it had once clung to life stood up from the surrounding ground by about four metres. Neil led the way, picking a path through dense vegetation and Gutierrez brought up the rear, obliterating any signs of our movement through the forest. After several minutes we stepped up onto the bald rock. By now, the sky had begun to lighten with impending morning and from the top of the rock we had a commanding view of the surrounding forest. Far below we could even see the indentation where we knew Goncalvez's compound stood. From my vantage point at the base of the tree I looked east. The green jungle stretched away unbroken to the hazy horizon in faraway Brazil.

"What else did the diary say?" Neil asked.

"It said that if we head in the direction that this limb points, we'd find the cave."

"How far?"

"I'm not sure but I have the impression from what I could make out in the diary that it's not far at all, maybe five or ten minutes from here."

"All right," said Neil. "We might as well give it a whirl."

The going was tougher now that we had plunged into the jungle again without any semblance of a path to follow. Rather than cutting the undergrowth, Bobby and McSweeney led and simply pushed, lifted and ducked under the foliage. I sent up a silent prayer of gratitude for their good hearts and big muscles.

True to Cecilia Wardley's notes, in ten minutes we came upon a pucker in the earth's surface that rose up on our right toward the foothills of the Andes. Below to the left the ground sloped gently before falling away precipitously into green oblivion. Giant ferns lolled from the upward slope, interspersed with looping vines and the sound of trickling water.

I heard Juan Carlos say something behind me as he pushed aside vegetation. The others, edging up toward the cliff face, poked and hacked with their knives. *It has to be here somewhere*, I thought, stabbing viciously through the vines when my blade clanked hard against the rock sending a painful jolt up my arm.

"Oww!" I said, rubbing my shoulder and attacking it once

more with vengeance.

This time my arm plunged straight into nothing.

CHAPTER THIRTY-THREE

By now, we were deep in the earth. The dry air had a chill that defied the above-ground jungle heat. Somewhere out there, Goncalvez and his henchmen had probably roused and now roamed the jungle paths searching for us. My throat tightened at the thought of Marco with that band of thugs. Drawing a deep breath I closed my eyes for a second. *I can't think about that right now.*

Juan Carlos, the expert at finding tracks, was also skilled at making tracks disappear. Not only had he obscured the cave opening after cutting away just enough vegetation to force an entry but he had also backtracked and obliterated any traces that we had diverged from the obvious path. Hopefully, Goncalvez would suppose that we would either head for the river for a quick getaway by water or that we would head back by the way we had come.

Not much more than a slit between two slanting rock faces, the cave entrance forced us to wedge ourselves through in single file. Neil pushed through first to look around then beckoned the rest of us. I followed, easily slipping through the fissure. Bobby squeezed through next with McSweeney bringing up the rear. Juan Carlos followed several minutes after the rest of us.

Inside, we followed a slightly larger passageway for about a dozen feet then the cave ballooned into a dry, high-ceilinged room. No light seeped through the opening so both Neil and I switched on flashlights to check around. *Thank goodness the bats haven't found this place,* I thought. The floor slanted away to the left and sloped downward into the gloom so far that we could not see the back of the enclosure.

"Let's head down here," Neil suggested, leading off. "Most of us have been up all night so I think we should take a nap before we try to figure out what to do next."

On a level spot beyond a bend in the corridor we dropped our packs and sank to the dusty floor of the cave. Within minutes the others had fallen into heavy sleep. I lay down and for a long while simply stared into the blackness. As exhausted as I felt, sleep had been displaced by the anguish I felt every time I remembered meeting Marco's eyes. I rolled onto my side as desperate prayers escaped my dry lips.

I had no idea how long I had been asleep when I woke with a start from a dream. In it, Marco walked beside me in my garden, his arm across my shoulders and his lips brushing my hair. As consciousness returned, I could almost smell his after-shave and feel the warmth from his body next to mine. We had spent many days throughout the summer doing just what the dream had portrayed, walking hand in hand, or sitting on the porch swing planning our lives together.

I remembered travelling with him throughout Europe after we had met in Madrid the previous spring. There had always been something mysterious about him, the very something that I felt drawn to from the start and still found irresistible.

Eventually, I slid into a troubled sleep again, this time with nightmarish dreams of guns and snakes and danger. When I woke for the second time, I could hear McSweeney and Neil talking. I checked my watch. "I'd like to do a little exploring of this cave," I heard Neil say. "If the Wardley diary mentioned this place, there is a chance that the glass dolphin may have been hidden here."

"What's your reason for wanting this artifact?" McSweeney inquired. "I know Goncalvez demanded it to spring Jimenez but now that he's gone turncoat on us, why don't we just hightail it out of this sweatbox of a jungle and leave him to his choice?"

Horrified at that thought, I lay still and listened as Neil explained the situation regarding the code.

"Quentin, if nothing else," he added, "we owe it to Jill to get him out."

"I guess you're right," McSweeney muttered. "She's probably hurtin' pretty bad anyway."

"Now, about the dolphin, you know as well as I do that the ancients had technology that we've only begun to discover. Finding the ring of stones and discovering what they meant proved to me that my hunches were correct and that there are more discoveries like that to be found. I was already putting together an expedition to Peru to search for a particular site of ruins. I'd heard rumours during previous journeys and have come across clues in my studies. I hadn't quite planned to end up here but God seems to have had other ideas."

"Are you telling me that you think this glass dolphin is connected to some kind of ancient tech stuff?" McSweeney probed.

"Yes," Neil replied, "I do. I don't know how yet but I'm pretty sure that the crystalline structure of the artifact described in Miss Wardley's diary has something to tell us. If we can keep it out of the hands of Goncalvez, we might be able to find out what that is."

"What about this guy named Sharp that Goncalvez mentioned?" McSweeney asked. "Isn't that the guy in Paris that you and Moss here, went to see? I thought he was a friend of yours."

"Same guy, and I thought so, too. Something weird was going on when we talked to him. Jay and I used to work together and always got along pretty well but he had a penchant for wanting to know the market value of anything we found. I never actually caught him dealing in black market antiquities but there was something devious about him that I could never quite put my finger on. I guess I shouldn't be surprised to find that he's mixed up in this somehow." Neil went silent for a few moments. "I never pegged him for the kind to get hooked up with a guy like Goncalvez though."

I heard Bobby cough. "Hey," he said, "you guys up already?"

"I'm awake, too," I said, sitting up and switching on my flashlight.

"Oh good," said Neil. "I don't know how much you just heard, Jill, but since we're on the subject of Jay Sharp, why don't you tell McSweeney what your impression of the man was."

I glanced from Neil's face to McSweeney's in the thin flashlight beam. I could barely see Bobby's dark face. "I had the feeling that he was hiding something. No, it was more like he was lying or deliberately trying to deceive us. He acted cagey and…smug, like he knew something we didn't and he felt pretty self-satisfied about it. Arrogant, superior; oh, he was kind of a jerk. Do you think he's behind Marco's kidnapping somehow?"

"Don't know," Neil answered. I could see his shoulders shrug. He switched on his own flashlight and squinted at his watch. "It's three o'clock in the afternoon. I suggest we get moving."

I scanned around the interior of the cave with my feeble flashlight beam and was about to get up and gather my things to go when I realized something. Juan Carlos Gutierrez was nowhere to be seen.

CHAPTER THIRTY-FOUR

As we set off to explore the cave, it didn't take long to discover that we had inadvertently stumbled upon an ancient tunnel. The walls, rather than solid rock like a naturally-occurring tunnel, had been built with blocks stacked evenly one upon another, with finely bevelled edges; the same kind of stone blocks that made up what is believed to be the Inca ruins in Cusco and Machu Picchu. Neil believed that an advanced civilization had pre-dated the Inca by at least a thousand years. He believed that these people were the real builders of the fabulous cities and earthworks that were now in ruins. With advanced technology that still baffles most scientists, this race of master builders had left their mark all over Peru.

Neil explained that Juan Carlos had left to see if his son was all right. After a brief and scant meal from our kitchen raid at Goncalvez's compound, we had set off. Sticking together with one flashlight glowing at a time, we advanced slowly. The tunnel sloped downward at a gentle angle then dropped several feet by way of a carved stone staircase before levelling off and continuing. It travelled straight for a while then angled to the right before climbing sharply. Great swooping swaths of spider webbing cloaked the walls and hung across the expanse that measured about two metres wide and three metres high. Scorpions scurried into the corners. The front man – in this case, Neil – had the unsavoury job of knocking down the cobwebs to make way for the rest of us following on his heels. Still, it didn't take long until my hair felt sticky from the strands and I expected any moment to feel the creep of little furry feet down my neck.

After perhaps an hour of feeling our way along, I suddenly stopped.

"Can you hear that?" I whispered. I stretched out my hands to stop the others. "Listen."

"I don't hear nothin'?" McSweeney grunted. "Do you, Bob?" Bobby stood still head down and tilted. Then he shook his head.

"Are you sure you're not imagining the sound?" Neil asked, barely disguising the skepticism in his voice.

"Listen," I hissed. "It's a high-pitched tapping, almost like the ticking of a clock, only faster. I'm not imagining this. My hearing is just better than yours."

Everyone went silent. That's when I saw the first glow of light. "Look!" A moment later, through a veil of cobwebs a faint green glow flickered to life down the dark passageway, emanating from a translucent stone globe on the wall. "Look! That light just came on."

Neil plunged toward it, swinging his machete, now thickly draped in grimy cobwebs. In seconds, we stood below the light, which was situated high on the stone block wall.

"Can you hear it now?" I asked, giving Neil a nudge with my elbow.

"It's a vibration," Neil said, staring up at the light, a quartz prism mounted in a stone sconce. "This is phenomenal! Amazing! It produces light on its own."

"It's like it heard us, or felt us, coming," I said, gaping at the glowing prism. "How does it work?"

"No idea. It must react to sound waves or something. I would think that we were too far away for body heat to activate it."

"It vibrates," McSweeney told us. "I'll bet sound sets off the vibration and the vibration causes the quartz to glow."

Neil gazed at the crystal, examining it from every angle. "I have read about crystals that can be activated by sound to produce light. I've just never heard of it happening outside of a physics lab."

As we moved away from the strange glowing light into almost darkness we discovered that another light up ahead began to glow softly too, so that the corridor now had lighting either from behind or before us at all times. With no daylight, it was difficult to tell what time it was but I was getting hungry so I surmised that it must have been getting late. We had been edging our way along for quite some time. After what felt like another hour we turned a corner into the shadows and came to an abrupt stop.

Before us stood a solid wall of stone. For a moment no one spoke.

McSweeney turned on his flashlight and broke the silence. "Well, I'll be!" he said, scratching his beard. "Why on earth would someone put a wall up here?"

Neil flicked on his flashlight too, and inspected the wall. "One piece," he observed, thumping it with his hand. "How did they get it in here and fitted into place?" He pulled a small trowel from his pack and tapped the wall in several places. It definitely sounded like one solid piece.

"Does this mean we have to go back?" I asked, sagging against the gritty wall.

"Not necessarily," Neil replied. "It might be a door, and doors are made to open."

"Where's the handle, Neil?" Bobby asked, slouching to the floor next to where I stood. I sat down beside him. He gave me a gentle smile. "It's going to work out, you know," Bobby whispered, reaching over and giving my hand a squeeze.

"Thanks-you, Bobby. I need to believe that right now," I answered, "but it's not easy."

I leaned my head back and gazed up into the shadows. The ceiling stood perhaps twenty feet in height at this point and the stone barrier reached all the way to the top.

How could anyone have brought that slab of stone in here and set it up, I wondered. *And why? Why build this massive tunnel that must run for miles underground and then end it with a wall?* It made no sense. From where I sat I flashed my light around the high walls, looking for anything out of the ordinary.

Neil had enlisted McSweeney to examine the edges of the stone and I watched as the two of them ran their fingertips around its perimeter and brushed at the seams in the surrounding walls. When Neil had reached as high as he could, Bobby jumped to his feet and easily hoisted him up on his shoulders to extend his range. McSweeney was down on all fours scrutinizing the floor stones.

"Aha!" Neil shouted, startling me. "Clever fellows, they were," he cried with childlike glee. "I think I've found something. I saw it the instant your flashlight beam hit it, Jill, so keep the light on this spot. Hand me a knife, will you, Bobby?" From his perch on Bobby's shoulders, he wedged the knife blade into a narrow slit between two rocks. At first nothing happened, then a grinding roar broke the echoing silence of the tunnel, as stone on stone, the massive barrier wall began to move. Leaping to my feet, I back-peddled out of its path.

"Get me down," shouted Neil. Bobby leapt backward, too, turning and bending at the same time and landed Neil on his feet beside me. He threw out a hand to grab the wall. "Quentin, get out of the way," he hollered but Bobby had already grasped McSweeney's jacket sleeve and jerked him toward us. We ran backwards up the tunnel, watching the edge of the colossal stone as it ground toward us.

With flashlights trained on it, the right side of the slab of rock grated inward, opening like a bedroom door, and moving of its own accord. Breathless, we watched, as it swung open on invisible hinges, until at last it stopped against the wall. Creeping forward we looked out through the opening the stone door had revealed and gazed at the moonlit panorama before us. We all stood and stared.

"Oh…my…goodness," I whispered. "Where are we?

CHAPTER THIRTY-FIVE

When we emerged from the tunnel we could make out shapes, looming out of the blue moonlight – pyramids, stelae, pillars, statues and hulking, unrecognizable forms. Our weakened flashlight batteries offered little in the way of illumination of whatever lay before us. The tunnel had ended on the threshold of a vast bowl bordered on all sides by hulking highlands. A wide, stone staircase descended from where we stood, into the vast basin full of wonders.

"I think we'd better stop here and take a rest," Neil suggested. "We can't do anything more tonight and we're all dog-tired. It's too dangerous to venture down there in the dark." Grunts of agreement followed. It was hard to believe that we'd spent an entire day and part of a night inside the cavern, exploring the tunnel. Part of that time, we had been sleeping but it still seemed impossible that twenty-four hours before, we were escaping from Goncalvez's compound and into the night. I used my flashlight to check the time. It was 2:45 a.m.

"I'm grabbin' somethin' to hold that door open," McSweeney announced, "in case that tunnel is the only way outta here." He snooped around in the overgrowth near the tunnel's mouth and came up with a stout length of fallen tree trunk. Wedging it between the open door and the opposite wall, he stood back and surveyed his work then grabbed a couple of heavy rocks from outside the tunnel opening and jammed them against the base of the stone door. "There, now I can relax," he said. Tossing his pack on the ground, he flopped down on the floor of the tunnel entrance and propped his head on it. Three

205

seconds later, he was asleep.

"I guess he relaxed," Bobby commented dryly, surveying his snoring friend. "We might as well do the same."

Dawn had just sent its first tentative slivers of periwinkle light over the tops of the canopy above. Stars, bleached out to mere pinpricks in the fading night sky had all but disappeared and the morning birds, waking to a new day, twittered unseen out in the forest somewhere.

Now, even though dawn was already stealing over the scene below, the men were still all asleep so I closed my eyes again and wafted back into a dream. When I awoke later, the sky had been transformed into a lavender bowl suspended over a veritable salad of greenery. For a while I just lay there and stared at the sight before me, my head propped on my lumpy backpack. It felt good to be alone with my thoughts.

I reviewed each moment of our harrowing escape, from the time we had been ushered into the compound at gunpoint, to that thoroughly weird meeting with Mr. Goncalvez, to the sweltering cell where we'd been locked. Then Bobby and McSweeney had rescued us. But we had failed in our attempt to rescue Marco.

As I watched the morning light tint the dark greens of the forest with gold and lime. McSweeney wrestled himself to his feet, muttering something about finding a bathroom. That woke Neil and Bobby who yawned and stretched, scratching and adjusting their clothing. Neil stood to his feet and surveyed the city below.

"No idea," he murmured. "I had no idea that this was here. Wherever 'here' is." He pulled out his satellite telephone and poked it with an index finger. "I was so off course..." he muttered to himself. "That's weird. I can't get a fix on our location."

"Good morning to you too," I said. "What's for breakfast?"

"What happens next?" Bobby asked, appearing from the

shrubbery. "Are we going to look around a while before we get out of here?" His right eyebrow rose slightly as he watched Neil, who gave him only a sideways glance.

"Look at this, you guys," Neil said, reaching for my hand. "It's a lost city. There really is one." The sight was thrilling beyond compare. I followed his gaze over the city below. Two towers made of what appeared to be single blocks of pale stone formed a gate at the base of the staircase that advanced down the slope from where we stood. The towers, completely encrusted in intricately carved designs wore capstones of elongated heads with fierce faces carved from black stone. Vines coiled up the sides of the towers and draped the surfaces with glossy leaves and deep pink blossoms. The effect was at once beautiful and terrifying, clearly meant to cause any visitor to think twice about continuing.

Beyond the gates, a broad passageway led straight through the city and disappeared in the overgrown ruins near the distant edge of the bowl where the land sloped up again toward the mountain peaks. From the high vantage point where we stood, we could see evidence of an advanced civilization rising from the foliage. Walls of intricately cut stone topped with slabs or no roofs at all, streets and walkways, plazas and watercourses crisscrossed the expanse. It was as though at some time in the past, the people had just moved out and the jungle had moved in.

"I know this is a big moment," Bobby said, bringing me back to the present, "but I'm kind of hungry. What have we got to eat?"

Reminded of our stomachs, we fetched our food stores from our backpacks and shared, nibbling on slightly bruised fruit and squashed bread, which tasted delectable, given our circumstances. I sat on a low shelf of rock and watched the morning sun light the sky.

"Here's the plan," Neil said, brushing crumbs off his filthy, cobweb-covered pants and standing to his feet. "We'll head down this alley and see where else it leads. Let's stay together. For all we know there may be booby traps – though, to be honest, I doubt we'll encounter anything like that." We gathered up our breakfast leftovers, hitched packs on our backs again then set off.

The broad stone staircase, made from individually carved blocks, consisted of more than sixty low steps and descended at a gentle angle down into the city. We trooped down the steps like a group of children on the first day of kindergarten – awestruck, excited and apprehensive. Palpable stillness seemed to cover the entire place, as though it existed in a bubble, part of, yet separate from, the surrounding jungle. The rays of the sun, now shooting over the edge of the bowl, seemed to shimmer in the tranquil air above the city. There was something almost magical about the place.

Neil led our procession forward, stepping over tree roots and pushing aside looping branches and trailing vines. The scent of flowers, heady and sweet, permeated the still air. An insect buzzed in a blossom overhead. Walls on our right and left, made of stone and carved with designs of creatures and beings, some with wings, towered over us. A doorway, at least eleven feet high, its lintel formed from one massive slab of stone, opened to our right and I peered into the dark interior. Deserted eons ago, the jungle had moved in and claimed it, leaving the floor heaped with the debris of rampant vegetation.

"This is amazing," Neil breathed, picking his way along.

"It's somethin', ain't it," McSweeney agreed, his hand resting lightly on the handle of his machete.

"And just imagine," I commented, stepping over a sprawling tree root. "We're probably the first people who have walked these streets in centuries."

"Well, you might be," said a voice behind me, "if it weren't for me."

CHAPTER THIRTY-SIX

The woman stepped out from the shadow of a large-leaved tree that lolled over the recessed doorway. Short, grey-haired and smiling, she wore a brightly-coloured embroidered dress and turquoise, rubber flip-flops.

Extending her hand to Neil she said, "Welcome. I'm Dr. Mildred Standish. Everyone here calls me Millie. Who might you be?"

It's rare that I've seen Neil nonplussed but for several moments he simply stared, his mouth hanging open. Then he said, "Forgive me. I didn't expect to find anyone here. I'm Dr. Neil Bryant. I do a bit of archaeological digging from time to time." He extended his hand.

"Ah, yes. I have heard of you," Dr. Standish responded, her pale blue eyes nearly disappearing in the folds of her smiling face. "You're the one who unearthed that ring of stones with the three impossible languages on them, aren't you? Didn't your daughter have something to do with that?"

Neil shook his head. "My niece, actually." He reached a hand toward me and drew me forward. "Meet Jill Moss, artist and, I guess you could say, intrepid adventurer," he said with a doting grin.

"You'll want to see what we're doing here," Millie suggested after introductions had been made. "This is indeed an ancient ruin but it's not everything it seems. Since you have appeared on my doorstep, I'm assuming that the Father sent you?" She searched our faces.

Neil's eyes flickered in my direction and an eyebrow rose as we followed the woman into the nearest structure. *A kindred*

209

spirit? I wondered.

"By 'the Father' would you mean God?" I asked.

"Of course," she said with a short laugh.

"We can't think of any other explanation, ma'am," Bobby answered. "In any case, we're here."

"That will do for now," Dr. Standish replied as she led us through a short hallway, lit by the same kind of lights we had encountered in the tunnel. At its end, she pushed open a heavy wooden door and we followed her into a sizeable room, lit by skylights and powered by solar panels, which could only be described as a stunning marvel. The room held a state-of-the-art laboratory, like something out of a futuristic movie, and reminded me of the underground lab in Israel that Neil was involved with. Massive computer monitors hovered over desks, some piled with fragments of bones, stones or pottery; some heaped with papers or graced with microscopes and glass test tubes. Machines that I didn't recognize lined the walls. Besides us, the place was empty of people.

"Everyone went to town today," she said.

Town? What town? And who is 'everyone'?

Before I could ask, McSweeney spoke up. "What's going on here anyway? I thought this place was some kind of lost city, never seen for thousands of years."

Dr. Standish smiled. "Well," she said, "it was lost until my parents discovered it about forty years ago. You see, we were a missionary family to the tribes hidden away here in the forests of the Andean cordillera. Back then we were about the only white people to venture into these parts. While I was not born here, I grew up among these people groups. My folks are gone now, moved on to be with the Lord," she paused briefly, pushing her fingers through a mass of salt-and-pepper curls, "and so has my husband. I have spent nearly my entire life in these forests, with the exception of my university years."

"But how did you happen to find these ruins?" Neil begged,

still agog. "I've been looking for a place like this for most of my career. In fact, I was about to mount an expedition into this area based on a rumour of such a find when we had a bit of a family problem to deal with. As it turns out, it landed us here anyway."

"As I said, since you've managed to find the place, I'm assuming that God has sent you here. You came through the tunnel?"

"Yes, we found the entrance from the directions in an old diary," I said, wondering if I just had revealed too much.

"That wouldn't have been Lady Cecilia Wardley's diary, would it?" Dr. Standish asked, her eyes glowing with excitement. "We've known about that diary forever. The tribes here told my parents about Miss Wardley years ago and said that she had kept a detailed diary of her travels in these parts. Now, when was it she came through here? 1830 or '35?"

"1835." I replied.

"I remember my mother having a great deal of curiosity about her travels since she was one of the first women to explore these parts."

"Wait," McSweeney said. "What're you doin' here? What's with all this, this lab stuff? Ye're in the middle of nowhere."

Millie grinned up at him. "I suppose 'the middle of nowhere' depends where you're measuring from. I prefer to think that we're exactly where God has placed us."

"If I may ask," I interjected, "who is 'us'?"

"Graduate students, mostly. They come from all over – computer scientists, engineers, archaeologists and historians. We have a strict entrance policy and anyone who comes here is sworn to secrecy for life. Right now we have only three besides myself. That's not counting Consuelo and Arpad who, you could say, help out around the place."

Bobby now spoke for the first time since meeting Dr. Standish. "Ma'am, it's obvious you're doing some kind of important work here. May I ask what you have in place for security?"

"Don't worry about that, my good man," she said patting Bobby's arm. "We have more than enough security here. We have to." She led us toward the far end of the room where another door stood open.

"And why is that?" Neil asked as we walked.

"The giants, of course," she replied. I glanced at Neil and he returned my glance with a knowing look.

"What giants?" he ventured cautiously.

"Remember David and Goliath? That kind of giants."

Neil observed her through narrowed eyes. "Are you saying that there are giants here, like in the Bible?"

"Of course," she answered, pushing open the door and beckoning us to follow. "I assume you'll be staying for a day or two at least. I'll show you where you can put your things and where we sleep and eat. The kids should be back before dark so you'll get a chance to meet everyone."

"What kids?" McSweeney asked.

"Oh, I mean the students. They are all so much younger than I am that I can't help thinking of them as kids. My own children are old enough to be their parents so it stands to reason, don't you think?" She smiled and the corners of her eyes crinkled up again. "Right this way, please."

"If you don't mind me saying so, Dr. Standish..." Neil began.

"Millie."

"Millie, yes, you seem awfully casual about our arrival. Aren't you afraid that we might have harm in mind for you and your operation?"

"Oh, goodness no," she replied, waving away the idea. "I knew you were coming; I just didn't know exactly when."

The accommodations reminded me of summer camp except that the "cabins" had thick walls of stone carved by some ancient people thousands of years before, and air conditioning cooled the interiors. Private cubicles had been created within the larger chambers and included single beds, all neatly made, and small wardrobe cupboards. Bathroom facilities, located in another building down a narrow street, featured the latest in plumbing and design. *How on earth did they bring all this in here?* I wondered.

After we had been assigned lodgings and washed up, I got my chance to find out. Dr. Standish – Millie, I corrected myself, had gone on to the dining room and invited us to join her for a late breakfast. I arrived before the men. When I entered the spacious room, set with six round tables covered in white tablecloths, I could see Millie standing in the doorway to what I assumed led to the kitchen. As I neared I could see that she was talking with another woman. While the dining room had no windows, the area where the roof had once been was now covered with solar panels that let in a soft light and powered the air conditioners. I stepped up beside Millie and with a jolt I realized that I recognised the other woman.

"Dr. Hannah? Is that really you?"

The lady spun around and the moment she saw me, her face broke into a wide smile. "Oh, my dear, my dear," she cried, rushing to throw her arms around me. "How lovely to see you again. Imagine you coming here."

"Imagine you being here yourself? The last time I saw you, you told me that you had retired and planned to live out your days at your lovely little place on Cozumel."

When Neil had summoned me to pick up the pieces of a Mayan artifact earlier that year, one of people to whom he had sent one had been Consuelo Hannah, a long-time archaeologist, along with her late husband, Charles. Together they had studied the connections between Biblical and Central American history and archaeology. After picking up the stone in her possession, I had never expected to see her again.

"Oh, that was ridiculous," Consuelo explained. "I couldn't retire. You were right, you know, when you told me to get back up and get out there, doing what I love to do. Before long, Millie called me and asked me to come and work with her. So, here I am!" She flung out her arms and hugged me again.

"Well, doesn't this beat all?" Millie commented as Neil and the others strode in.

"My friend, Neil," Consuelo said, her voice thick with affection as she embraced him. "How is it that you ended up here today?"

"It's a long story, Connie," he replied.

"Oh, my. If it isn't the polite Mr. Buckingham," Consuelo cried, throwing her arms around Bobby as a grin spread across his features.

"It's lovely to see you again, ma'am," he said, patting her shoulder before introducing McSweeney.

"We've spent the past few days and nights trekking through the jungle," Neil explained, looking around at all of us, "working to free Jill's husband-to-be, Marco, from a disreputable thug by the name of Goncalvez. He was kidnapped the day before he could show up at his own wedding."

"Why, that's terrible!" Dr. Standish cried. Then with a voice as brittle as glass, said, "Why would he do that? What did Goncalvez want?"

Neil hesitated but I blurted the answer out. "An ancient artifact known as the glass dolphin. Do you know it?"

The two doctors shared a solemn glance. "Yes," Millie answered. "We know of it. I've heard of it all my life, living here in Peru. But it is only recently that we think we may have discovered its whereabouts."

CHAPTER THIRTY-SEVEN

Down an ancient corridor, a carved stone bench sat warming under the morning sun near an antediluvian street corner, leaving the others in the dining room. I dropped onto it and leaned my head against the hewn rock wall at my back. Everything had happened so fast that I felt like my world had tilted and I couldn't quite get it back upright. Seeing Marco with a gun pointed at my head at Goncalvez's compound had been like a kick in the gut but there had been no time to feel anything more than the terror of the moment.

I knew what I needed. The only real source of comfort and hope I could count on was God. I reached into my bag and pulled out my Bible, flipping the pages at random. As I scanned the text, my eyes fell on a familiar verse. "I will lift up mine eyes unto the hills," the psalmist had written, "from whence cometh my help. My help cometh from the Lord, who made heaven and earth."

In response, I lifted up my own eyes. Glancing up at the sky, I again marvelled at the shimmering quality that seemed to envelop the ancient city. It looked almost iridescent, like the inside of a soap bubble. In the sparkling morning light, I could barely see the glowing peaks of the mountains to the west. I knew that my help didn't come from the mountains themselves, rather from the God who made the mountains.

"Aha. I thought I'd find you sooner or later," Neil said as he stuck his head around the corner of the building. "Brunch is ready in the dining room." He held out a hand for me to join him. "We're having a meeting with the others. You need to be there."

"All right," I said, rising to my feet, "though I'm not very hungry."

"Hunger is not a requirement," he assured me, tucking my hand into the crook of his elbow. "We need to discuss some plans for getting our hands on that glass dolphin and for getting your man back. You're good at strategizing."

The dining room tables, to my surprise, had now been set with silver, crystal, and china. An array of dishes filled an oblong table at the side of the room and the others had already begun to fill their plates by the time Neil and I walked in. Soon we had all taken seats at a round table.

"Where's the other fellow you mentioned?" I asked, looking around for the man Dr. Standish had mentioned earlier.

"Arpad? I called him but he's out in the back of beyond hacking at vines and didn't want to stop," Millie explained with a dismissive flip of her hand. "What we need to discuss doesn't require his presence anyway."

As I picked at a fruit cup and nibbled on a muffin, the others conversed, talking mostly about the ancient city and the scientific work that Dr. Standish and Dr. Hannah had been doing here. While it was all immensely interesting, particularly from an archaeologist's point of view, I was sure, I had a more pressing reason for being here in the jungles of Peru. Finally, in a lull, I spoke.

"Where is the glass dolphin and how do we get it? The safety of my fiancé is dependent on us finding it." I looked from face to face.

Millie dabbed at the corners of her mouth with a blue cloth napkin then spread it across her lap. "We have heard the legends surrounding the glass dolphin," she began. "The local people have known about it for as long as I can remember and I recall my parents talking about it more than once. The tribal people among whom it originated believed that it held special powers, as I'm sure you're all aware by now."

216

"But does it actually still exist?" I wanted to know.

She held up a hand. "I'm getting to that, dear. I believe that it disappeared over a hundred years ago but no one is quite sure why, nor where it went. Sometimes with these superstitious spiritual practices, something happens and people become afraid so they do things out of the ordinary. I know that your Lady Cecilia Wardley travelled through this area and at that time it was still in use as a mystical symbol, used by the leaders of the clan to claim power."

"But the thing hasn't got any power, has it?" McSweeney interjected. "Isn't it just a lump of glass that happens to look something like a dolphin?"

"Well, yes, and no," Millie answered. "As far as spiritual influence goes, as you know, many objects are worshipped as having divine connections or power which has been bestowed on them by whoever creates the idol. Doing this opens the door for evil spirits to enter the culture. The more the spirits are worshipped, the stronger they become and the more havoc they create. Satan's purposes have always been to deceive people into believing anything except that God loves them and sent his Son to die for their salvation. In the absence of the gospel, people will often grasp at anything that seems to give life spiritual meaning. That's why my parents came here to work and why I've stayed."

"I see it time and again in my work," Neil said.

"The glass dolphin is one such artifact. In a sense, it is a lump of glass but was seen as having or bestowing spiritual power, so it became an idol. However, from the lore that I've heard over the years and from my own investigations, there is a little more to it than that. You see, the 'lump of glass', as you call it, Mr. McSweeney, also contains a most remarkable crystal."

"You can see it in the drawing in Miss Wardley's diary," I said, grabbing my bag from the floor and pulling the book out.

217

"Take a look at this." I flipped the pages until I found the drawing and spread the book open for Millie and Consuelo to examine.

"See how the shape changes right here." I pointed with the nail of my little finger. "You can see the crystal shape in the body of the dolphin. And down here," my finger traced the tiny handwritten lettering, "she mentions the presence of this crystal shape. Do you think that is significant for some reason?"

Millie leaned back in her chair. "After we're finished eating, we'll show you around the compound that we have built here," she replied, "but to answer your question, yes, it is significant. We believe that the crystal is actually a key component in some ancient technology."

I glanced at Neil and he winked back at me. I was surprised he could sit still. The study of ancient and buried technologies was his passion and I knew he had to be twitching with excitement to hear Millie confirm his suspicions about the glass dolphin.

"What technology might that be?" McSweeney asked, his furry eyebrows drawn together. For all his gruffness, I knew that his fascination with the topic almost equalled Neil's. It was fun just to watch the two of them.

"We've made a lot of discoveries in this city," Consuelo answered, "but we have one great mystery and we, Millie and I, think the glass dolphin holds the key to unlocking it."

By this time we all sat in rapt attention. "And that is?" Neil prompted.

Millie's gaze swept around the table, resting on each person for a second. "Understand," she said, "we don't know this for sure."

Until now, Bobby had sat eating his meal, the most relaxed person of the group but now he leaned forward and blurted, "Just tell us, please, ma'am, before I choke on this bun thing."

Millie laughed. "All right. We think we're about to unlock

the science behind acoustic levitation and we believe that the glass dolphin may conceal a vital clue."

"Behind the who, what?" McSweeney said.

"The process by which matter is transmitted from one location to another using high frequency sound waves," I answered. Every head turned to stare at me.

"How did you know that?" Neil asked, the corners of his mouth turning up in a grin.

I sat up straight and tilted my chin up. "I read."

CHAPTER THIRTY-EIGHT

Neil and I hung back from the rest of the group as Millie led us on a tour of the facilities. "What makes Dr. Standish think that the glass dolphin crystal has any connection to acoustic levitation? And if it does, so what?" I spoke quietly so we would not be overheard.

"Think about it," Neil answered. "For centuries people have speculated on how the Inca, or whoever it was, built such amazing edifices as Sacsayhuaman and Machu Picchu. They've come up with theories on how the ancient Egyptians built the pyramids but no one is sure. And think about those megalithic stones in Lebanon that make up the ancient ruins of Baalbec. They're saying now that these ruins prove the existence of aliens from other planets or solar systems."

"Fishing for explanations?"

"Of course," Neil agreed. "When man makes the choice to ignore God, he has to make up his own theories to understand the world. These theories, as you know, frequently become religions, which over time lead in a downward spiral to destruction."

"What about the giants? Millie thinks they exist and apparently are not far from here."

"I'm convinced that they are real and that they could very well inhabit this area. You know already that the Bible describes these beings as the offspring of fallen angels and human women. I don't have to tell you about how often their images occur in ancient art. We just tend to assume that the difference in body size is due to perspective or artistic license. But no one wants to believe that the beings that appeared to be two or three times the size of regular people actually were."

"I hadn't thought of that before," I commented, thinking about the art history I had studied, "but I suppose there has to be some explanation. The sheer magnitude of the art and artifacts indicates that there must be at least some truth to the images. There are just too many examples spread over too long a span of time for the concept that giants lived alongside regular people for it all to be just the figment of someone's imagination. But how would they have ended up in a far-flung place like this? It's a long way from Mesopotamia or Egypt."

"If you'll recall, when Joshua and Caleb scouted out the land God had promised to the Israelites after their exodus from Egypt, they found giants in the land. All the other spies were terrified and advised against going in, but Joshua and Caleb knew God and claimed that, in spite of the giants, they would be well able to take the land, which they did. The beings there were either killed or they scattered, or they managed to hang about the fringes because Goliath showed up before David became king. You know the story."

I nodded.

"These beings, called the Nephilim or Rephaim in the Bible, were a highly intelligent species, massively strong and completely evil. When God scattered them in the face of the oncoming armies of the Israelites, I believe that these giants used their technical know-how to disseminate around the globe. Throughout fairly modern history, like in the past few hundred years, remnants of these peoples have been discovered and many skeletons have been unearthed that verify their existence. As a race, they are degenerative, meaning that each succeeding generation is worse or less than its predecessors, yet more evil."

"Do you think they will present a problem for us?"

"I doubt it. Do you?"

I shuddered. "I hope I have no opportunity to find out. The sooner I'm out of this jungle the better."

Neil strolled quietly beside me for a few moments, his hands clasped behind his back, looking up to the sky above the colossal carved stones of the ancient city. "See that sky," he said, stopping. "Did you notice that it looks different, kind of pearly?"

"Yes, it's weird," I replied, pausing beside him. "What's going on with that?"

"It's a hologram."

"Seriously?"

"I talked to Millie earlier and she told me that they have projected a hologram that covers the entire city from one side to the other." He swung his right arm in a wide sweep to indicate the entire circumference of the bowl. "From above, it looks exactly like the surrounding forest. That's why no one has found it."

"That's amazing. But holographic images are fairly new technology. It couldn't have been in place forever."

"You're right," he said, resuming walking, "or you might be wrong. I have come across evidence that indicates that ancient civilizations may also have been aware of holograms. The evidence is not conclusive so I've avoided broadcasting my findings. In the archaeological world it's pretty easy to be branded a crackpot if you suggest anything too far outside the 'party line.' However, until recently, this city was buried in the actual jungle, overgrown with brush so thick that for anyone to find it they'd first have to stumble into the valley. That would be no mean feat in itself. Then they'd have to slash through centuries' worth of growth even to recognize that there was something here. It was a completely lost city for generations – no, ages. Millie's parents stumbled upon it, probably with God's help, and rather than invite a horde of archaeologists, tourists and hangers-on, they excavated it themselves with the help of a few trusted colleagues. The scientists that they invited built the labs and created the holography to camouflage the entire site."

"That's amazing," I murmured. "How does that hologram work?"

"I'm no expert on the subject, but basically it involves lasers, diffraction, and light to create a three-dimensional image so that no matter from which direction it is viewed, it appears real. It's not really an image but that's the easiest way to describe it. The rest is beyond me."

"I wondered why the sky here looks so unusual, like an iridescent bubble."

By this time the others had disappeared through the door to the lab and as we caught up, Millie was in the middle of describing their complicated and advanced computer systems. At this, Neil stopped and listened intently. This place bore an uncanny resemblance to the secret lab I had visited with him in Israel in the spring.

"One of the main tenets of our study here is with magnetic fields," I heard Dr. Standish explain. "We are hoping that the glass dolphin holds the key or at least further information to unlocking the ancient technologies that account for the amazing architecture that surrounds us here in this ruin."

I gave Neil a jab with my elbow. "She sounds just like you," I whispered.

He grinned. "I know. Isn't it great?"

"The problem," Millie went on, giving Neil a meaningful look, "is that while we have a general idea of where the glass dolphin is located, we don't have a specific lock on its location. We could spend decades looking for it and even then we may find that it doesn't do what we think it will; that we've been mistaken all along."

"In other words," Bobby ventured, "to find out if it works, we have to first find it."

"That's right, unfortunately," she replied.

"Where do you think it is?" I asked, stepping closer. My motivation for finding the thing was personal, so anything I could do to speed up the process sounded pretty good to me.

"We believe that it is right here in this city somewhere. We have found evidence in carvings and various artifacts that mention its existence. The problem is, we have yet to figure out exactly where it is. Since at its peak we estimate that this city had a population in excess of 20,000 people, it could be anywhere, in any one of the over four hundred individual buildings."

"I thought the glass dolphin originated in a later time than this city appears to have," I said, frowning slightly. According to Cecilia Wardley's diary, it wasn't adding up.

"We agree," Consuelo Hannah interjected, stepping from behind a bank of computers where she had been working. "But the tribal people who acquired the glass dolphin appeared to have spent time in this city. For some reason, though, they also appeared to have left abruptly or perhaps had been chased out. That's another reason we believe it is still here."

It crossed my mind that a mean and nasty local giant population might be a good reason to leave but I didn't mention it. "So now we just need to find it," I said, looking from Millie and Consuelo to Neil.

"That's right," Mildred answered. "However, the clues that we have discovered have not been sufficiently conclusive for us to zero in on a definite location. I am hoping the four of you can help us figure out the puzzle. With Dr. Bryant's background and whatever the rest of you can offer, I'm hoping that we can find it before…" she hesitated and looked away. "Well, before long. We don't think we have much time."

"Before what?" I said. "I want to get my fiancé free and get out of here. If there is something going on, I want to know what it is."

Dr. Standish reached for my hand and gave it a squeeze. "I understand your urgency."

"Doctor, we need you to tell us what's on your mind," Neil

said. "If we're to work together, we need to have no secrets. I know that my crew here is completely trustworthy as is Dr. Hannah. If we're in danger, we need to pull together."

Millie nodded. "You're right, of course. I hesitated to mention this earlier because we have so little hard evidence but we've heard rumblings that the giant people are getting restless."

McSweeney fixed her with a narrow-eyed stare. "You're sure these creatures exist, are ye?"

"Oh, yes, Mr. McSweeney. They exist. Make no mistake. I've seen them more than once during my years here in the jungles."

"We passed through a village on the way here," I said. "The place was deserted but we found some huge footprints. They had six toes."

"Juan Carlos, our guide, was petrified," Neil explained to the others. "He rushed us out of there at lightning speed."

"Do these 'giants,' as you call them, want the glass dolphin?" Bobby ventured.

"Oh yes," Millie Standish answered. "They want anything that will give them added power. They have most certainly heard the legends surrounding the artifact and probably have some suspicion that it has a connection to ancient technologies. These beings are ruthless beyond belief and will stop at nothing to get what they want."

Consuelo Hannah stepped forward. "My late husband and I have done extensive research on biblical archaeology, including the existence and history of the giants mentioned numerous times in the Bible. They existed then, and I believe they exist now. There is a grand and devious plan being developed by our enemy, Satan, for his final take-over of God's creation. He won't succeed in the end, of course, but that doesn't stop him from putting his plans into place. He will use and subvert anything he can to bring his plans about. Much of it has already begun. We need to pay attention, to watch and pray, yes, but also to be informed. This is not a time in history to bury our heads in the sand."

"In other words, we'd better get our roller skates on and find that thing," I said, glancing at the others for agreement. Every head nodded.

"If we all work on it," Millie stated, "perhaps we can speed things up. Follow me."

"I know what I'm going to do," I announced, falling in behind Dr. Standish as she led us down a narrow alleyway, into the ancient city. "I'm going to pray and find out what God has to tell us. Without him we won't get far."

CHAPTER THIRTY-NINE

By evening the sky had clouded over and the dome above the city took on the shades of an abalone shell's interior, deep grey swirled through with sparkling ribbons of colour in emerald, garnet and sapphire. "The kids," as Millie called her graduate student assistants, had not returned from Cusco, in fact, had emailed to say that there was a festival on and they had decided to stay a few more days to enjoy the revelry. As our focus had narrowed to discovering the location of the glass dolphin, we were happy to have no one else around to distract us, or for that matter, to cause problems.

Millie led the hunt through the overgrown streets of the ancient city. At times, passage was nearly impossible and we were only able to hack a path through the vegetation wide enough for us to pick our way through single file. After about a half hour of strenuous exertion we stopped for a break and water replenishment. As we stood in the small cleared section, we were all startled when a man stepped through the doorway of a roofless structure, carrying a shovel in his hand. He was my height, or maybe a bit taller, had thinning brown hair and looked to be around fifty.

"Oh," Millie said, fanning herself with her hand. "This is Arpad Morris. Dr. Morris is an engineer of just about every kind – mechanical, electrical, civil, geological – you name it."

"But mostly a shoveller of dirt," Morris added with a grin.

"We're off to find the glass dolphin," Millie chirped as though we were simply skipping along the yellow brick road in search of the Wizard of Oz. "Would you care to join us?"

"Not right now," Dr. Morris answered. "I've just uncovered

227

part of the water system and want to keep digging."

I saw Neil's eyes light up and could tell he was itching to investigate so I gave his sleeve a tug. "Down, uncle. We're on a mission here." He shrugged and promised Dr. Morris that he would stop by later to explore his findings.

The magnitude of the ruined city astonished me. While few structures had roofs any longer, as they had probably been made of perishable materials like wood and thatch, the carved walls of stone rose from the cobbled streets at exact angles. Over the centuries many of the stones had tumbled, often pushed out of place by encroaching plant life. In places, massive trees grew directly out of floors or streets, their limbs elbowing aside anything in their paths – mere roots dislodging slabs of flooring stones. Verdant vines trailed over collapsed walls, their probing fingers penetrating into every crack and fissure. The walls that remained standing displayed such precise masonry cuts that they put even the ruins around Cusco to shame.

"How did they do this?" I asked, to no one in particular, as I ran my fingertips along the flawless seam of adjoining stones, cut in polygonal shapes.

"No one is sure," Millie replied, "but I have a hunch that the glass dolphin may hold a clue for us. Please follow me," she continued, pushing aside a branch festooned with orange trumpet-shaped blossoms. "The place I'm looking for is not far now, unless I've taken a wrong turn. It's easy to get lost in this jumble."

When we finally stopped thrusting our way through the overgrown alleys, and up and down stairways, we found ourselves in a small square, like a miniature plaza, which showed evidence of having been purposely cleared of debris and flora. Several fairly intact buildings skirted the open area and in the centre stood a monument. It was like nothing I had ever seen before, either in person or in photographs. The structure stood about ten feet in height with a square base, wider at the bottom than the top, tapering upward at a gentle angle. This in itself was not remarkable as it simply resembled an obelisk from which the top and been knocked off. The structure was now crowned with a tropical plant, which had no doubt self-seeded in the humus layered down from surrounding growth.

What was peculiar about this edifice was that it was made up of hundreds of tiny blocks no more than roughly two inches in diameter each yet no two were exactly the same shape. Not a single one was a perfect square, and the colour variations made each unique. It reminded me of a puzzle or a mosaic made with hundreds of perfectly fitted fragments.

"This is amazing," Neil said, running his fingertips across the smooth surface. Like unpolished jewels, the stones glowed in a myriad of subtle kaleidoscopic colours. I stepped to my right to view another side and saw that the colours changed depending on the angle of the light.

"It's incredible, isn't it?" Millie said. "But the colours are not the most remarkable thing about this monument. It also sings." I saw McSweeney raise a skeptical eyebrow. Millie continued, "We have yet to figure out what sets it off but it seems to be associated with certain slants of light. We've taken turns sitting in this square and recording everything we can think of but have yet to determine what causes the high-pitched sounds."

"What does it sound like?" I asked.

"It's a cross between flute music and angels singing," Millie answered, "– though I can't say I've ever heard angels singing. It usually occurs toward evening. If you'll look around this square you can see that some blocks are highly polished, almost like mirrors." She pointed out one near where she stood. "At certain times of the year the sun strikes one or another of the blocks and causes this structure to emit sounds."

"Then what happens?" Neil asked over his shoulder as he examined the stone's coloured faces.

"The colours are brighter, like they are lit from within. After a while, after the sunlight no longer strikes the mirrors, it stops. It's quite a show."

McSweeney, who until now had been walking around the statue from a distance like he was casing it, said, "So where's the glass dolphin? Is it in this thing?"

"Besides the legends that I've known about since I was a child living in this area, we have found other clues that point to this location. Only recently have we been able to work out this information based on the jumble of clues we've found in the city."

Neil now looked like a dog about to be handed a new bone. "What sort of clues?" he demanded. "Where did you find them?"

Between them, Millie and Consuelo filled us in on their findings. Apparently, the city itself held many clues, the most frequent being the image of a dolphin. The popularity of the image carved into stone lintels and painted on shards of pottery convinced the team of the veracity of the glass dolphin legend, or at least that there had been some connection. As the city itself lay several days' trek from the ocean, a sea creature like the dolphin seemed an unlikely myth for a people group this far away to adopt as a talisman.

Looking up and out to the bluffs surrounding the city I could see that the multi-coloured stone tower stood almost exactly in the centre of the natural bowl where the city had been built. Its obvious features – the beauty, the craftsmanship and the sound phenomenon – according to Millie, displayed only one aspect of its importance.

"We have come to believe that the glass dolphin is entombed within this structure," she said. "Everything we've found so far points to this location."

"And do you know how to remove it," Neil asked, "without a sledgehammer?"

A look of horror crossed Consuelo Hannah's face before being replaced by a wry grin. "Stop that, Neil," she said, cuffing him on the arm. "As you can see, the structure is created to be like a puzzle. We've taken hundreds of digital photos and studied them from every possible angle looking for the way in. We believe that there is one piece that acts as a key and will reveal its interior but we don't know which one it is."

Neil stood back and rubbed a hand over his chin, his favourite cogitating gesture.

"What do you think, Jill?" he asked, settling a hand on my shoulder.

"How would I know?"

He gave me a look that exempted him from actually saying, "Well, duh."

"Why don't I ask the Holy Spirit?" I suggested in my perkiest voice, catching on.

"Yes, why don't you?" Neil said, grinning broadly. "It's bound to save us time, something we don't have a lot of right now."

I dropped my head and pressed two fingers on a spot between my eyebrows to help me focus, while at the same time turning away from the group and wandering a short distance away down a rock-cluttered alley. I asked God to show us what we needed to know and focused on listening with my heart. I could hear the others talking in the background and heard Millie suggest that they all have a seat while they waited. Deliberately tuning out their sounds, I pulled my concentration inward, downward, deep. For a while, I paced back and forth over a fairly clear space of this ancient street, absent-mindedly nudging debris out of my way with my toe. Whispered prayers floated up from deep within my soul. I knew in my heart that this glass dolphin was important somehow, and though my longing was to free Marco, there were bigger stakes involved.

It was slow in coming. Or, maybe it just took a while to

quiet the clamouring in my brain so I could really listen to the Spirit. I was about to give up and go back to where the others waited when suddenly the image of a glowing, lavender blue spot burst across my mind's eye. I stopped walking. *What does that mean?* The answer came back just as suddenly as the lavender blue spot formed into a distinct shape, similar to a crescent moon. Then I felt a slight pressure on the top of my left hip. I waited a while longer but nothing more came.

Rushing back to the square, I could barely breathe. "I don't know what this means," I said, my voice trembling, "but I believe God has shown me something." Everyone turned to stare at me as Neil sprang to his feet.

"What I saw in – I suppose was a vision – was a purplish-blue crescent-shaped stone. I think it's located at about my hip level."

Before I had even finished talking, Neil and McSweeney were on their knees examining every stone on the monument at that level.

"I think it's a bit higher," I told them as the sense grew and they both moved their search up to the approximate the level of the top of my hip. "Look for lavender blue," I added, bending at the waist to hunt alongside Neil.

The sky had filled with clumps of cloud earlier and now dappled sunshine poked through the scattered cover. Suddenly, a streak of light pierced the shadows, reflected off one of the mirrored tiles high up on the wall of a stone partition, and shot a beam of light onto the column. Instantly, a lavender blue stone blazed into startling brilliance.

It had the shape of a crescent moon.

CHAPTER FORTY

Certain moments in life transcend others; they stand out in memories years down the road, after the day-to-day remembrances have faded into the grey mists of obscurity. What happened in the next several minutes seemed wrapped in that sparkle of the miraculous to such an extent that I doubted the images would ever diminish from the corridors of my memory.

A wall with stones so finely cut that the individual blocks appeared to have been scored from one massive slab, featured a single palm-sized tile fixed high on the exterior. The brilliant shaft of white sunlight, reflected from the mirror-like inlay, shot through the still air like a laser beam. It struck a single stone on the mosaic of tiny, carved nuggets that made up the pillar standing in the centre of the ancient square. The beam was so fine that it struck only one single stone, and it was lavender blue and crescent-shaped. Exactly like the impression the Holy Spirit had imparted to me, mine for the asking.

Then, nothing happened. We all held our collective breath, expecting, who knew what? It dawned on me that this action with the light probably happened every day, or every month or even if it happened only once a year, it had probably been going on for centuries, with or without the hologram covering the city.

"Push on it," I said to Neil, who was closest. "See what it does."

Neil placed his thumb on the glowing stone and applied pressure.

Nothing.

I stood there continuing to think, praying quietly and listening intently for any further instructions from the Holy Spirit. Suddenly, I had another strong inner sensing. Vividly, the conversation we had had earlier regarding acoustic levitation came back to me and that Neil had a particular interest in the possibility that the massive cut stones found at archaeological sites all over the world had actually been moved into place by the use of sound waves.

"This might seem a little crazy," I said, looking around the group, "but I have the feeling that sound has to be involved in this somehow. So, I'm going to sing up the scale by tones and semi-tones and we'll see if anything happens. It may have something to do with combining sound with light so I'd better hurry."

"It's certainly worth a try," Neil agreed with a grin. "It doesn't seem to want to budge using pressure and I'd hate to have to dismantle it piece by piece if we don't have to."

I cleared my throat and began at the lowest note I could comfortably reach, somewhere in the neighbourhood of a low D. Thankful for those years of voice and piano lessons I had endured and the opportunity to be worship leader at my church, I drew in a deep breath. Opening my throat wide, as I had been taught, my voice rose in tone, note by note, as it ascended the scale. I had run out of breath and reached the highest notes in my range when I was about to give up. Heaving in one last quick breath, I sang out the highest note I could comfortably reach without my eyes popping.

And then something happened. The lavender stone cracked in two and toppled to the paving stones at Neil's feet. Everyone gasped. What occurred next was equally shocking. The structure had been held together, apparently, by this one keystone and with it in pieces on the ground, the rest simply collapsed in a circular pile around the central tower.

We couldn't help but gape at the sudden change and stare at

the structure standing before us. The stone tower had been completely lined with a glass sleeve. As the outer stones were only about two inches thick, this crystalline casing was only slightly smaller in size than the exterior coloured block structure, and now stood glistening in the rays of sunshine. Within the glass casing stood a slender, white stone pillar and on top of the pillar rested a figurine that could be none other than the glass dolphin. We all fell into a hush of absolute awe, staring at it, as though struck dumb.

Finally, Neil stood to his feet, as did McSweeney. Millie and Consuelo moved in for a closer look. Bobby gazed in wonder over Neil's shoulder.

The figure itself glowed a pale, clear aquamarine, the glass swirls almost artistically arranged around the base so that it really did look like a surging wave. The dolphin shape rose from the furrowed base in a high arcing leap, its body curving exactly like that of the animal itself, soaring from the sea in playful ecstasy. While the figure had clearly not been polished or ground into the shape of the animal by any tool I knew of, it still managed to depict the personality of a dolphin with all its elegance and grace. Its size was about equal to my forearm, just as Cecilia Wardley had said.

We had found the glass dolphin at last.

"What on earth made you think that singing would do the trick, Moss?" McSweeney asked, almost in a whisper, clearing his throat as he gazed at the artifact.

"It had to be the Holy Spirit," I said. "The idea began to come on me so strongly and seemed more supernatural than anything I'd experienced before."

"It's a good thing you're a soprano," Neil remarked. "It was that high note that did it."

"*Es hermoso,*" Consuelo murmured. "It's beautiful. Look at how it sparkles in the light." Indeed, where the sunlight struck the contours of the glass, it reflected back an ever so subtle aqua glow. But there was more to it than that. Within the outside shell of glass that actually created the dolphin shape, I could see when I examined it more closely, that it contained the most peculiar phenomenon – a perfect inner crystal column that shot beams of colour in all the hues of the rainbow.

"It is breathtaking," I said. "No wonder ancient people believed there was something special about it. What do you think, Neil?"

"I think we need to find a way to get it out of here without breaking anything," he answered, standing back and surveying the pile of rubble with the glass tower standing before him. Curiously enough, when the stone casing had toppled in a heap around the base of the column, the plant growing on top of it remained intact, as though unmoved by the monumental discovery hidden beneath its roots.

"Perhaps if we get those stones away from the base we can lift the glass sleeve right over the top," Millie suggested. I could tell that she found it difficult to pull her eyes away from the glass dolphin's magnificence.

Just then, Arpad came around the corner of a narrow street pushing a wheelbarrow. At the sight of the glass dolphin, he halted, mouth open.

"Ah," said Millie. "Just the man I want to see."

"I thought you might need this when I heard the, uh, the crash. My, my, that's a remarkable artifact, isn't it? Never seen anything quite like that before." Without taking his eyes off the artifact, he pulled a spade from the wheelbarrow and held it out to Neil. "Um, sorry, will this help?"

"Immensely," Neil replied. "Give it to one of those guys over there. They're just standing around doing nothing anyway." Turning he added, "But be careful. We'll want to catalogue all of these stones."

McSweeney, still agape over the find, and no doubt, sensing as we all did, the presence of something breath-taking all around us, stuck out his hand. But before he could take the shovel from Arpad, Bobby grabbed it and began to gently lift and tip the stones into the wheelbarrow, carefully edging the tip of the spade beneath each shovelful so as not to disturb anything else. Everyone else pitched in by hand, touching each stone delicately and stopping to gape at the glass dolphin every few seconds. Within a few minutes the paving stones around the base of the glass tower had been cleared of the rubble of coloured blocks.

"Now comes the tricky part," Neil explained. "We have to see if we can lift these cobblestones and find the bottom edge of the glass." Consuelo offered to accompany Arpad back to the main building to fetch some digging tools, trowels and even stiff artist's brushes for removing all traces of soil. A short time later they were back carrying a tool bag filled with various implements. As I was the only artist in the group, I offered to do the brushwork and plunked myself cross-legged on the cobbles to begin.

It took us well over an hour, each working on a small section of the paving stones, to clear the area at the base of the glass column. Once the stones had been removed and the sandy soil brushed away, it became clear that the glass casing had been created in one piece.

How did an ancient civilization create such a masterpiece? I wondered. Before I could voice my unspoken thought, Neil answered.

"Most people believe that civilizations that existed prior to the great flood had to be primitive, especially in remote areas like this one. However, nothing could be further from the truth. My work has revealed again and again that the cultures that existed prior to about 3000 - 4000 B.C. had advanced technologies, some of which modern man has yet to discover or understand." He sat back on his heels and I could see him warming to his favourite subject. "I have come to the conclusion that there are many facets of technological understanding that we are only beginning to grasp."

"How do you suppose this glass tower was made? It's so perfectly symmetrical and polished." I asked, not wanting to be here in the dirt all night listening to Neil lecture.

"I'm not a glass worker," Neil admitted, "but it was probably created in a glassblowing furnace, much the same way that glass is blown today. Where the sand came from that was used to create the glass in the first place is another question."

He nudged the tip of a trowel under the edge of the glass on his side of the structure and invited the rest of us to find purchase beneath the smooth edge. With many hands to steady it, he said, "Let's see if we can lift it straight up and over the top. I don't think I need to mention not to knock the glass dolphin off its perch, do I?"

On the count of three, it came loose from the base. Surprisingly heavy, and with that plant quivering on its top, the hollow glass column rose steadily. Slowly, slowly, we guided it over the top of the glass dolphin where it stood on the pale stone pillar and then gently set it down several metres away.

Once the glass dolphin was free of its casing, the full effect of its glittering beauty emerged. It was dazzling, stunning, and awe-inspiring.

"Well, what now?" McSweeney inquired, one hand on his hip and his head tilted sideways to better view the figure. His face wore a grin that wouldn't quit. Even his eyes sparkled.

Neil beamed, as though he could not contain his anticipation. "I can't get over the fact that we – you guys, us – we found this artifact that has been sought after for eons. Thanks be to God." He looked around the circle of faces. "I guess now we need to figure out what all the fuss is about."

Chapter Forty-One

I will always wonder if it was God's design that Bobby, standing quietly in the background throughout all the exclamations of admiration and wonder, took a step backward and tripped on a fallen stone block. When he flung out his arm for balance, he accidently swiped the trowel from his back pocket. It went spinning through the air.

Fortunately, the flying trowel caused no harm either to the implement or to anyone standing nearby, or, thank God, to the glass artifact that we were so ardently admiring. It was the sound, however, that caused what happened next. The trowel hit the cobbled street surface with a sharp clang and in that instant set off a chain reaction like nothing I have witnessed before.

A high-pitched note began to emanate from the figurine and we stared, wide-eyed, as the sound grew in volume and timbre. At the pinnacle of pitch, when it had reached dog-whistle tone and was almost impossible to hear, a vision appeared before it. I'm tempted now to say, "I kid you not," because it was the most far-fetched apparition I have ever encountered. I would doubt it too, if I hadn't seen it with my own eyes.

What appeared before us is nearly impossible to compare to anything else I know of except to say that it was like a transparent blackboard, completely covered in script that looked like mathematical equations or language. The image glowed a soft aqua blue that faded in and out as the sunlight sifted through the lightly overcast sky above. None of the writing on this transparent screen made any sense to me.

Glancing at Neil, I asked, "Do you see what I see?" He

proceeded to describe it in detail while the others nodded in agreement.

"What just happened?" Bobby asked, staggering and bug-eyed.

"It seems that Dr. Standish was right about the acoustics," Neil murmured. "When the trowel clinked on the stone over there, it must have been exactly the right frequency to activate the…this…"

"It looks like an extremely sophisticated hologram," Mildred said. "I've never seen anything quite like it before and this has been my field of study for years. It's fascinating, just fascinating."

"Any o' you guys know what it says?" McSweeney asked.

"I've never seen this particular script before," Neil admitted. He turned to the other scientists. "Is this familiar to any of you?" All shook their heads.

"I'll bet I know who would be able to read it," I said mostly to Neil and McSweeney. "Dr. Silverman." Turning to Dr. Standish I explained. "He's one of the world's foremost experts on ancient languages. It's just too bad he's not here." Dr. Silverman had been one of the scientists to decipher the languages on the ring of sixteen stones that we had discovered early that same year.

"I'm quite sure that we have nothing in our lab to decipher this code, and a code is what it appears to be," Millie said. "Whatever could it mean?"

"That's something we will eventually find out," Neil answered. "I'm sure Doc Silverman can help with that but not without the assistance of our super-computers at the lab in Israel. The real question is how to transport this artifact from here to there. What do you think, Bobby?"

An adrenalin-fuelled jolt of panic shot through me, jerking me back to the present. "Whoa! No, no, no!" I cried. "This thing has to be used to get Marco back. If it leaves the country, what's going to happen to him? Goncalvez could kill him!" Protecting what I saw as the only leverage to save my fiancé, I moved toward the glass dolphin and reached out my hand to touch it. When my fingers penetrated the hologram, it vanished.

"Oh…nooo," I whispered, biting my lip. "I've wrecked it. I'm so sorry." For a moment, no one said a word. Then Neil wrapped an arm over my shoulders and pulled me close.

"Listen, Jill. This artifact will be used to get Marco back. Just maybe not in the way you'd prefer."

"What are you talking about?"

"Marco is smart, clever, and highly trained. Remember, he was with Israeli special operatives only a few years ago. He hasn't lost his edge. Sometime between now and when we get this 'thing,' as you called it, out of the country, you're going to see your man again. I promise."

Only slightly mollified, I nodded. "I'm assuming you have a plan and it had better be a good one."

"Before we left England, and after you discovered the diary, I contacted my colleagues in Peru's Ministry of Culture to obtain permission to remove the artifact from the country for the purposes of study only, should we be fortunate enough to find it. It would be returned to the people of Peru. The paperwork is all ready."

"That's not what I mean," I said. "How are we getting from here back to Cusco while at the same time letting Marco know that we've got it so he can get out of Goncalvez's clutches? And how do you intend for us to slip past Goncalvez and his guards?"

I saw Neil shoot a glance across to where McSweeney stood, his thumbs hitched in his belt. The look on Bobby's face confirmed that the three of them had been making plans without me. I swung back toward Neil with narrowed eyes. "Okay, you guys. Let me in on it, whatever you've been cooking up. Tell me," I demanded.

"What do you say we cover the dolphin with the glass casing again and throw a sheet around it for now." Neil checked with Millie, who nodded in agreement. "Then we're going to all sit down and map out a strategy. Yes, while you were off praying, the three of us sketched out a plan but we'd never do anything without consulting you. Each one of us is vital to the operation, especially you."

Over cups of good, strong Peruvian coffee half an hour later, the discussion began. Within an hour we had prepared a workable strategy. The plan was to crate up the glass dolphin, which would not be difficult to transport in a backpack, as the size was no bigger than a child's doll. Rather than travelling back through the jungle by the way Neil and I had come, we would make our way down toward the river following a route similar to the way that McSweeney and Bobby had come. The major obstacle was that Goncalvez's compound lay between the ancient city and therefore the cave entrance, and the river dock. But so did Marco. I wasn't leaving this country without him.

"I haven't quite figured out how we will find the way without a guide, now that Juan Carlos is no longer with us." Neil looked around the table, clearly hoping for a suggestion.

"God will show us the way," I said. "The Holy Spirit will lead us. He's done it numerous times before. We can count on him."

Neil spread his hands and nodded in agreement. "You're better at that than I am so I'm going to leave it up to you to lead us."

"We have to let Marco know," I said. "If we can get a message to him, he can give Goncalvez the slip and meet us. Before anyone knows what has happened, we'll all be gone, along with the glass dolphin. Any ideas?"

After some debate, we agreed to set out right away so that we might emerge from the tunnel entrance into the jungle once the sun had begun to descend. That way, we could travel under the concealing shadows of late afternoon. When we came into the vicinity of Goncalvez's compound, Neil and Bobby would infiltrate it and find Marco. By then it would be dusk so they should be able to sneak in and out again without detection. Once Marco joined us, and the two of us were re-united, our entire group would carry on to the river. Using Dr. Standish's lab's satellite internet connection, McSweeney contacted Henry, the boatman, to have a boat waiting to meet us just upriver from where he had dropped Bobby and McSweeney previously.

The plan seemed simple enough. Too simple, actually. I tried not to think about what could go wrong. Aside from venomous snakes, anacondas, jaguars, poisonous frogs, crocodiles, caimans and piranhas to deal with, the possibility of breaking a limb or two, falling into a gorge, running into patrols of Goncalvez's men, or getting shot trying to rescue Marco, there was the little matter of a race of vicious giants roaming the forest. And if that weren't enough, we'd be doing most of it in the dark.

We had one hour before departing. Neil and the others had gone off to crate up the glass dolphin while I went to pack and do the only thing I could that I knew would make a difference. Call on the name of the Lord for help and protection.

CHAPTER FORTY-TWO

Even though the sun had already started to lean into the shoulder of the Andes, its rays sent needles of pain into my eyes as I emerged from the narrow opening of the cave. After saying our good-byes to Mildred Standish, Consuelo Hannah and the elusive Arpad Morris and taking a final look at the magnificent secret city, we slipped single-file through the stone slab opening from the ancient city into the magically-lit tunnel. Now that we knew where we were going, we lost no time in retracing our steps through the tunnel and cave, jogging most of the way.

We stumbled into daylight with dilated pupils, shielding our tender eyes with upraised hands. Bobby had emerged a good ten minutes before the rest of us, concealing himself until his vision adjusted, and acted as lookout. He informed us that with his dark skin, he blended with the shadows much better than the rest of us. One by one, we stepped out of the cool cave interior into the steaming jungle, which had been freshly dampened by another tropical downpour. That meant the trail would be muck and our tracks as easy to conceal as if a tank had ploughed through the underbrush.

It couldn't be helped. Time was of the essence. At this moment the glass dolphin lay packed securely in cotton wadding and foam chips – the latter included so if it should land in the river it wouldn't sink out of sight – and riding in a pack on McSweeney's back. Neil had argued that he should carry it but had been overridden by McSweeney's logic. He was bigger, stronger, and wouldn't be sneaking into the enemy compound this evening. He also claimed to be meaner than Neil, a claim none of us wanted to argue. If by some stroke of evil, Goncalvez discovered us, and realized that we had found the coveted glass dolphin, we had to be prepared to make tracks, no matter how deep in the mud or obvious they might be.

We set off in silence, led by Neil, whose years trekking through jungle terrain in Mexico and Central America at least gave him the edge on what to watch out for. I followed right behind him, listening intently in my spirit for direction from the Holy Spirit and informing Neil when I sensed anything. McSweeney came next and Bobby took up the rear. Bobby's years in security work and surveillance meant that we had a hyper-vigilant rear guard.

At first the going was rough. We had come to the cave entrance from a direction that to me seemed quite different from the way we now advanced. Ordinarily, I'm pretty good at not losing my way but the forest offered no markers at all by which to navigate. In the failing light, one tree began to look identical to the next and everything else just appeared leafy, soggy and foreboding. To my reckoning, with the fading sun on my left shoulder, when it by chance was able to cut through the canopy, I knew that we were going roughly north, toward the river. Trudging through the stream with the coffee-coloured water gave me slight orientation but I had no way of knowing if this was where we'd passed before. For one thing, the daily torrential downpours would have long since washed our tracks from the previous jaunt away and could have easily changed the appearance of the stream itself.

A steep downward grade with a path that curved in repeating switchbacks alerted us that we had to be nearing Goncalvez's complex. Sliding and skidding down the slope, I grasped at low-hanging branches to keep from landing on my backside. Neil held up his hand at a bend in the path and we clustered around him under the cover of a plant with leaves as big as parasols. It didn't help that a light drizzle had started up, adding to the difficulty.

"If you'll remember," he said in a harsh whisper, "at the bottom of this hill there's another stream. It's fairly wide and shallow but fast, at least in this area. Once we spring Marco, we'll head back this way and follow the stream down to the river. I'm not sure but I think we might be only ten minutes or so out from Goncalvez' place now. What do you guys think?"

The other men nodded and grunted agreement.

"Jill, are we on the right path? Do you concur?"

"It seems right to me," I answered. "I'm not getting anything that tells me otherwise, so I say we carry on as planned." I couldn't let on that my heart was beating so fast I thought I might faint. After all that I had been through over the past week, my emotions had been so strained that now I didn't know whether to look forward to seeing Marco, or to give up hoping that things could ever come to a happy conclusion. As we set off again, a vision of Marco swam into my mind, his dark eyes warm and his hands cupping my face. Taking a deep breath, I purged the sweet image from my mind and plunged ahead through the punishing brush.

A few minutes later, the trail widened into a flat area and as Neil stepped left around a rotting tree stump with a fern growing from its fertile core, I stepped right around the fronds, directly into the biggest spider web in the world. Its sticky strands grabbed at my hair and face. I swung my arms and spun around to free myself. Then I felt a weight plop onto my left shoulder.

I froze.

Sliding my eyes sideways I could see the massive, hairy, repulsive arachnid with legs longer than my fingers. A high, thin wail escaped my throat. "Heeeelp!"

Thwap! The thing vanished and a big hand yanked me backwards.

"Get a grip, Moss," McSweeney muttered under his breath.

"It's only a spider. Get goin'."

Oddly enough, McSweeney's gruffness calmed my jangled nerves. By this time Neil had disappeared around the next bend and the rest of us had to jog to catch up.

Climbing down the steeply angled banks of a tumbling stream, we picked our way across it on the tops of protruding rocks. A slip could have sent any one of us crashing down the gully, carried away by the force of the water. On the other side, we scrambled up the steep bank, clinging to roots and vines.

A few minutes later we topped a small rise and found ourselves looking down at the compound. It seemed like only hours before that Goncalvez had captured and imprisoned us in that roasting, grubby cell in a back corner of one of the sheds we could now see beyond the fence surrounding the complex.

Where is Marco now? I wondered, searching the open area in the centre court. Concealed behind thick shrubbery, we surveyed the expanse before us. All was still. By this time the sun had scaled the heights of the Andes to the west and glided over to the Pacific side, leaving the eastern slopes in deep shadow. Suddenly, a figure separated from one of the shops below and strode across the yard toward where the house stood. A moment later, a dog followed, loping beneath the circular glow from a light high on a pole.

"Dogs!" I whispered. "I thought Juan Carlos got rid of those."

"Looks like they had spares," McSweeney retorted.

"I'll look after that," Bobby added, his eyes not wavering as he scrutinized the tableau before us through binoculars. "Ma'am, you stay here with Mr. McSweeney, all right? If you see us come tearing out of there like a posse is on our tails, get back to that stream and head downhill, okay?"

"Got it," McSweeney answered.

"I'll lead out now," Bobby instructed. "Neil, you follow and do whatever I say. Agreed?"

Neil nodded and prepared to set off.

"Wait," I whispered, grabbing both men by the shirtsleeves. "I'm going to pray for you." It took only seconds for me to say, "Give these men success, Lord. Please send your warrior angels with them. We pray that God will prevail on our behalf, in Jesus' name." I released their sleeves as the tears choked my throat. "Bring him back to me, okay?"

With solemn nods, Neil and Bobby set off at a lope toward the gate of the compound. I pulled a little pair of binoculars out of my pack and watched them until they disappeared in the jungle, not to emerge until just in front of the gates. *What will Bobby do about that dog, or dogs, if there are more?* I hadn't been able to ask what he had in mind but now as I watched, he reached into his backpack and drew something out, reached through the locked gates and set it on the ground on the inside. Then he and Neil melted back into the jungle next to the compound wall. I heard the faint call of a jungle cat and within seconds, the compound erupted in a cacophony of barking as two powerful canines tore toward the gates. The barking stopped abruptly as the animals began sniffing whatever Bobby had deposited on the ground. I surmised that it must have been pieces of meat from Consuelo's kitchen. The guy thought of everything.

In the same instance, I also saw Bobby edge into view and with a flick of his wrist send a missile into the nearest hound who yelped, stumbled, then wandered a short distance away and fell to the ground. In another second, the other dog had suffered the same fate, a blade to the neck. Now he and Neil had to get inside.

I knew that Neil had borrowed a pair of bolt cutters from Arpad back at the ancient city compound and after Bobby had emitted the cat's cry again to make sure no more dogs were on the prowl, Neil snapped the locked chain off the gate. Sliding it open slightly, the two men glided between the gates and disappeared into the shadows inside.

A gust of pent-up breath escaped my lungs as relief washed over me. They had overcome the first couple of obstacles. But would they find Marco? Was he still there? *Oh, please, God,* I prayed, *let them find him quickly. Let him be all right.* What I didn't add because I didn't even want to acknowledge my doubts was, *Let him want to come back to me.*

Now all we could do was wait. I took a step closer to where McSweeney stood. He stood at an odd angle to me and as I turned to look at him, I saw that he had raised his hands above his head and a scowl contorted his craggy features.

From the shadows behind him I heard a voice growl, "*No mueva,*" then add in heavily accented English, "Don't move."

CHAPTER FORTY-THREE

There comes a point after all your nerves have been stretched as tightly as an overloaded clothesline in a Chinook wind for far too long, when something just snaps. When you just get too blamed tired of being afraid and running on adrenalin and you just say, "That's enough."

Feeling that gun in my back brought me to that exact point.

"What do you want?" I demanded, sounding like someone's high-strung, ticked-off mother.

"Who are you?" the voice wanted to know. "What are you doing here?"

"Why should we tell you?" I snapped back.

"Calm down, Moss," McSweeney muttered through clenched teeth. "You want to get us killed?"

"Señora Moss?" the voice asked, surprise evident in the tone. "This is Señora Moss? And Señor McSweeney?"

I turned stiffly toward our captor. In the darkness I could barely make out the man's features. It was Juan Carlos Gutierrez.

"Señor Gutierrez?" I pushed his gun away from my belly and peered at him. "Is that you? What on earth are you doing here?" I demanded.

While McSweeney slowly lowered his hands and turned, Gutierrez explained. "I am so sorry, Señora and Señor. I have wait here from since I found my son safe. I come back to help get Señor Jimenez free from this *serpiente*, Goncalvez." He stopped and spat on the ground at the mention of the name. "But where is Señor Bryant and Mr. Bobby?" he whispered.

McSweeney gestured with a tilt of his head. "They went in to get him."

"Okay," Juan Carlos said, with a decisive nod. "I go too. I have guns and knives." He patted various lumps on his body. "I think they need me, *si*?"

For the longest time after Gutierrez scampered down the mountain with his personal arsenal, nothing happened. The jungle had switched into night mode and instead of going silent, the humid night air fairly came alive with sounds. The night birds had wakened from their daytime slumbers, monkeys hooted somewhere farther away, and insects set up a persistent and extremely annoying onslaught, buzzing in swarms around our heads. Slapping mosquitoes was out of the question because the sound would give us away, so swiping at them continuously was our only option.

McSweeney offered to keep watch so I could at least sit a while but finding somewhere dry proved nearly impossible. Finally, I took out my knife, one that Consuelo Hannah had loaned me, and sawed off a big leaf from a nearby plant, shook the water from it and used it as a ground cover.

How long has it been? It felt like more than an hour but when I tugged on McSweeney's pant leg and tapped my wrist at him, he shushed me and held up five fingers three times. *It has to have been more than fifteen minutes,* I thought. I couldn't bear the waiting and not knowing. I stood up again and peered through the foliage.

For a few minutes all was still other than the humming of the maddering insects. It seemed like nothing at all was going on down there. Suddenly, two shots rang out followed by a volley from an automatic weapon.

"That's it," snarled McSweeney. "I ain't standin' up here waitin' for those guys to get outta there. Come on, Moss. Let's roll."

He took off at a dead run straight down the slope, ignoring the switchback path and scything the foliage with a lethal machete. I leapt after him, struggling to keep up, skidding and sliding in his wake. Where the land evened out, McSweeney hesitated and looked back.

"I'm still here," I panted as I jumped to my feet. "Let's go find Marco."

At the gates to the compound, McSweeney stopped. "Look," he said in a low voice, "I'm gonna stow this artifact in the bushes here so no one can kill me for it. But if I don't come out alive, you know where it is." He hastily dug a shallow indent in the soft earth under a voluminous fern and stuffed the backpack into it then heaped dead ground cover over it. Grabbing my arm, he propelled me back to the gate while whispering in my right ear. "The first chance you get, tell any or all of our guys where that thing is. I'll do the same. Neil will have our hides if we lose it after all this."

"You've got that right," I muttered as I crept forward in the dark. Slipping through the parted gates we stepped over the dead dogs and kept to the shadows along the wall, heading in a sweeping curve past the pool and toward the house. All the yard and patio lights had been turned on and flickering reflections glinted off the water. McSweeney and I paused behind a prickly shrub and surveyed the area. Suddenly, the sound of voices emerged from somewhere near the largest shed, the one that held the mining excavators. Shouts, followed by muffled bursts of command or orders. Running feet.

"*Oh, God, where are they?*" I pleaded silently. "*What has happened to Neil and Bobby? Where is Marco? Please God, let them be all right.*"

McSweeney nudged me with his elbow and jerked his head to the left, indicating for me to follow. We crept around the far side of the pool and along the only wall of the house that lay in shadow. An open, screened window spilled light in a long polygon over the mass of low, leafy plants that covered the area. The terrain sloped gradually down, in the direction of the river.

The sound of voices pulsed from the interior, strident and heated. An argument between at least two men — no, three. Creeping up to the window, I motioned for McSweeney to keep watch while I stood on tiptoe and peeked over the sill. My jaw dropped and my eyes popped wide.

In a loose circle in the middle of the vast living room, Goncalvez and Jay Sharp stood nose to nose, shouting at each other in Spanish, arms waving and neck veins bulging. Off to the side only a few steps away stood Neil. With arms crossed over his chest, he scowled at the two men who, when he tried to interject, paid no attention to him.

If I can only catch his eye. Reaching behind me, I flicked McSweeney's sleeve and motioned him closer with my hand. After a swift look, he pulled me away from the light. Fading into the bushes with him I whispered, "What shall we do now?"

McSweeney ran a hand over his beard and in the dim light I could see his puckered brow. *Okay,* I realized, *he doesn't have a plan either.* Suddenly, the words of Jesus to his disciples dropped into my mind: *Watch and pray.* Gripping McSweeney's arm with all the ferocity I felt, I motioned for him to stand still. Then I began to pray silently, as hard and as fast as I could. I keenly sensed pressure building and knew that something was about to happen — something cataclysmic, though I had no idea exactly what that might be.

The shouting continued for a few more minutes then the pop-pop-pop of gunshot burst through the night air on the far side of the house and the voices ceased. Someone shouted something and I could hear the sound of running feet across the yard. *Where in the world is Marco?* Sweat prickled my palms and trickled down my spine. McSweeney and I stood our ground and waited. I prayed harder, if that was possible.

"I'm surprised at you, Jay," I heard Neil say evenly. "A guy like you with your credentials, stooping to petty crime."

Sharp snorted. "There's nothing petty about this, Bryant.

You can have your credentials and your journal articles. There's a whole lot more to this glass dolphin artifact than just a hunk of glass to stick in some obscure museum for people to take their snotty-nosed kids to look at on a rainy Saturday. Since you're going to be dead in a few minutes, I don't mind telling you the significance of this artifact."

"Be my guest," Neil answered. I thought I could hear him smile. "I have been wondering what the excitement is all about, why you and your friend, Señor Goncalvez here would go to such great lengths to get your hands on this 'hunk of glass' as you call it. By the way, where is Mr. Jimenez? I hope no harm has come to him or you will never see the glass dolphin."

Goncalvez muttered something in Spanish, which I didn't catch and wouldn't have understood anyway.

"You'll be surprised to find that your Mr. Jimenez is not quite as loyal to you and your cause as you suppose," Sharp sneered. "He made it perfectly clear to Señor Goncalvez that he had much more interest in our plans than in yours."

I drew a sharp breath in and covered my mouth with my hand. McSweeney dropped a hand on my shoulder and gave it a squeeze. Even though it couldn't be true, hearing the words spoken that Marco would betray Neil, or me, still seared.

"Hang tough, Moss," McSweeney whispered behind my ear.

Neil's voice broke the silence again. "Please, do tell me about your version of the glass dolphin's value. I'm curious."

"Let's just say that it fits nicely into our plans."

Neil interrupted with a laugh. "What plans are those, Jay? Overthrow the government? Of which country? Or are you going for total world domination? Perhaps a new religion at the same time? That would be novel."

Why are you baiting the man? I wanted to scream. I took a step forward but McSweeney stopped me with a firm grip on my arm and a soft, "Ssh."

"You won't be laughing when we've taken over," Sharp

claimed with arrogant scorn. "You have no idea what's been going on behind the scenes."

I knew this was not true. Neil's associations with select leaders in powerful positions around the world had placed him in a unique situation. Not even I knew the extent of his dealings on international levels.

"And who is 'we'?" Neil asked politely.

"Right now, I'm a leading member of a secret society with connections around the world. Our plans are moving into place as we speak. You will not recognize the world within a year."

"Ah," commented Neil. "So it *is* world domination you're after."

"You and your religious claptrap," Sharp spat. "I've been following your movements. I know that you think there is a link between ancient technologies and things like anti-gravity and I know that you're trying to figure out how the Inca moved those massive stones around. You think the Bible is a source of real knowledge. Seriously, Neil. I thought you'd have more brains than that. You're wasting your time. With the glass dolphin in my possession, I'll be able to do that and more. And with the spiritual power that we've tapped into, you and your pitiful little band of Christian believers will soon be wiped off the face of the earth. You think your religion has power? I'll show you power."

In spite of the heat and oppressive humidity, I shivered. The man was evil. When we had met with Dr. Jay Sharp in Paris I had known that something was not right. In spite of his cool, urbane demeanour, the gut feeling, or actually, that warning of the Holy Spirit down inside, told me that he was not to be trusted. I thought about standing in his plush, cold apartment and staring down at the tiny square below. For a moment, I was back there. *What was it that had set my teeth on edge?* Something did not fit the picture that I had just viewed as I'd peered through the window before me now.

The cast!

Jay Sharp had been wearing a cast on his leg when we had seen him only a few days before in Europe. Did he have one in his closet that he clamped on when the need for deception arose? Or perhaps he had just had it removed. I turned my attention back to the scene before us.

"Oh, so you are going for a new religion, too," Neil pressed.

"The whole enchilada. Well, Jay, you always were a greedy one." Neil gave nothing away. "And what do you think of all this, Señor Goncalvez? Did you know about your partner's plans?"

Goncalvez let loose a stream of rapid-fire Spanish and I had the distinct impression that Sharp's scheme was news to him. *Very clever, Neil,* I thought, *playing one villain against the other.*

"Pay no attention to him," Jay Sharp countered. "He's expendable. Just like you are."

CHAPTER FORTY-FOUR

When I learned that Sharp had been behind Marco's kidnapping all along, livid fury coursed through me. Not only had this man thoroughly messed up my life by kidnapping the man I loved on our wedding day but he had also jeopardized the lives of several people I loved.

"We know," Sharp had said, "that the glass dolphin contains ancient secrets. It's the key we've been looking for to unlock the power to bend time. You clowns, petty little archaeologists and bumbling scientists, have no clue how far advanced our studies are," he boasted. "With the ability to intersect time we can change the future, and we will. The power will be in our hands to do whatever we want."

"Interesting. Tell me more," Neil pumped.

"Oh, no. These mysteries have been guarded for centuries through societies of utmost secrecy, waiting for the right moment. Our great leader is about to unveil his ultimate strategy. Your so-called friend, Lord Wardley, has been part of this, too. He doesn't know it, but he played right into my hands."

I swallowed. *Did Sharp know about the diary?*

In the next moment, I had my answer. "Wardley had a relative, a spinster woman, who travelled and explored in these parts almost two hundred years ago. Rumours confirm that she found this glass dolphin. Unfortunately, Wardley himself knew nothing about it, the old fool." I thought of the diary still safely stowed in the pack on my back and vowed that Jay Sharp would never lay his hands on it.

Neil seemed to be buying time and though I tried to be still,

I found myself shifting from one foot to the other, antsy. The tension in the air had ratcheted up like a balloon about to burst. Something was about to happen. I could feel it.

It didn't take long. First a shout then a volley of shots split the darkness. A scream of utter terror escaped someone's throat. Running feet and more screams, shouts, and yelps of pain followed. I grabbed McSweeney's arm and dragged him with me to take another look into the house. The place where the three men had stood was now deserted.

Running around the side of the house, we skidded to a halt at the corner and looked cautiously around it, crouching low and hidden by shrubbery. Collective terror had struck the compound, gripping all the participants in common panic.

Sharp and Goncalvez burst from the house and both men sprinted into the yard to investigate. I saw Neil step from the doorway and look around. Now was our chance! A low whistle from McSweeney's lips brought Neil's head snapping around. He melted into the shadows and re-appeared at our sides.

"Where's Marco?" I asked in a frantic whisper. "Where is Bobby?"

"I'm not sure," Neil answered, "but I think they're together. Marco was guarding the house when Bobby found him."

"What's goin' on out there?" McSweeney jabbed a thumb in the direction of the vast compound yard.

"Let's go find out." Neil led out, hugging the wall of the house and sliding silently toward where the yard lights flooded the main open area. There we stopped, clustered together and hidden behind an extremely convenient bush. *Thank-you, God.*

The sound of thunderous blows reverberated through the night and we watched in a kind of abject horror as an entire section of the compound's rock wall crumbled in a scattered heap. Over the debris came the most terrifying sight I have ever encountered. Ragged, hairy, filthy men leapt over the stones. Giant men, many nearly nine feet tall, pushed each other, and came stumbling through the opening. In the glow from the yard lights, they stopped and looked around, shielding their eyes with gnarled hands. At the same time, more deafening thuds emanated from another section of the wall and in moments it too disintegrated, allowing more giant creatures through it and into the compound.

Goncalvez's men screamed in terror and ran like ants that have had their nest poked with a stick. Shots rang out and I saw one of the giant men swipe at his leg and hobble a few steps; he didn't even slow down. There had to be fifteen or twenty of them. Even though men in the compound outnumbered them, crazed as they were with panic, almost no one seemed to be about to stop and think long enough to point a gun and shoot.

Both Sharp and Goncalvez began shouting orders, their quest for the glass dolphin momentarily forgotten. Dashing back into the house, they each emerged with automatic weapons and began strafing the oncoming hoard with bullets. This seemed to galvanize their men who hid behind anything they could find, including, oddly enough, the lampposts. From these vantage points, shots aimed at the invading giant hoard began to have an effect. It seemed to enrage the beast-like men even more and with unearthly howls they attacked as though gripped with fever.

One giant, with a face like a baboon, including long canine teeth, plunged an arm into a thicket and yanked out a cowering outlaw. With a guttural screech, he broke the man's arm and flung him aside like a toy. I watched in terror as another massive creature, with one swipe of a hair-covered arm, bashed the side of a man's head so hard that he flew through the air, like a petulant child pitching away a rag doll.

"I think it's time we made our exit," Neil whispered calmly.

"But what about Marco and Bobby," I gasped, grabbing the front of Neil's shirt with both hands.

"They know what to do," he replied, prying my fingers

away. "Come on, let's go."

We headed back around the house, away from the light and horrific combat. When we got to the corner near the pool I stopped. "Wait," I said. "We've hidden the glass dolphin." Before I could tell him where to look in case anything happened to McSweeney and me, another volley of shots rang out.

"Tell me later," Neil said, taking off toward the next clump of bushes.

The compound gates stood open, one of them hanging at an angle from one hinge where the invading tribe had bashed through.

"This way," McSweeney muttered. "Let's keep as far away from those creepy critters as we can." Neil and I followed on his heels as he dashed through the gloom and mottled shadows. Within moments we had the main gates in sight again. Now all we had to do was get through that last patch of light. We could grab the pack containing the glass dolphin and disappear into the jungle night.

Creeping forward on silent cat's feet, Neil whispered, "When I say 'Now,' we run for it, okay?"

The bulk of the invaders had scattered toward the farther reaches of the compound and at this side of the space it seemed almost quiet. Casting about in all directions, I could see only one man lurking behind a length of culvert near one of the sheds and he suddenly leapt up and began to run into the dark.

Neil shot a swift glance behind him to McSweeney and me then with a quick nod said, "Now."

The three of us erupted from the bushes.

"Going somewhere?" Jay Sharp's voice spoke out of the gloom.

I skidded to a halt and smacked right into McSweeney's back. Peering around his shoulder I could see Sharp's profile. And a machine gun barrel pointed directly at Neil's chest.

"Where is it?" Sharp snapped.

Neil looked not the least bit rattled. "Where's what?" he asked.

"You know what I'm talking about," Sharp snarled. "The glass dolphin. Where is it? I know you have it."

"I haven't the faintest idea," Neil replied casually. "Not that I would tell you if I had but the fact is, I don't know where it is."

"Tell me or I'll kill you now."

"That wouldn't help much, Jay, and you know it. Now we're leaving so put your gun down and get out of the way."

Sharp raised the barrel of the gun until it pressed against Neil's throat. My heart rate rose correspondingly.

"Where's all that power you were talking about, Jay? How are you going to take over the world if you can't even find a little artifact like the glass dolphin?"

For goodness sake, I thought, *don't taunt him! The guy is a nut case. Who knows what he might do?*

My eyes widened as his finger moved on the gun's trigger. I stepped out from behind McSweeney before he could stop me.

"Where is Marco?" I demanded. "You said if we turned over the glass dolphin, Marco would be released. Where is he?"

Sharp swung his gaze toward me and gave a hollow laugh. "It's too late for that, sweetheart," he replied. "Marco is dead."

CHAPTER FORTY-FIVE

A scream rose in my throat. "No, no, no!" I wailed, crumpling against McSweeney's arm. Anguish coursed through my body, followed by fury and loathing for this evil man standing in front of me. Never before had I wanted to kill a man, but right now the desire to destroy him swept over me with such force that I could see nothing but red-hot hatred.

My muscles tensed, ready to spring but before I could move, a figure bounded from the shadows and with one swift kick sent the gun flying from Sharp's grip. It was Bobby. Sharp howled and swung around as the attacker's other foot slammed into his face. In a second, it was over and Sharp lay sprawled on the ground, his head twisted strangely away from his body.

"Come on," Bobby commanded, speeding off toward the compound gates. I felt a hand grab my arm and yank me into motion. With a sob, I ran too. Behind us I could tell the tide was turning on the giant ones and heard their bawls and moans as bullets found their marks. The rumble and roar had turned and was now headed back in our direction.

Within seconds we had dashed through the gates. "This way," Bobby said, turning right toward the river.

"Wait," I cried. "What happened to Juan Carlos? We can't leave without him."

"He'll catch up, Jill," Neil answered, towing me forward. "He knows his way around the jungle."

From the corner of my eye, I saw McSweeney dive beneath the plant where he had buried the glass dolphin, fling the pack over one shoulder and spring after the rest of us. Into the night we ran, through slapping leaves and snapping branches, leaping over downed trees and puddles that left me sodden to the knees. Behind us I could hear giant men crashing through the forest.

At one point Bobby stepped aside and allowed Neil to take the lead. When I caught up to where he waited, he fell in behind me.

"Keep quiet," he said as he took up the rear. "We might be able to lose them."

Behind us I could hear the heavy, thudding footsteps of our pursuers. Clearly, we hadn't given them all the slip and the terror of being caught, shot, or worse, kept me going.

A scrap of silvery moon winked through scudding clouds but gave little in the way of light. We ran on, stumbling, flinging aside foliage and still running. I tripped, fell flat and skinned my chin on a tree root but scrambled back to my feet and tore on. My leg muscles burned and my breath came in panting gulps. Energy flagged as I toiled through the dark. At times I could see McSweeney up ahead, or Neil, then I lost them. I knew Bobby was somewhere behind me. I came to a fork in the trail and could see nothing and no one. There was no time to consider the best choice, no time to think even. I dared not call out and reveal our location.

Then I heard voices up ahead, hushed urgent whispers and a moment later, I nearly crashed into McSweeney, Bobby and Neil. Somehow Bobby had gotten ahead of me and now they had stopped to wait for me to catch up. But there was a problem. We had run out onto a point high above a gorge. Below us the stream that we had traversed earlier had become a raging torrent, swollen by rains at higher elevations. To go back meant to run straight into the net that Sharp and Goncalvez had cast for us or clash headlong with the giant tribesmen who surely hunted us with more cunning and jungle knowledge than any of us possessed.

A thin veil of moonbeam sifted downward and highlighted

the rugged jumble of rock on both sides of the gash.

"We have to cross here," Neil said, gasping for breath.

"What? Climb down the rocks?" I huffed, bending over with my hands on my knees.

"There is a bridge."

I squinted into the darkness. "What bridge?"

"It's a rope bridge," Bobby answered, stepping forward and reaching into the gloom. Giving the invisible structure a couple of good yanks and stepping gingerly out into black nothingness, he pronounced it sound. "McSweeney, you take the lead," he said. "It's not far, maybe only ten yards. When you get across, whistle and the next one can start. If you think it's strong enough to hold more than one of us, whistle part way across."

"Aye, aye, Captain," McSweeney answered. "Single rope on the bottom. One rope above. Hang on tight," he reported then disappeared into the darkness.

Oh, no! Not another rope bridge. I groaned inwardly.

"I'll take the rear," Bobby said, "behind Jill." Neil set off. I could hear the crashing of runners through the jungle, getting ever closer.

"We've got to hurry, Bobby," I whispered, placing my hands on the rope above my head and giving it a tug. I could barely reach it.

"Go," Bobby said. "I'll be right behind you."

Finding the bottom rope with my feet, I splayed them out sideways and set off with hand over hand grasping the upper rope. Wind gusted down the canyon over the river and I could feel the tug of its velocity against the ropes. A whistle sounded from the jungle up ahead but before I had gone more than ten steps the rope strands bounced with Bobby's weight and he called out in a hoarse whisper.

"Hurry, ma'am, they're almost here. Go, go."

Picking up the pace, I scrambled to keep ahead of the advancing threat from the jungle at our rear. In the darkness, my arms flailed to find the rope with each overhand then my right foot missed the bottom rope and I hung dangling by one hand. Between the motion caused by the wind and the rebounding spring from Bobby behind me, my body spun and twisted as I grasped air. Then my other foot slipped from the rope and my one hand could not hold my entire weight. With a cry, I felt my throbbing fingers uncoil and slide from the rope. Flailing my arms, I grabbed for the bottom rope on my way down. It caught under my left arm and jerked me to a stop. Flinging my right arm up to catch it, I held on while the rest of my body dangled below.

"Someone, help me!" My cry sliced through my throat like dull razor blades.

"Hang on, Jill." I heard Neil's voice call from the darkness. But it was too late. From the corner of my eye I saw dark figures appear on the bank we had just left. Shots rang out and a bullet sang through the wild air. Bobby's body twisted like a corkscrew and he drew a weapon, cracking off a couple of shots before the swaying rope bridge sent him twisting the other way.

The rope cut into my underarms. My legs flayed the air as I tried to swing a foot up and over the rope but the bridge bounced so violently that it was impossible to time it right.

Then Neil called from the far side of the gorge.

"I'm coming, Jill. Hang on."

"No," I cried. "It can't hold us all." How I knew that, I don't know. I just did.

Bobby had been able to take another couple of shots from his position up the ropes from me and I heard more shots ring out from McSweeney or Neil as our pursuers strafed the banks with bullets.

Something whizzed past my left ear. *What was that?* Another, then another, flew passed me. Then something hard struck my shoulder. Someone upstream was pitching rocks at me! With a mighty heave of my legs, I wrapped my ankles around the rope and began to crawl, upside down, as fast as my limbs would move.

It was not fast enough.

I felt, rather than saw, Bobby's body lurch as he yelped in pain. He swung out from the rope and dangled for a horrifying moment before spiking his body back toward it, catching the cable with a foot. Even with his strength, he could not get purchase and his balance was off. Bobby dangled by one hand from the top rope but he must have been too injured to hang on. Then I felt the top rope snap past my head. It had been cut and I watched in utter horror as he dropped from sight into the abyss.

My entire weight had been suspended from the lower rope. I felt the repeated reverberations of steel striking the cords. With stomach-turning recognition, I felt the last strand break free from its moorings.

"Help me, Jesus!" I screamed, as I felt myself plummet downward, into darkness and the thunder of the river.

CHAPTER FORTY-SIX

Through the leaves fanning my face I could see slivers of winking light. Then it went dark again. A while later – I didn't know how long – I opened my eyes to find that the coming morning had begun to paint the ink-black sky with the faintest shades of midnight blue. Water dripped on my cheek. Lying on my back, I turned my head and winced. Lifting my hand, I felt the spot over my right ear where a lump had formed and blood and hair had crusted into a tangled knot. That's when it all came back to me.

I remembered standing outside the house listening to the conversation inside between Neil, Jay Sharp and Luis Goncalvez.

Where am I, Lord? I prayed silently, lifting my head to examine my surroundings. A persistent roar filled my ears and as my vision adjusted I could see nothing but branches, leaves and juts of rock. Somewhere the cry of a night bird going home to roost broke through the booming din.

Get up, the voice of the Lord spoke into my dazed mind. That was all. I rolled onto my side and felt a stab of pain in my ribs but pushed myself up on my elbow in spite of it. Another fat drop of water plopped on my head from above. In the gloom, I looked around me but could see almost nothing. I felt around with my hand, touched the damp earth and felt the sharp-edged rocks.

The crash of the cascading water below me brought me sharply to my senses. I could tell that it was nearby, that I had somehow landed on a ledge of rock above the main stream. *How long have I lain here?* I wondered, pushing myself painfully to

267

my knees and peering through a dangling fern suspended from a rock above me. I felt around with my hands to discover that the rock ledge was only about as wide as a piano bench and only slightly longer. Leaning back into the wall of rock seemed like a good idea since when I looked below I could just make out the raging stream crashing over boulders in a tumble of rapids. *Best not to go there,* I decided.

By now the sky had lightened just enough for me barely to make out the far side of the canyon. The jagged rocks dripped with ferns and vines and I could now tell that the chasm was not that deep, maybe thirty feet in total but given the vertical nature of the gorge's sides, climbing up out if it seemed impossible. Twisting my body while hanging onto the rocks behind me, I stared up the wall at my back. *No hope there, either.* It rose through the foliage in an almost sheer wall without even finger holds – at least none that I could see in the feeble light. My options for getting out of there seemed pretty slim.

Get up, said the voice of the Spirit again.

"Okay," I mumbled. "I'll get up." Clinging to the rocks, I pulled myself to my feet and pressed my back against the canyon's side. My head and shoulders emerged into the open above the fronds and I looked around. Upstream, a small waterfall plunged over a jagged ledge and the water rushed past below my feet. Unless I slipped, I was in the only safe place on this rock wall.

Squinting upwards into the half-light, I could see a short length of the twine bridge hanging limply on the far side of the gorge. Frowning, I remembered that last, near-fatal plunge as the footbridge had given way. When I leaned out slightly, I could see its remains hanging from the same side of the chasm as where I stood, a little farther upstream. Our attackers were nowhere to be seen.

Where is everyone? I thought, looking around. Suddenly, the previous night's scene shot vividly through my mind. Like an ice pick through my heart, I suddenly remembered Jay Sharp's last words to me. *Marco is dead.*

I couldn't think about that now. I had to get out of here.

I scanned the banks in both directions as far as I could see. Not far downstream, a jut of rock pushed the water out of sight around a bend. Suddenly, a shrill whistle pierced the air, above the roar of the water. Looking up, I could just barely see Neil, standing on top of the outcropping of rock, waving his arms. He motioned for me to stay where I was.

Like I have anywhere else to go, I thought, as I watched him dash along the edge of the chasm toward me and disappear from sight above where I stood.

Five minutes later the remains of the twine bridge unfurled from overhead, its ragged ends smacking me on the shoulder.

"Ouch," I said, as I grabbed at the swinging rope.

"Come on. Climb up," I heard Neil call.

You've got to be kidding.

One more scan of the area confirmed that Neil's plan was my only option. Tying the twine around the tops of my thighs, I gave it a tug. Miraculously, my backpack still clung to my shoulders, though now it sagged a bit. Gripping the rope with both hands and bracing my feet against the rock, I reached the top in a couple of minutes and lurched over the edge and into Neil's arms.

"Come on," he said, yanking the rope off me and looping it over his shoulder. "We've got to get to the others."

"Wait," I panted. "Where are they?"

"There's a pool farther down. McSweeney is waiting there. He'll be glad to see that you're fine. You are fine, aren't you?"

"I had kind of a nasty bump on the head and my ribs hurt when I breathe but otherwise, I think I'm in one piece."

"Good. Come on. There's no time to waste."

"Where's Bobby?" I asked, limping along behind Neil as he jogged along the edge of the precipice.

"He fell and we have to rescue him."

"Is he okay?" I panted.

"He'll make it but we have to get out of here. No telling what's going on up the hill."

When we reached the spot where the rock protrusion sent the river water whipping around a bend, I could see McSweeney below us. A small pool, whirling with foam, had formed where the canyon widened. Neil dashed nimbly down a jumble of rocks and I followed, with far less agility. The plan was for McSweeney to tie the rope around his body and wade or swim across the swift stream. Bobby, lying on a pile of rubble one the far side of the gorge, had shown signs of consciousness but none of us knew the extent of his injuries. Given that the woods might still be full of men – or half-men – with weapons, we needed to be quick and quiet.

The rescue went exactly as planned and, to our relief, McSweeney found the water around the edges of the pool reached only to his chest and was less turbulent than expected. He carried Bobby back across the pool on his back, no easy feat, while Neil and I hauled on the rope. McSweeney laid him down in a patch of soft moss.

"Bobby, can you hear me?" I said, kneeling at his side and brushing a leaf off his forehead. Neil, meanwhile, performed a first aid inspection and, thankfully, found only numerous bruises, a few cuts, and a broken wrist, nothing worse.

"Yes, I can hear you," Bobby answered with a crooked smile, opening his eyes.

"Where are you hurt?" I wanted to know, ignoring the ache in my own side.

"Here and there. My wrist hurts. That was a wild ride."

"I know."

"More excitement than I bargained for."

"Agreed."

"Bobby," Neil broke in, digging into his pack, "we're going

to bind up your wrist and if you are up to walking, we really have to get out of here."

"He better walk," McSweeney said. "There's no way I'm haulin' that carcass all the way down to the river."

"There's no telling if those guys are still looking for us," Neil continued. "McSweeney's still got the glass dolphin, so unless their numbers have been decimated, Sharp could be mounting another search as we speak."

"He might have a bit of a migraine this mornin'," McSweeney observed, "given that kick to the head that he got last night."

Bobby grinned as he rolled on his side and McSweeney helped him sit up then grimaced as Neil wrapped his wrist in surgical tape.

"All the same, I don't want to hang around and find out who is awake up there." Neil and McSweeney hauled Bobby to his feet, checked his legs for sturdiness and set off down a narrow game trail along the bank of the stream.

"What's the plan from here?" I asked after we had not gone far.

McSweeney answered. "I gave Henry, the boat guy, a shout on my sat phone, which, miracle of miracles, still works. He's going to meet us down at the estuary."

Morning sun lit up the sky by degrees until it suddenly burst into full glory, awakening half the jungle. It was going to be another beautiful, hot day but I had a bag of tears around my heart and didn't care. All I wanted now was to go home.

We followed the course of the stream, which flattened out and widened the closer we drew to the main river. The terrain alternated between rocky outcroppings that we climbed and stumbled over, with swampy flats buzzing with insects, which we skirted as much as possible. The prospect of encountering quicksand, caimans, water snakes or lurking anacondas made our passage through the swamps swift and silent.

Wet and exhausted, we all found the heat out in the open punishing and whenever possible, clung to the shoreline under the canopy. We reached the riverbank by around noon. Good to his word, Henry's boat lolled on the shore while its captain lolled in a hammock slung across the deck. When we emerged from the dense brush along the bank, he rolled to his feet and leapt off the gunwale to the sand.

"You made it," he said, grinning and pumping our hands. "Let's get you all on board and out of here. I don't want any repercussions for helping you guys, if you know what I mean. I like my boat too much."

He lobbed our packs on board, with the exception of the crate holding the glass dolphin, which McSweeney insisted on keeping in his own protective custody. "I've got it this far," he claimed. "I'm not takin' any chances now."

Henry had just put his long limbs into pushing the boat off the sand when a commotion erupted from the forest and Juan Carlos scampered out of the trees.

"*Quiero venir también*," he panted. "I come too."

After a nod from Neil, Henry reached down and grasped Gutierrez's arm. "Come on, then." With one swift yank, the little man vaulted to the deck. A brisk conversation between the Spanish-speakers followed as Henry pushed away from the muddy bank and hopped aboard.

"What?" I said, giving Neil's shoulder a shake. "What's he saying?"

"He says we don't have to worry about being followed by Goncalvez. He's dead."

"Did Juan Carlos kill him?"

Neil shook his head. "No, but we don't have to worry about him anymore."

"What about Sharp?"

Neil shrugged. "He has disappeared."

CHAPTER FORTY-SEVEN

"Are you serious?" Holding the cordless telephone to my ear I paced back and forth across my living room carpet, listening intently.

"It looks like part of their plans involve EMPs," Neil went on.

"What are EMPs?" I asked, trying to concentrate.

It had been more than a week since Bobby, McSweeney and Neil, along with the glass dolphin, had flown out of Cusco. Neil's destination was the ultra-high-tech science lab located under a mountain in Israel that employed some of the most brilliant minds in the world. With the goal of breaking the antediluvian code that had appeared from within the depths of the glass dolphin crystal, the scientists there had gone to work. Bobby had accompanied him as security since, even though he had a broken wrist, he didn't consider his job to be finished until the glass dolphin had finished its journey. McSweeney had flown back to Florida.

"It stands for electro-magnetic pulse, a blast of electrical charge designed to knock out the power grid of entire cities, shutting everything down faster than a hurricane or flood."

"Oh. You mean that Sharp and his evil cronies intended to use the glass dolphin for something like that? Would it work? Is that its purpose?"

"Well, we're not sure yet whether it could add any power to what is already available out there since with the right technology that could happen any day anyway. I think he had no idea what the glass dolphin crystal was all about since no one knew about the hologram until we uncovered it. No one, that is, except the people with whom it originated.

"Who were they? Have you been able to figure that out?"

"Well, our Lady Cecilia Wardley didn't know and as far as we know there are no other written records, though it is possible that Dr. Standish and her crew may unearth something as they excavate the hidden city. It's my belief that the story of the glass dolphin is not the real one. The simple fact that the technology it displayed is so advanced points to a society that also had the ability to cut those massive fitted stones and move them into place with more precision than a jigsaw puzzle, and do it over vast distances. What we have figured out is that the formulas that we've been able to decipher may be able to offer an explanation to big questions like *how* the stones in the ancient monuments were cut so precisely and *how* those people were able to move them into place across valleys and to the tops of mountains when modern man hasn't figured out how to do it yet."

"And?"

"We're not entirely sure yet but it has something to do with sound waves and magnetic resonance, special high-frequencies – like Millie said, acoustic levitation. It will take us a while to get to the bottom of it but everyone here is pretty excited about the findings so far."

"Thanks for letting me know, Neil," I said.

"And how are you doing?"

"Um, okay. I guess I just have to forget about Marco and get on with my life. Impossible as that seems."

After Henry had rescued us all with his boat, we collapsed in bedraggled heaps on the deck, all too tired to move. My head ached as a result of its collision with a rock face, my ribs hurt with every breath and every muscle in my body cried out for rest. My heart longed for the oblivion of sleep. In an hour or two, I had awakened. The hot sun had steamed the moisture out of my sludge-soaked clothes, which were now stiff and scratchy. I lay still, with my head on my pack and watched the riverbanks slide past my view. I never wanted to see this place again. The hope of recovering Marco's body faded more with each passing moment.

Back in Pillcopata, we managed to procure a helicopter to fly in and pick us up. Getting out of the country quickly with the artifact was paramount. No one knew what had happened to Jay Sharp, if he was still alive, or if he might turn up at any moment with a squad of thugs armed with automatic weapons.

Neil prevailed on some of his archaeological buddies in Lima for assistance. As he had previously arranged, they were more than happy to help facilitate the movement of the glass dolphin for study purposes with the assurance of a safe return to its home country.

Cecilia Wardley's diary had described the trek of the ancient tribe from the jungle interior, through the mountain passes to the sea where their lightning ceremony and the creation of the glass dolphin itself was thought to have begun. As it turned out, the glass dolphin held many more secrets than Cecilia Wardley knew. We had yet to discover how and why it was able to deliver messages from the deep past and what those messages had to tell us. And the cause of her mysterious death would have to remain just that, a mystery.

I had hugged my uncle good-bye at the airport in Cusco and boarded my plane for home. The flights were long, gruelling and with too many stopovers. When I arrived, my daughter picked me up at the airport, brought me home, fed me a bowl of chicken soup and put me to bed. That had been days ago.

Now, as I placed my phone back in its cradle, the doorbell rang. Before I could answer it, Julia strode in, dumping her overstuffed handbag on the hall table.

"Mom, guess what? We're invited to a party." Her eyes sparkled with excitement.

"Hello, Julia. Thanks for stopping by," I said, kissing her

cheek. "I don't want to go to a party, sweetheart. I've just been on the phone with your great-uncle, Neil."

"What did he have to say?"

"The usual. We foiled international disaster again, by a narrow margin."

"Oh, good," she replied, rolling her eyes. "I can't stand international disasters. Local ones are more than enough for me."

"I think I'm done with disasters for a while," I said. "They're exhausting."

"Forget about that. You have to come to this party. It's starting in half an hour. I'll help you get ready."

"I'm not going. Whose party is it anyway?"

"First of all, you have to go. It's in your honour. The ladies at the Ivy Tea House are putting it on. It's kind of a memorial slash wedding party. They want to make you feel better. A whole bunch of your friends are coming too."

"For goodness sake," I said crossly. "Why didn't someone ask me if I wanted a party before they went ahead and planned one? This is ridiculous."

"Of course it is," Julia chirped. "It's just what you need, so come on, you have to put on your wedding dress. I'm going to wear my bridesmaid's dress, too."

I sighed deeply. "I'm *not* traipsing down the block in my wedding dress, Julia. Everyone in town knows that there was no wedding. It's macabre."

She gave me a push. "Get up those stairs," she ordered, "and put on that dress. My car is right out back and no one will even see you. You have to let your friends do this nice thing for you."

Twenty minutes later, I stood before my bedroom mirror with my hair pinned up, fresh lipstick on and Julia fussing with my simple, cream-coloured dress. Julia wore her chiffon dress, looking as fresh as a spring tulip. I was the saddest looking bride I had ever seen.

"Come on," she said. "You look lovely. Everyone is waiting."

We parked the car at the restaurant's front door so I had only to step from the curb into the building. Inside I found, to my surprise that my parents had also shown up. My mother gave me a hug, looking weirdly cheerful under the circumstances, before trotting off on her high heels to the vine-shaded terrace. My father put his arm around my shoulders.

"You look just as beautiful today as you did a few weeks ago," he said, kissing my forehead. "Be happy, okay?"

"I'm trying." My heart felt like a stone.

"I'll walk you in. Grand entrance, you know."

I sighed. "Okay. If we have to." From somewhere, music flowed into the room and my father took my arm and led me toward the doorway to the terrace. I could see friends seated at tables around the room, dressed up for afternoon tea, smiling and laughing. Julia grabbed a bouquet of flowers from a table just outside the tearoom door and thrust a second bouquet into my hands before waltzing ahead of me. Inside, I groaned. I so did not want to be part of this charade.

When my father and I stepped into the tearoom doorway, everyone in the room rose. The tables had been arranged as before with a centre aisle leading to a flower-bedecked dais. I could see the smiling faces of my dearest family and friends filling the room and my eyes brimmed with tears. It was like a replay of the horrible wedding that wasn't. I couldn't do it. I could not go through with this joke because the joke was on me.

With a sob, I glanced at my father, whose face wore a bright smile, too. He tipped his head toward the front of the room and flicked a glance that way. What was he doing? I thought. This whole thing was such a terrible idea. Then he did it again and with supreme reluctance and shoulders sagging, I turned my head and looked up the aisle toward the front. That's when time stood still.

From the right side of the dais a man stepped forward. He had the tenderest look in his eyes that I have ever seen. They were the very eyes I thought I would never look into again.

Marco reached out both hands toward me and started down the aisle to meet me. A cry tore from the bottom of my soul as I dropped my father's arm and ran toward my love. In a second, I was in his arms and his lips were on mine.

I couldn't stop crying. Gradually, I realized that the room was filled with applause and cheers. Mopping my cheeks, I tucked myself under Marco's arm as he led me towards the altar. Julia stood to the left of the dais and my son, Tim, waited on the right side.

"Oh, Marco," I said. "They told me you were dead."

"Who told you that?"

"Jay Sharp. He said you were dead. That's why we left."

"And you believed him? The man is a criminal and a scoundrel. Men like that are known to be liars."

"But how did you get away? How did you get out of the jungle?"

"I walked out, down to the river then caught a ride with a guy named Henry, the boatman."

I laughed in spite of my tears. "It was so terrible, believing that you were gone forever. I didn't know how I was going to live without you."

"And now you don't have to."

"Wait a minute. How did you set all this up from Peru?" I looked around at the pop-up wedding that surrounded me.

"I tried to call you and tell you I was coming but there was no answer, so I called Julia. This was her idea." He grinned and winked at my daughter. "She pulled it all together in only a few hours." Right on cue, the pastor from my church appeared and opened his Bible.

"Oh, Marco," I said, "I love you so much."
He kissed my hands. "Let's get married, shall we?"
And so we did.

EPILOGUE

"Did Neil say anything else?" Marco asked from his position on a cushioned lounger as I pressed the button on the phone and set it down. The remains of our breakfast, including a last cup of coffee, lay scattered on a little table next to the balcony railing. From our hotel room, we could hear the sound of the waves licking the pale sand and hear the seabirds squabbling over the day's catch down the beach. We were having our honeymoon on the sugar sand beach after all.

"He talked to Lord Wardley. There was this sleazy character that Neil and I met in a little antiques store near Wardley Hall. Anthony Sims was his name."

"Okay," Marco replied, lazily nibbling a spear of pineapple.

"It turns out that he was in cahoots with Jay Sharp, dealing in stolen antiquities. Cardy used his connections to have his antiques operation looked into and they discovered the connection to Sharp. I guess when the pressure was on, he squealed like a weanling piglet."

"No honour among thieves."

"That means that the authorities are onto Sharp's nefarious activities. I don't think we'll have to worry about him any time soon."

"And did your esteemed uncle have anything else to add?"

"Well, I hate to mention it at a time like this but he did say something."

Marco's left eyebrow lowered in an apprehensive frown and he gave me a sideways look. "You might as well tell me now. I'm going to find out anyway."

I chuckled as I reached over from my own lounge chair to

run my hand through his dark coils of thick hair. "McSweeney told him that he has come across a sunken wreck that he wants us to explore with him."

Marco sat up straighter. "What kind of wreck? Where is it?"

"Something ancient, of course, and somewhere in the Caribbean. He didn't elaborate. I told him we're a little busy right now."

"We're not busy."

"Yes, we are. We're on our honeymoon and when we're finished lounging on this fabulous beach, eating too much seafood, and getting too much sun, we have to go home and be a normal married couple."

He reached over and took my hand. Kissing my fingers one by one, he said,

"You're absolutely right, *mi amor*," he murmured. "We are far too busy. McSweeney and his wreck can wait."

THE END

Wendy Dewar Hughes

Also by
Wendy Dewar Hughes

Picking up the Pieces

The first Novel in the
Jill Moss Adventures series.

www.pickingupthepiecesbook.com
Also available at Amazon.com, Amazon.ca,
Smashwords.com and
wherever e-books are sold.